Bob Pritchard has been writing all his life, but since he retired from the corporate world in 2019, he has dedicated his time to his two passions, theatre and writing. His first published work was the play *Front Porch Steps* (YouthPLAYS).

During COVID-19, he completed his first novel, *Her Puerto Rican Smile* (available on Amazon Books). *The Man Who Wanted to Be Cary Grant*, a comic story of love, identity, and Hollywood, is his second novel. *The Silver Paladin and The Man Who Wanted to Be Tom Brady* are finished and a mystery novel titled *Parole Board, A Gabby Rameriz Murder Mystery* is in the works.

Bob lives in Florida.

To my mother, who always believed in me.

Bob Pritchard

THE MAN WHO WANTED TO BE CARY GRANT

AUSTIN MACAULEY PUBLISHERS™

LONDON * CAMBRIDGE * NEW YORK * SHARJAH

Ordering Information
Quantity sales: Special discounts are available on quantity purchases by corporations, associations, and others. For details, contact the publisher at the address below.

Publisher's Cataloging-in-Publication data
Pritchard, Bob
The Man Who Wanted to Be Cary Grant

ISBN 9798889107644 (Paperback)
ISBN 9798889107651 (ePub e-book)

Library of Congress Control Number: 2023923218

www.austinmacauley.com/us

First Published 2024
Austin Macauley Publishers LLC
40 Wall Street, 33rd Floor, Suite 3302
New York, NY 10005
USA

mail-usa@austinmacauley.com
+1 (646) 5125767

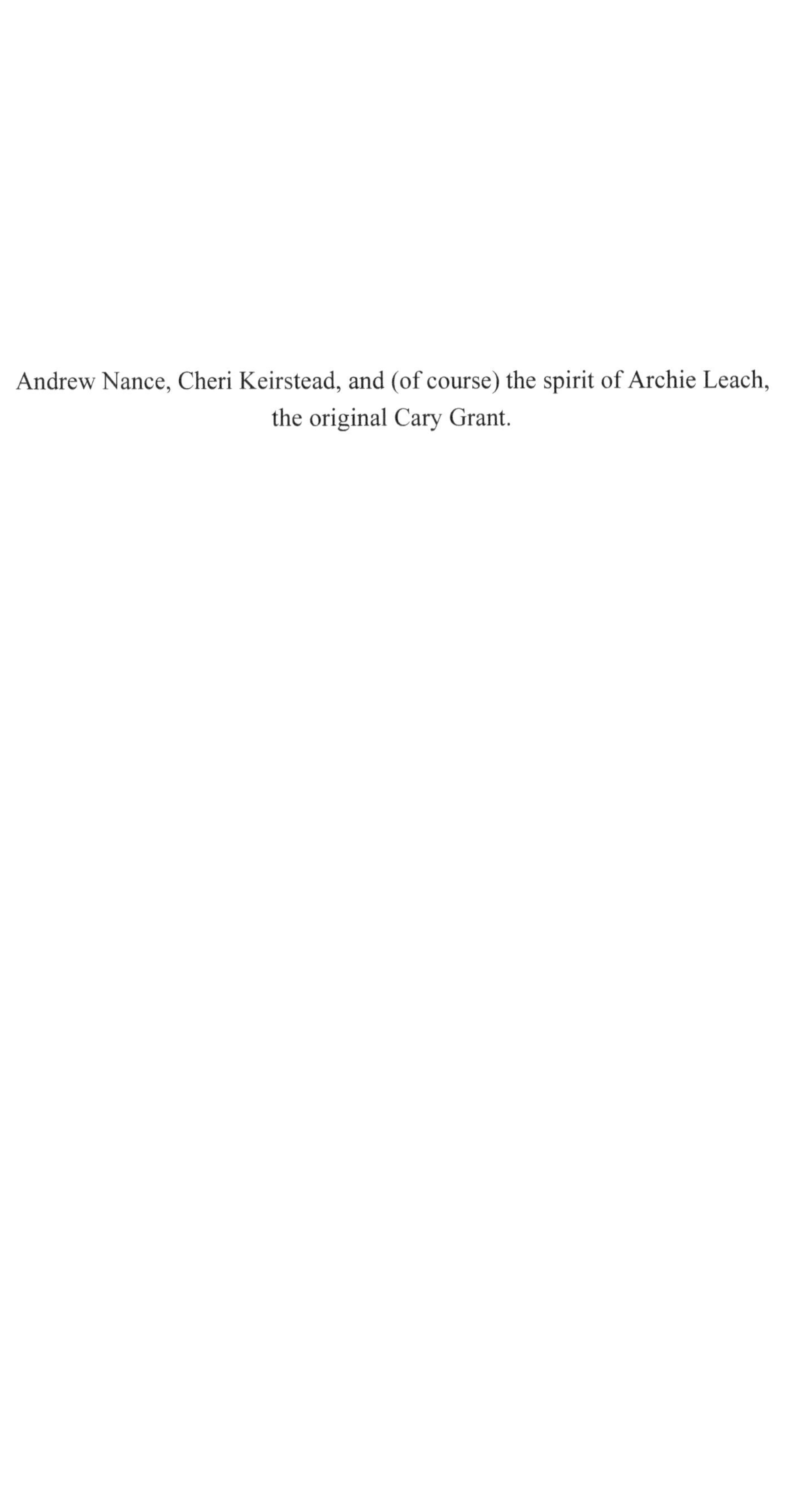

Andrew Nance, Cheri Keirstead, and (of course) the spirit of Archie Leach, the original Cary Grant.

Table of Contents

Chapter 1: Every Time a Bell Rings   11

Chapter 2: The Peer Review   16

Chapter 3: Meet George Dudley   24

Chapter 4: Thanksgiving Day   33

Chapter 5: Home Again   43

Chapter 6: Of All the Gin Joints   47

Chapter 7: George and Mary: Catching Up   51

Chapter 8: The Return of Archie Leach   57

Chapter 9: George and Mary: Sitting in a Tree   63

Chapter 10: The Matinee Idol   67

Chapter 11: On Set with Bradley Cooper   71

Chapter 12: Spielberg and Jennifer Lawrence   76

Chapter 13: My Fair Gentleman   85

Chapter 14: Tut, Tut, Tut   94

Chapter 15: I Think He's Got It   97

Chapter 16: Bradley Cooper—Take Two   102

Chapter 17: Happy Birthday, Oprah Winfrey   106

Chapter 18: The Heir Apparent   113

Chapter 19: Reporting In   117

Chapter 20: The Afterglow   121

Chapter 21: The Morning After   124

Chapter 22: New York State of Mind   134

Chapter 23: Till Death Do We Part. Or Whatever   142

Chapter 24: It's Valentine's Day… Again   154

Chapter 25: #Onhisass   161

Chapter 26: We're Getting the Old Band Back Together   167

Chapter 27: Everybody Loves Ryan   172

Chapter 28: At Least Someone Is Happy   183

Chapter 29: Can Chris Pratt Play First Base?   186

Chapter 30: Rainy Days and Mondays   192

Chapter 31: Divine Intervention—In Action   197

Chapter 32: ET Live at Jurassic Park   206

Chapter 33: Cary and Kay   211

Epilogue: The Man Who Wanted to Be Cary Grant   213

Chapter 1
Every Time a Bell Rings

He was enjoying his retirement. There was plenty to eat and drink (not that it was needed); there was music and parties every night; and the company was glorious. Everyone who was anybody was here. Well, mostly. There were a few who were missing, but that did not surprise anyone. Not anyone who knew them. When they were alive, that is.

So, when Clarence Odbody, Angel First Class, requested Cary Grant's presence at the big house, he could not refuse. Kay Kendall, his pretty personal assistant, held the door open as Cary Grant entered the office. Clarence's impressive wings, on full display, fluttered behind him, blowing papers off his desk. "Oh, so sorry, Ms. Kendall. I did it again. Still getting used to them."

"No problem, Mr. Odbody," Kay said, crawling on the floor of the grand corner office, picking up the sheets of paper. She placed them on Clarence's desk and used a copy of *Tom Sawyer* as a paperweight. She took a seat next to Clarence's desk, crossed her shapely legs, which were on generous display under her lavender pencil skirt, opened her small notepad, and waited, the picture of modesty.

"Mr. Grant. Mr. Grant," Clarence said taking Cary's hand in his. "Well, this is a great pleasure. A great pleasure indeed. Big fan. Oh, yes. Seen all your movies. Well, most anyway."

Cary nodded.

Clarence continued. "Yes, sir. Wait till I tell the wife. She will be so jealous."

Cary Grant looked at Kay Kendall and shrugged. He got used to this kind of reaction on Earth, but it always surprised him up here. "Well, enough of that; have a seat," Clarence said checking his wristwatch. "Right on time. A good start. And how are you this fine and glorious morning, Mr. Grant?"

"Please call me Cary. Very good, thank you, Clarence," Cary replied. "Though I usually don't get up this early anymore, you know."

"Yes, yes I know. You were more of a night owl in your day, eh?" he said, with a chuckle.

"Old habits, you know," Cary said and sat down in the very plush chair across from Clarence's large mahogany desk.

Clarence Odbody slipped on a pair of reading glasses he kept around his neck with a fine-linked white gold chain and picked up a plain manila folder. Cary could easily see his name handwritten on it in a beautiful Florentine script.

"Not a very thick folder, is it?" he asked.

"What's that? Oh, tut-tut-tut, this isn't your life story, Cary," he explained. "It's only a Class D directive. Came in last night from 'you-know-who'." He looked over the top of the folder and added, "He likes to keep his hand in." Clarence folded his wings in, crossed in front of Cary, and said, "We usually assign an intern to deal with these, but it appears this one concerns you directly."

"Me? What did I do?" Cary asked, alarmed that God wrote a memo about him.

"Well, it's not 'you' exactly, more your…" he paused and waved his fingers searching for the right word, "your legacy. You know that persona you created when you were on Earth? Well, it still resonates with people down there, even after all these years."

"That's the truth," Miss Kendall said crossing her legs.

"Please, Miss Kendall, do try to control yourself," Clarence said.

"Sorry, sir," Kay Kendall said, slowly recrossing her legs. She looked directly at Cary, hooked a loose strand of her dark brown hair, and leisurely placed it behind her ear. *Oh, I may be dead, but I know that look*, Cary thought.

The phone on Clarence's desk rang.

"Oh, oh!" Clarence clapped and smiling said, "Someone just got their wings."

"It's just the phone, sir," Kay said.

"I know it's the phone," he said, picking up the receiver. "Hello?"

"He does that every time someone calls," Kay whispered to Cary. "When he's having a bad day, I'll call him from my office. Cheers him right up."

"Yes, sir. He's here now," Clarence said into the phone. "I know, sir. Top priority. And God bless you too."

Clarence sat down. He looked at Cary and said, "You see? That was Saint Peter. He never calls this early. This is his fishing time. So I hope you are beginning to see how important this is to everyone up here."

"I'm beginning to see the light, sir," Cary quipped.

"How's that? Oh, another joke. Very good, now listen. It seems there is someone on Earth who is thinking seriously of changing his assigned plan," Clarence said seriously. He picked up the folder. "It says here, he has been thinking about it for years, most of his life actually, ever since he saw one of your old movies."

"Probably *To Catch a Thief*," Kay Kendall added, recrossing her legs a third time.

"No. Not that one," Clarence said. "We showed that one on movie night a few years ago, but Michael made us turn it off. Gave the wrong message you know. Glorified criminal and all," he said primly, "and the 's-e-x' scene," he spelled out slowly. "Couldn't very well show that, you know," he said and began chuckling to himself.

"Yes, I totally understand," Cary said. "Then which one was it?"

Clarence scanned the sheet again and then said, "*Monkey Business*. Oh, yes that one. With Ginger Rodgers. What a sweet lady. Runs the Arthur Murray Academy up here. Not that she did much dancing in that one. Funny, though." Kay Kendall audibly scoffed.

"Not a fan?" Cary said.

"I prefer the Hitchcock ones," she said leaning closer. "*To Catch a Thief. North by Northwest. Notorious,*" she said the last one overly annunciating every syllable, before licking her lips.

"Miss Kendall," Clarence said sharply, admonishing her. "If you can't control yourself, you're going to have to wait outside."

"Sorry, sir," she said meekly. "I apologize Mr. Grant." Cary Grant just smiled, used to it.

"And that is why I called you in, Cary. It appears," he consulted the folder again. "This, Mr. George Dudley, wants to be you. He is very unhappy with his life and believes if he could just be like 'Cary Grant', all his problems would go away."

"Well, maybe the world needs a new Cary Grant," Cary said, flashing his hundred-watt smile.

"Do you think this is funny, Cary?" Clarence Odbody said dropping the folder. "Do you think I rearranged my entire morning to banter jokes with you?"

"Clarence, I'm sorry. I just don't understand what the problem is."

Clarence held up a finger to silence him then crossed the room to a tall, plain white filing cabinet. He opened the top drawer and extracted a two-inch thick folder, wrapped with a large rubber band to keep its contents from spilling out.

"Do you know what this is?" he said, dramatically.

"My movie reviews?" Cary said.

"No, Cary, this is a list of every man currently alive on planet Earth who wishes daily that they were you," Clarence said seriously.

Cary looked at the single folder and said, "Well, that doesn't look like that many."

"This is only the letter A—Aaron through Adams," Clarence shouted and thrust the folder back into the cabinet and banged it closed.

"Sir," Kay Kendall said. "Your blood pressure."

Clarence took a deep breath and tried to regain his composure. "Sorry. Sorry," he said and made his way back to his chair. "You see Cary, this is becoming a—Well, he doesn't like it when we use the P word. *'There are no Problems, Clarence, only Opportunities'*. He's always spouting off axioms like that lately."

"That's God's truth," Kay Kendall agreed. Then she laughed at her own joke. Clarence silenced her with a withering look. "I will not warn you again, young lady."

She did not reply, but Cary saw that the smirk remained on her lips. He smiled too.

"I'm sorry, Clarence," Cary asked "But I still don't understand why you called me in this morning. What is it exactly you want me to do?"

"Do?" Clarence said, quickly rising from his chair. "Do? I want you to stop them."

"Stop them, sir."

"Yes. Stop them. Stop them from wanting to be you! They are diverting from His plan. We can't have everyone down there just going off half-cocked with their own ideas. And, before you protest, I do not mean free will. That is a given. No, they can have all the free will they want; that's what makes life exciting. What I am trying to fix is their obsession with you. This thing you created. Oh, you know what I mean."

"I do, sir," Cary said, "but I repeat, what exactly do you want me to do about it?"

"What I need you to do is go down there and observe Mr. George Dudley for, oh let's say, six months, that should do it. Then give me a report."

"A report?"

"Yes. A report. Follow him around. Watch him carefully. But just watch," he said, raising a finger in warning. "No interference. You'll be tempted, right, Miss Kendall? But that must be avoided at all costs. We've had some bad episodes over the years, trust me, I know from personal experience." He shared a knowing look with Kay Kendall, then cleared his throat, and continued. "The Man upstairs has laid down the law. Watch but do not touch. Got it? Good. Just observe, dear boy, then write down what George Dudley does. Find out why he wants to be you," Clarence concluded. "300 pages should do. Double spaced."

"Excuse me," Cary objected, "but did you say three hundred? That's not a report. That's a book!"

"Exactly. In a three-ring binder. For easy storage," Clarence said smiling.

"But sir, I've never even written a recipe before, much less a book."

"Oh, recipes are easy, Cary. Just follow the instructions. Do you need help with one? I make a wonderful chicken cacciatore."

"Um, no sir. But this book report…"

"Oh, don't worry. I'm not going to just throw you off a bridge alone. Miss Kendall will help. She's done this thing before. She has everything you'll need," Clarence said moving to his door and opening it. "Now get cracking. No time like the present. Goodbye, Cary. Have a blessed day."

Chapter 2
The Peer Review

"What the fudge was that?" Cary said when they were outside.

"Ah… Ah… Ah." Kay chastened him. "Watch that. No cursing here."

"Kay, I did not sign up for this," he said raising his voice. "I'm supposed to be relaxing. Enjoying the fruits of my labor."

"You didn't sign up for anything, Cary. You lived; you died; and now you're here. Not a lot of time for signing anything," she said. "Besides, this should be right up your alley. You played an angel before. *The Bishop's Wife.* Remember? I loved that movie. I wish I were in it."

"I've lived my life, Kay. I'm finished," Cary said. "All I want to do now is play volleyball with Gary Cooper, cards with Bogey and swim with Marilyn and Esther."

"Everything doesn't stop when you die, Cary. You must know that by now," she said, trying to console him. "Running the world is a full-time job. There's a lot of balls in the air to deal with, you know, and I don't just mean the planets," she laughed. "Get it? Balls in the air? Planets?"

"You really do find yourself amusing don't you, Kay?" Cary said, smiling.

"I may not have been in as many movies as you, Mr. Movie Star, but I was very funny in all of them," she said, her hands on her hips.

"I know, Kay. I am sorry. But this is all just happening so fast. And I haven't had breakfast yet."

"Here's a donut. I stole it off his desk. Now, you're going to need this." She handed him a thick folder. "This is George Dudley's file. You should read up on him before you make contact."

"Contact?"

"That's probably not the best word for it. Observe is more accurate," she said. "But just observe. You must remember that, Cary. Trust me on this."

He watched her carefully and then asked. "What was Clarence talking about? What bad experience was he referring to? That George Bailey business?"

"Hush," she said alarmed, looking around. "Not here." Then she placed her hand gently on his arm. "Listen, Cary, I've done about ten of these. It's really no big deal."

"Ten?" he said, raising an eyebrow.

"Observations. But it'll be easier to show you than tell you." She locked his arm with hers. "Tell you what, let's go to the peer review now, and I'll give you the tour."

"Lead on, Gunga Din," he said.

She laughed and said in a passable Indian accent, "Right this way, Sahib."

The peer review was in a plain concrete block house. You could pass it by a thousand times and never notice it. "Here we are."

She opened the wooden door and entered. The lights came on automatically. The inside was as plain as the exterior. Two chairs stood in the middle of the room about the size of a grade school classroom. The chairs resembled old barber shop chairs. In front of them was a low console with scores of buttons, switches, and levers. Above the console was a large 50-inch TV screen.

"Have a seat," she said, noticing his wide-eyed expression. "Don't be a scaredy cat." He never liked mechanical things, but she piqued his pride, so he sat.

"Now put this on while I calibrate this thing." She handed him a hat and visor.

"Wait a minute," he said, holding the thing in my hands. "This looks like a motorcycle helmet."

She stopped fiddling with the knobs and looked closely at the helmet. She tilted her head to the side and started to nod. "Funny. I never noticed that before. But we are not riding bikes, old boy; we are traveling much faster and much farther."

He put the helmet on and looked through the gray-tinted visor. Kay put on a similar helmet and took the chair next to him.

"You're going on this ride too?"

"The first time is usually a bit bumpy," she said, and he heard her clearly through speakers implanted inside the helmet. "Can you hear me, okay?"

"Loud and clear."

"Good, but remember, the microphone is overly sensitive. So try not to scream too loud."

Cary was about to reply when he was suddenly propelled like a missile into a black void. There was no wind, but he felt the wind. There was no sound, but he heard hurricanes. There was no light, but his eyes were seared. His skin tingled and then burned. He screamed.

And, as quickly as it began, it stopped.

He was still in blackness, and he floated. He could feel the helmet on his head and the chair under his bum but nothing else. His stomach gurgled, and he heard Kay in his ear.

"Don't throw up," she said.

Cary took a deep breath, held it, waited until his stomach settled, and then let it out slowly.

"Sorry about the scream," he said, trying to regain his sea legs.

"I was ready for it. I muted you. Now tell me what you see."

"See? I see nothing; it's all black," but as soon as he spoke the words, a dusky cloud passed in front of him, like thick smoke, dark, gray, and swirling.

"See the smoke?" Kay asked.

"Yes. What is it?"

"The veil dear," Kay said blissfully. "It still gets me every time. Now wait. It will start to blow away in a moment."

"This is like an expensive special effect. Hitch would love this," he said, marveling as a surge of color infused the cloud: yellows and burnt orange, and there was a hint of cyan.

"Do you see any buildings yet?" Kay Kendall asked.

"Yes, an entire street actually. High rises. Just below me. I could walk on their roofs. This is marvelous," he said.

"Now focus, Cary. Concentrate, then say his name out loud."

The wonder of it all had taken him and he wanted to float in it forever. *What was Kay talking about? Say what name? How can I turn her off? She's distracting me.*

"Cary. CARY!"

"What? Stop screaming. You hurt my ears."

"You need to say his name, Cary. Right now," Kay Kendall said. "Before we lose the connection."

Something is... wrong. That sounded like Kay, he thought, but he could barely hear her. "Kay. Kay! What name? Where am I? What is happening?"

The apartment buildings were obscured again; a silvery fog had formed; and he felt a tug in his gut like someone had wrapped a rope around his insides and was pulling him backward.

"Cary. Hurry. Say his name."

Then it came to him. Through the fog and the clouds. The name, 20 feet high, made of incandescent lights, emblazoned on a theater marquee.

"George Dudley!" he shouted, and like a Cecil B DeMille epic, the clouds parted, the sun was ablaze, and a face instantly filled his vision, so close he could see specks of amber in the eyes.

"Pull back," Kay said clearly. "Pull back before he sees you!"

"Sees me?" Her voice filled his helmet and equilibrium returned. Or at least as much as could be hoped for in a spiritual void. "What do you mean, see me? You said we were just going to observe?"

"It's my own personal theory," she said quickly. "My last time inside I got so close to my subject. I could have sworn she sensed me. Her eyes opened wide, and she took a swipe at me. It was very disturbing. When I pulled back, all was fine, but for just a minute there..."

Cary pulled further away from George Dudley and let him complete his morning shave in peace.

"Well, that was, totally unexpected," he said.

"Yea, the first time is always a gas," Kay Kendall said, her laugh returning. "We'll just make this a short jump today, okay? So here's what we're going to do. Pull back a little more." He pulled back another twelve inches.

"A little more, Cary. Keep going. That's good. Little more. Perfect."

He was about twenty-five feet away from Mr. Dudley, now. Commonly known as a wide shot in his previous life.

"What do you see?" she said into his ear.

"I see a man shaving his face with an electric razor."

"Good. What else?"

This was amazing. He felt like the cameraman 'and' the camera, all wrapped up in one. He could zoom in with thought and dolly or track just by moving his eyes. He could even hover or slip underneath if he wanted.

"What did you say, dear?" Cary said.

"What else do you see?" she said, louder this time, annunciating each word slowly.

"Everything. And in Panavision!" he said, the wonder back in his voice.

"Try to concentrate, Cary. It's easy to get caught up in the big picture. You need to focus on George Dudley, and only George Dudley; otherwise, your point of view will keep bouncing around so much you'll get dizzy and confused. But if you keep George Dudley's name, and only his name in your head, you will see everything he sees, hear everything he hears, and believe it or not, hear what he thinks."

"I'll hear his thoughts too?" Cary said, incredulous.

"It takes a little practice to filter out the nonsense, the mind is an amazing thing, but yes, you'll be able to hear what George Dudley is thinking. You will know everything he knows. The whole point of this exercise is to determine motivation. Why does he want to be you? Hearing his thoughts will make that easier."

Cary was still grappling with it all when he heard a voice inside his head.

"What did you say, Kay?"

"I'd didn't say anything," Kay said. "Hey, I think you just made contact. Focus. What's he thinking?"

The voice he heard was more like a sequence of musical notes, up and down the scale in a low baritone. He could not make it out, but somehow, he knew they were words. Hundreds. Thousands of words flying around, a constant jumble.

"Get anything yet?" she prodded.

"Lots of noise. Like static but, pleasant. There's meaning just outside my… wait… wait a minute, it's getting clearer. Murdoch? And Moscow? No, not Moscow, Moskowitz. Yes, that's it. Bobby Moskowitz. And a… meeting… this morning… He's worried about something." Chills went through Cary's body. "This is amazing, Kay. It's like listening to a Shakespearean monologue."

"That's good, Cary. Now, I want you to do one more thing before we leave."

"Leave? Why leave? We just got here."

"First time is always overload, Cary. You need time to process," she said. "But one last thing. Reach out with your hands. Can you feel the console?"

He did as she asked and touched the table in front of him.

"Can you feel the large lever on the right?"

"Um… yes. It's right here." It was within easy reach and fit comfortably in his hand.

"That's your recording switch. When you want to start recording, just pull it toward you. When finished, push it back. I'll show you how to review, rewind, and store the memories later. Trust me. You'll never remember it all. This will help you understand what's going on with Mr. George Dudley."

"Got it," he said.

"Okay. That's enough for the first time. Ready to go back?" she said, and he felt her hand on his arm.

"Yes, but how do we…" And, before he could finish the thought, they were back in the Spartan room.

"Oh, returning is much easier," he said, gratefully.

"Yes, it's just like Dorothy clicking her heels. Just think 'There's no place like home', and you'll return instantly."

They removed their helmets, and she spent the next half hour showing him how to operate the console. When she was satisfied, he could work it by himself, she said. "Well done, Cary dear. Most people never hear thoughts their first time."

He nodded his thanks, but then he looked hard at her. "Tell me what happened with Clarence."

"Oh, that." She sat back down in the chair and took a deep breath. "You must never repeat this to anyone. Only four people know about this. It took some serious divine power to clean things up."

"Well, you've got my attention now. Give."

She looked around the room and said, "It all started here. St. Peter showed Clarence, who was an Angel third class back then before he got his wings, how the peer review worked. He showed him this Bailey guy's life and instructed Clarence to go down and help him."

"I know the story, Kay. Heck, they made a movie about it down there. People watch it every Christmas."

She looked down at her hands, took another breath, and said, "Yes, but that was not the whole story. What you saw was the cleanup."

"Clean up? What happened, Kay?"

"St. Peter sent another angel down to help Bailey before Clarence. Someone a bit more, how should I say this… creative?" She was lost in thought again, and Cary waited patiently.

"You see this other angel decided, on his own mind you, that the best solution to George Bailey's problem was to make him rich. So, when he found him on the bridge planning suicide, he put a million dollars in his bank account." She snapped her fingers. "Poof. Just like that. Then he returned here. Turned in his report and went back to whatever he was doing before."

"Oh my."

"Oh my indeed. The consequences were immediate. The bank examiner found the money."

"George had no explanation. The IRS got involved. Bailey was arrested and thrown in jail. His uncle Billy got drunk and hit a kid with his car. His wife and kids were left destitute. The bank bought out his Building and Loan. People were thrown out of their homes. And on and on and on. You see Cary? The consequences of interference didn't affect just one person. It destroyed an entire town."

"I had no idea," Cary said.

"So a reset was ordered. Only the third in history. But, after it was done, Bailey's problem still remained, so St. Peter chose the simplest, kindest angel to help Bailey. That was Clarence. And he did. The 'see your life if you were never born' gambit was just the ticket. Bailey didn't kill himself. He went home and discovered God does move in mysterious ways. But all of this is way above my pay grade. Just remember, no interference. You have no idea what the consequences would bring."

"No interference," Cary said, nodding agreement. "Got it."

She got up from the chair and took his shoulders in her hands. "I think you will be able to start tomorrow. Get a good rest, and don't get drunk tonight, hangovers are counterproductive, trust me. I know. From personal experience."

"Good advice."

He walked her back to her home. She lived on the second floor of a lovely high-rise condo on a beach. "I'll meet you at the peer review tomorrow morning to set you up and answer any questions that you might think of tonight. Okay?"

He took her hand and kissed it gallantly, "You were a marvelous instructor. What can I ever do to repay you?"

She moved closer again and said in her best Mae West, "Why don't you come up and see me?"

"I believe I will," and he took her in his arms.

Kay Kendall accompanied Cary Grant three more times (in the peer review and her bedroom) before she felt he was ready to solo. He adjusted the console, donned his metal hat, and gave the start lever a confident pull. *George Dudley, here I come*, he thought. And started recording.

Chapter 3
Meet George Dudley

REPORT #1

He had a nice face. Oval with thick eyebrows, full lips, and squinty eyes. But that was before he put on his glasses, which were square and black, like something Jack Benny used to wear in the 1950s. His skin was pale, and his brown hair needed a cut or at least a nice trim. It hung unfashionably long over his collar, curled out around his ears like an extra pair, and he was constantly pushing a handful out of his face. He did it so often, and unconsciously, along with pushing his glasses back up his nose, that they had become afflictions, not just habits.

His eyes, however, were a warm shade of brown, and when he would look up, which he rarely did, preferring to perennially search the ground for God knows what, they were quite striking. But the feature that people noticed the most when they first met Mr. George Dudley was his smile. It was dazzling. Perfectly white even teeth, broad and friendly with a hint of dimples. He had one of those smiles that when fully engaged used the entire face, eyes, and cheeks, even his skin seemed to shine a bit. But he rarely smiled these days, preferring to keep his lips together, grinning or smirking. Life had not been good for George Dudley. Not horrible, but not very good either, just average.

When he moved to New York nearly twenty years ago, he was ready to set the world on fire. His writing style was praised by editors and readers alike, a simple, clear style that found the truth beneath the rhetoric. He worked his way up from beat reporter to lead financial writer by the time he was twenty-nine. But his big break happened when he caught the scent of a major new player making waves and money on Wall Street. His interview with Bobby Moskowitz launched him into the big time. And his cover story when

Moskowitz was named 'Forbes Man of the Year' brought accolades, an overdue raise, and major writing awards.

Fame and fortune brought many things to George Dudley except the two things he always desperately wanted, lasting respect and happiness. There was some respect after the article came out, but it didn't last. Everyone was waiting for the next big thing, but George never found it. And there was happiness at home with Darcy; the new upper east side apartment made her extremely happy, especially when she would throw a party, which she did with more and more frequency, but that happiness faded too into complacency. They attributed it to a natural evolution of marriage. But George knew she didn't look at him the same way anymore and she had lost respect for him that hurt more than the regular rebuffs in the bedroom.

He pulled open the small utility drawer next to the sink. It contained his dental floss, an extra toothbrush, anti-itch cream, an unused Bic razor, and a box of band-aids. Underneath was a heavily creased black and white photo. He unfolded it and stuck one end into the edge of the mirror. Looking back at him was a headshot of a young Cary Grant, one of the many studio publicity stills Hollywood used back in the late 40s. His head was tilted to one side; his black hair was perfectly trimmed; his smile was big and dazzling; and his eyes were staring right at George.

"Good morning, Cary," George said. His eyes flicked to the side to take in his own reflection next to the photograph, and he flashed his own big smile.

"Good morning, George. How are you, my boy?"

George's eyes went back and forth between the photo and his own image trying to imitate Cary's smile exactly. "I feel marvelous, old boy," George said.

Dudley was startled by a loud banging on the bathroom door.

"George," came a high-pitched female voice from the other side of the door. "Are you going to be much longer? Your breakfast is getting cold."

"Just a second, Darcy," he said, folding the photo and slipping it back into the drawer. "Can't rush perfection."

"Oh, God, George. No jokes this early, I truly can't handle it," Darcy Dudley said before walking back to the kitchen.

He scrutinized himself one last time in the mirror and picked up a hairbrush but then shrugged, satisfied with the overall look. And then he displayed that Cary Grant smile before hiding it away, slopping his shoulders and shuffling out to face the world.

"Don't slouch dear," Darcy said, glancing up from the magazine she was reading as Dudley entered the kitchen. "I tell you that every day. Please sit, your eggs are cold."

She was an attractive woman, in a sharp, magazine fashion ad way. Even at 7 am, she was already put together and polished. Her shoulder-length blondish white hair was pulled up and away from her face; her cheeks were sunken; and her neck stuck out of the collar of her turtleneck, cashmere sweater as if it were two sizes too small. Her porcelain skin was flawless, and her makeup was minimal but expertly applied. She was a totally made-up woman. Even her voice was made up, hiding the Mississippi drawl of her youth with an affectatious faux-British lilt she picked up by watching too many hours of *Downton Abbey*.

"The children will be here tomorrow. Decey says she has news," Darcy said, resuming her reading.

"Is she bringing, him?" Dudley asked, poking at the scrambled eggs on his plate.

"He has a name, George." Then she lowered the magazine and said in excited hushed tones, "I think Decey and Gabriel are going to have a baby. Isn't that wonderful?"

"What do you mean, you think? Didn't she call you when she found out?"

"I think she wanted to make a special announcement at Thanksgiving dinner tomorrow. She does love her theatrics. You of all people should be able to appreciate that," Darcy said. "She must have gotten it from you."

"And the sarcasm and willfulness she got from you," he mumbled as he took a bite of toast.

"What was that dear?" Darcy asked from across the breakfast table.

"Hmm? What?" Dudley mumbled. "I didn't say anything."

She rolled her eyes and then continued. "Paulie will be here at noon. Alone, naturally. And Decey said they'll arrive no later than two, so we'll eat then. But then they have to rush off again for a late party at the Stanton's."

"Oh joy," he said. "I'll rearrange my schedule to make sure I can squeeze them in."

"Now don't be smart dear. You know how hard she's trying. Gabriel's parents were not thrilled with their son's choice for a bride, so she's bending over backward to get on their good side. She spends almost all her free time with Mrs. Stanton now. I hardly ever see her."

"I guess if I had won the Pulitzer instead of just being nominated that would have won them over, huh?"

Darcy Dudley put down her magazine and stared at him. "It amazes me George how you make every situation about you. That was five years ago. And you were not nominated; your name was suggested to the nominating committee."

"Thanks for reminding me, dear," he said, dropping his uneaten eggs into the trash.

"I'm sorry, dear. That was uncalled for. You should have been nominated. Your article on Bobby Moskowitz should have won you the Pulitzer. It was beautifully written. But what have you done since? It's as if that loss took all the fire out of you. I miss that fire," she said sincerely.

"I've written things since then," he said. "Better things."

"Really George? Like what, the emerging Bitcoin trend, which you predicted was a passing fad, or that piece you did on the President's son, which resulted in a million-dollar lawsuit."

"That was not my fault. One of my sources lied to me. He was a plant by a political rival."

"Or this," she said sliding the magazine down to his side of the table. "You actually wrote a glowing obituary for Moskowitz?"

"He was a great man, in his day," Dudley said, defensively.

"He ripped off billions of dollars from his investors, George. And his friends. Like us!" she said, her voice rising.

"He helped me get my start," he said weakly. "You remember that."

"I do, George," she said, not unkindly, "Then he used you like his little bitch for fifteen years to prop up his own business. Which turned out to be the biggest Ponzi scheme since Madoff."

"He could be very charming, sometimes."

"How did Elliott even allow you to get that obit published?" Darcy marveled. "In the Sunday Times no less?"

"He was out last week. I don't think he saw it," Dudley said, sliding the magazine back toward his wife. "Betty just rubber-stamped it like she does all my stuff."

"Betty Marsh is a sweet old lady, George, but a lousy assistant editor," she said picking up the *Times Magazine* again. "This is going to piss off a lot of people, George," she said, genuinely worried.

Dudley's shoulders slumped even further, threatening to dip his tie into his coffee. "I gotta go. I don't want to be late for work. Murdoch is coming in."

"Rupert Murdoch? The owner? In person?" Darcy cried. "Oh, George. Are you worried?"

"He's not coming to see me," he said slipping on his suit jacket. "He doesn't even know I exist. And, if he was going to fire me, he would have sent an email, certainly not in person. I think there's a board meeting or something today." He opened the front door and picked up his briefcase. "Is there anything you need me to pick up tonight on the way home?"

From behind the magazine, she said, "A pumpkin pie. You know how much Paulie loves pumpkin pie on Thanksgiving."

"I like it too," George mumbled, as he dragged himself out of the overly expensive apartment on the Upper Eastside of Manhattan. It was not even 7:15 am yet, and he was already exhausted. It was going to be a long day.

But, as soon as he saw Fasir, the night security guard, his spirits rose. Fasir was leaning on the edge of his small desk by the lobby front entrance, a cup of coffee in one hand and a copy of the *Times Magazine* in his left. He was waving it when Dudley came out of the elevator.

"You keep writing stuff like this, Mr. Dudley. You're gonna end up wearing cement galoshes," he said laughing.

"Listen Fezziwig, I have to take that shit from the wife, but not some rent-a-cop wasting away his golden years in some gilded lobby," Dudley said in his best Bogart imitation.

Fasir smiled and hid behind his magazine, "Don't plug me, Bogie. I'm just repeating what the fat man told me."

Dudley pulled the magazine away from his face and said, "I'll let it slide this time, flatfoot, but you better watch your step or you're gonna get a fat lip."

Fasir raised his coffee cup and said with a wink, "Well, here's looking at you kid."

Dudley laughed and just before he left the lobby he said, "You know copper, I think this is the beginning of a beautiful friendship."

He could hear Fasir laughing as Dudley stepped out onto the busy sidewalk. He turned right toward the subway station, used his metro pass at the turn style, and soon after was speeding downtown to his office. The train was crowded, but he managed to find a seat. He placed his briefcase on his lap, opened it, and pulled out a hard-backed copy of *Evenings with Cary Grant* by Nancy Nelson.

Twenty minutes later, Dudley was in his office, looking at his computer. His phone rang, and he picked it up. "Mr. Moore would like to see you, Mr. Dudley," Betty Marsh said.

"Right now, Betty?" George said surprised.

"Yes, sir. They are waiting for you." She hung up.

They? George thought as he took the elevator up to the twenty-fifth floor. *Damn. It's got to be Murdoch. Okay, George. Just be cool. What's the worst that could happen?*

"Go right in," Betty said as George came off the elevator.

"Have a seat, George," Elliott Moore said immediately. He was an elegant man of fifty. He had worked for the BBC for twelve years before Murdoch offered him the New York job. He was professional, polished, and shrewd. He sat behind his enormous desk, which he consciously used to intimidate people. Betty Marsh knew that he had the legs lowered on the guest chairs, so people had to look up at him.

"Tell me what the hell you were thinking, George?" Elliott asked, pointing at the *Times Magazine* on his desk between them.

"I didn't think they'd put it in the Sunday edition, Elliott," George Dudley said.

"Not just the Sunday edition, Dudley," a new voice boomed from behind him, "they put him on the fucking cover!" This last explosion was followed by a half dozen copies of the magazine being thrown at Dudley's head.

"Mr. Murdoch," Dudley stammered, standing up. "I… good morning, sir."

"Oh, stop that shit and sit down," he barked. "What the hell happened, Elliott?"

"As I explained earlier sir, I was…" Elliott began.

"I know 'out of town'." Murdoch finished, shoeing him away from his desk and seating himself in Elliott's chair. He turned his gaze back to George, who was frozen in his chair.

"Listen, Mr. Murdoch…," George started, but Murdoch cut him off with a wave of his hand.

"There's really nothing to say, Dudley. You said it all in here," he said touching the face of Bobby Moskowitz on the desk in front of him. "Damn it, George, how could you write that shit?"

Dudley tensed up at this. "There is not a single false statement in that article, sir," he said with real passion.

"I don't give a fuck about facts," Murdoch screamed. "You make it sound like he was J.P. Morgan, Carnegie Mellon, and Rockefeller all rolled up into one."

"Well, he was responsible for…" Dudley tried again to defend himself.

A frustrated Murdoch stood up quickly. Elliott's chair went crashing to the floor. "Bobby Moskowitz was 'responsible' for stealing ten million dollars from me," he ranted. "And you, my employee, in my own fucking magazine write him a glowing obituary. I hope someone writes me an obituary like that when I go." Then he turned his full gaze back to Dudley and said, "But it won't be you, Dudley. You're fired."

"Rupert, I think…" Elliott tried to interject, but Murdoch turned his blazing eyes on him too.

"Or you either, Elliott. I want you both out of the building by noon."

With that, he headed to the door. "I left papers for you to sign with Mrs. Marsh. It's a generous severance package, considering. But there's a non-compete clause in there too. Don't violate it. I'd hate to have to kill you guys." With that, he walked out and slammed the door.

Elliott stared out his window. "I should have stayed in the Bahamas," he said blithely. "At least we had a good run, eh George?"

"You're taking this awfully well," Dudley said.

"Oh, Georgie, I was sending my resume out ten minutes after I read your article. You can't tell me you're surprised?"

"Well, I guess I didn't think it through."

Elliot laughed. "Same old George. Ah, well, I think I'll hop back over the pond to Bristol. Live the life of the gentry. Either that or go back to television. What about you?"

"Besides suicide, I don't know Elliott. Either I kill myself now or Darcy will do it for me when I get home," Dudley said.

"Oh, buck up, old boy, you'll bounce back. You're young yet," he said, then looking closely at George, said. "What are you, fifty?"

"I'm forty-two, Elliott," Dudley said.

"Really," Elliott said, genuinely surprised. "You look much older."

"And the hits just keep coming," Dudley said to himself. He stood up and without, even bothering to say goodbye, he left Elliott's office, took the thick

9 × 12 envelope Betty Marsh was holding out for him, and headed to the elevator.

"Hey, Georgie, watch where you're going," a young man said as Dudley entered the elevator. Dudley's head was down, and he bumped into Todd Mooney, a rising star in the editorial division. George's glasses fell to the carpet. "Better fix that prescription," Todd said as Dudley leaned over to pick them up. He gave Dudley a mean little push as he stepped out of the elevator.

Dudley stumbled and had to hold out a hand to not fall to the ground.

The commotion drew a crowd, and people stuck their heads out of nearby offices, laughing.

Dudley could hear a dozen or more hushed choruses of 'Loser'.

"Why is he still here?" and "Puke emoji. Puke emoji."

"Hey, Mooney, what's the big deal?" Dudley called out, but the doors had closed, and the two young women on the elevator stared at him.

"Who ya talkin' to Mr. D?" the shorter of the two ladies said in a heavy New Jersey accent.

"What? Oh, good morning Miss Jamison. I was talking to Mr…" But looking around, Dudley realized Mooney was not there.

"He must be talking to Harvey," the taller girl said.

"Who's Harvey, Caroline?" Miss Jamison said, puzzled.

"You know, Harvey. The six-foot invisible rabbit," Caroline continued. "From that movie?"

"With Jimmy Stewart and Josephine Hull. 1950," Dudley said automatically. "Miss Hull won an academy award for her performance. The movie was based on Darcy Chase's 1944 play of the same name. It won a Pulitzer Prize for Drama the following year."

Caroline and Miss Jamison stared at Dudley, then broke into laughter. "Oh, my God," Miss Jamison bawled. "You are such a nerd mobile, Mr. D."

"With a capital N," Caroline added, and they continued to laugh as the doors opened and they exited the elevator. "What a moron that guy is. And can you believe those glasses? He looks like Charles Nelson Reilly."

"Who's that?" Miss Jamison said, but before Caroline could reply, the doors had closed.

George Dudley just stood there and took it, a practiced, forced grin on his face. He waved dismissively to no one in particular, and when the elevator stopped at the basement level, he shambled down the hallway to the mail room.

"Hi, Cameron."

"Hey, Mr. Dudley. How are things in the nosebleed section?"

"Could be better," he said forcing a smile. "Can I get a couple of sturdy boxes? Need to move some things."

"Sure thing," Cameron Rogers said and then added, "Hey, I read your article in the Times yesterday. You're such a good writer. I couldn't put it down."

"Thanks, Cameron. Can I use you as a reference?"

"What?"

"Nothing, son. Thanks for the boxes. See you later." *Or not*, he thought.

When he was back in his office, he quickly packed up his personal items, including the signed, 8 × 10 framed photo he had of Cary Grant and Ingrid Bergman from *Indiscreet.*

"Why do people have to be so mean?" he said to the photo. *What would you do?*

REFLECTIONS ON REPORT #1

I'd have punched them in the nose, Dudley old boy. You're well rid of those losers.

Chapter 4
Thanksgiving Day

"George? Your mother's on the phone," Darcy called from the kitchen. She was checking the turkey inside the oven. Dudley entered, tucking in his polo shirt.

"If you keep opening the oven babe, it will never cook," he said.

"Oh, shut up. Is that what you're going to wear? Here, talk to your mom. I'll get your blue sweater," she said handing him the phone.

"Hi, mom. How are you?"

"Happy Thanksgiving, Georgie," his mother said. Dudley walked into the living room, picked up the TV remote, and turned on the TV. He muted the sound. The Jets were playing The Bears.

"Happy Thanksgiving, mom. What's up? We're about to sit down and eat. Decey should be here any minute now."

"I won't keep you dear," she said. "I just wanted to hear your voice. You know how much I miss all of you, especially on Thanksgiving. It was one of your father's favorite holidays."

A memory surfaced in Dudley's mind of a dining room table in a small home, overcrowded with bowls of carrot salad, stuffing, coleslaw, and of course a large butterball turkey dominating the center. Six people, two adults, and four young children sat around the table laughing, talking, and reaching over each other to grab bowls and fill their plates to overflowing. It was a happy time. *The past usually is*, Dudley thought.

"Minc too, mom. Is Connie coming over later?" he asked.

"Your sister has already been here and gone, Georgie. I am babysitting the twins. She had to show a home. On Thanksgiving," she said, shaking her head.

"Well, she is a single mother trying to make a living, mom. Jeffrey was a real prick."

"Language Georgie," she said reflexively. "Anyway, I must go. Just wanted to say hi. I miss you. You should visit more."

"I will, mom. Now that the kids have moved out, I'll hopefully have more free time," Dudley said and suddenly felt anxious knowing he had lots of free time now.

"Give my love to your family, Georgie," Elsie Dudley said.

"Bye, mom. Love you." He hung up. "Mom sends her love," he called out to Darcy.

"She's lonely," Darcy said. "She should get Connie to sell that place. Orlando is so crowded now. She should move to a nice condo in Tampa or Fort Myers. She can afford it. Doesn't her sister live in Ft. Myers?"

"Cape Coral."

"Same difference," she said. "Please turn that off George and open the wine. Decey and Gabriel will be here any minute now." She removed the turkey and placed it on the counter. "Cut this up for me dear. I'm going to finish getting dressed," she said and then threw him the blue sweater she retrieved from their closet. "And put this on. Try to be presentable at least one day of the year."

"Dressing up for my son-in-law?" he said slipping the sweater over his head. "Gabriel's family may be one of the richest in Manhattan Darcy, but the vetting process has passed. They're already married."

"Don't embarrass me, George," she called from down the hall. "Cut the turkey, please, and call Paulie again."

"Not necessary. I'm here," Paul Dudley said, vaulting over the back of the sofa and landing next to his father. "Hey, pop. How's it hanging?"

"Is that Paul?" Darcy said from the bedroom.

"Hi, mom. When's dinner ready?"

"Just waiting for Decey," she said loudly.

"Her Highness," Paul said, grabbing the remote from his father. "Who's winning?"

"The Bears. We fumbled on the one."

"As usual," Paul said, and they shared a smile. Paul then moved closer, looked over his shoulder to make sure his mother could not hear, and then said in a whisper, "Hey, pop, can you help me out?"

"I thought you were working?" Dudley said. "Don't you have a gig tonight?"

"Yea. First one this month. The holidays are pretty booked, but it's been slow," Paul said.

"You are so talented, Paul," Dudley said seriously. "Why don't get with a regular band playing covers for weddings, bat mitzvahs, even session work like you used to?"

"There's no real money there, Pop," he said, settling into the couch. "Plus, David and I want to write our own stuff."

He opened his wallet and took out five bills. "All I got is a hundred."

Paul took it, smiling. "That'll do. Thanks, Pop," he said and then slipped it into his pocket as his mother came into the living room. He hopped up and gave her a kiss on the cheek. "Happy Thanksgiving, mom."

"I'm so glad you're here, Paul. We hardly see you anymore," she said grooming his long hair.

Paul wandered over to the dining table and popped a deviled egg into his mouth. "Don't get uptown that much, mom. Busy you know."

"I thought you might bring that Puerto Rican girl. What was her name, Carmen?"

"We broke up back in July, mom," he said sitting down and scooping some stuffing onto his plate.

"Wait for your sister dear," Darcy said. "George! Cut the turkey. And turn that thing off."

Dudley moved behind the counter and started carving slices of turkey and placing them on a serving plate as the front door opened.

"Sorry, we are late," December Stanton said entering the home. "Parking is atrocious today."

"Had to use the Tower parking garage on 73rd," Gabriel Stanton said, entering behind her.

"Good afternoon, Miss Darcy," he said kissing her proffered cheek. "How do you look so lovely after slaving away in the kitchen all morning?"

"Hello, Gabriel," she said, enjoying the attention. "You look nice. Is that jacket new?"

"I got it at Macy's," he said. "Off the rack. Can you believe that?"

"Well, it looks nice on you," she said, touching his arm, caressing the material.

"Oh, Paul," Decey said, "What a surprise. The prodigal son returneth from the village."

"Better than slumming all day in the Hamptons, sis," Paul said, filling his plate with coleslaw.

"We live in Manhasset, old boy," Gabriel said casually. "It's a bit west of the Hamptons. Better schools and such."

"Speaking of schools," Darcy said and exchanged a look with Gabriel before blurting out, "We're gonna have a baby!"

Darcy Dudley screamed. "Oh, Decey, I knew it. I'm so happy for you." She threw her arms around her daughter. "Boy or a girl?"

"A boy," Gabriel said proudly.

"Well, this calls for a toast," Dudley said pouring chardonnay into the five wine glasses he had ready.

"A little boy," Darcy repeated. "Have you thought of a name?"

"Well, father is leaning toward Beaumont, but nothing is set yet," Gabriel said taking a glass from Dudley.

Darcy looked at December, the hurt visible in her eyes. "You told his parents already, Decey?"

She took the wine-filled glass from her father and moved to the table. "Mrs. Stanton insisted on coming with me to Dr. Adams last week, mother."

"I would have gone, if you'd asked," the room was suddenly chill.

"It all happened very fast, mother," she said. She took a seat and picked up the cloth napkin next to her plate and tried to place it on her lap, but it fell to the floor. "Oh, God, damn it."

"Hey," Gabe said, reaching to down to pick it up. "I got it."

She yanked it out of his hand. "Don't make a federal case out of mom."

"We'll talk about this later, Decey," Darcy said, her tone harsher.

"Well, I'm sorry, mother. What's done is done," December Stanton said, looking away. Tears were filling her eyes. "The food looks great by the way. We ate this way every year when I was growing up, Gabe."

"Looks quaint, honey. Like a Norman Rockwell painting," he said, sitting next to her.

"That's what we were going for," Dudley said, placing the turkey platter on the table. He then crossed to Darcy and placed a comforting arm around her shoulders. "C'mon, honey. Let's eat before it all gets cold." Darcy Dudley sat stiffly, and the only sounds were the serving spoons clinking against the food bowls.

"Looks great, mom. I'm starving," December said.

"You do look a bit thin dear. You should eat better."

"I will, mom."

"I have Tupperware ready if you want leftovers."

"Thanks, mom," Paul said.

"You too, Decey," she said, then through a sudden rush of tears, "Now that you are eating for two," and she leaped from the table and rushed to her bedroom.

"Oh, momma," Decey cried and rushed after her. Gabe rose but Dudley said, "Sit down son. Let them work it out."

"But—"

"I don't know a lot, Gabriel," Dudley interrupted him, "but I do know not to get between a mother and her daughter. Try the green bean casserole. It's delicious."

"I'll say," Paul agreed.

They ate for a while, then Dudley broke the silence. "The Bears are beating the Jets."

"I told father not to invest in them," Gabriel Stanton said, eating sparingly, pushing the food around on his plate and then into his mouth.

"Your dad owns the Jets?" Paul said shocked, spitting out food.

"Part owner. Silent. Doesn't like it known. I mean, Giants fans buy cars too, right?"

"Very diplomatic," Paul said.

"Practical is more like it," Gabriel Stanton said and then added, "Decey says you are in a band?"

"*God's Hammer*. Got a gig at the Gas Pump tonight in the village. You should come?"

"I hate that name, you know," Dudley said, his mouth full of cranberry sauce.

"I know, dad, Jesus."

"Got to take a rain check on that dude. Father's invited some people over for a late Thanksgiving party," Gabriel said. "Jon Bon Jovi's going to be there. Do you know him?"

"Sure do," Paul said sarcastically. "Tell him I said hi."

"I will," he said, oblivious. Decey returned to the table, wiping her eyes. "You all right pumpkin?"

"Oh shit, I left the pumpkin pie on the subway!" Paul said.

"That's fine, Paul. I picked one up," his father said. "Apple pie too. And ice cream."

"Thanksgiving is saved."

After the meal, Darcy, December, and Gabriel removed the plates from the table. Paul was still working on a turkey leg.

"Okay, everybody," Dudley said, clapping his hands. "Now that we're finished, I'll start up *It's a Wonderful Life*. We can eat pie in the living room and watch the movie."

"Oh, dad, I thought mom told you," December said. "We have to go."

"What? But it's a tradition," Dudley said in his best 'Tevye' voice and started dancing in a circle.

"Tradition! Tradition!"

"I gotta go too, dad," Paul said, standing up. "The gig's at 8:00, and I have to get my stuff and help set up."

"But... but it's Thanksgiving," Dudley said, helpless.

Decey kissed him, "Oh, dad, you're so sweet. Please don't ever change."

Gabe shook his hand. "Good to see you, sir. Wonderful meal, Mrs. Dudley."

"Don't forget, December June Stanton. You call me about your next checkup," Darcy Dudley said. "I am going with you. Just us!"

"Yes, mom," she said kissing her, holding back the tears.

Dudley stood by the DVD player, disc in hand, and watched as his children left.

"Bye, dad, you old savings and loan pal," Paul said quoting a line from the movie, and Dudley forced a laugh, but he couldn't hide how hurt he was. Decey noticed and went to her father and hugged him hard. When she pulled away, she slipped her hand into her pocket, pulled out an invisible flower, and showed it to him. "Look, dad. Zuzu's petals!"

He kissed her cheek and nearly cried, before pushing her gently out the door. "Get outta here you two. You're both getting lumps of coal for Christmas this year."

"Same as last year," Paul said. "Another tradition continues."

Dudley could hear their laughter as he closed the door. Darcy was loading the dishwasher and George went to the table to clear more dishes away.

"They're just growing up George. You didn't think things would stay the same forever, did you?"

"I don't like change," he said, sulkily. "But I was hoping for at least a couple more years," he said, cleaning his glasses with his shirt.

"Well, I'm not going anywhere. I'll watch it with you."

"Really Darcy?"

"Of course. Unless you want to watch that Jennifer Lawrence movie, I got you. You know the space one."

"Now that's a good idea," Dudley said.

"And I know how much you love her," Darcy said, adding more to the dishwasher.

"Well, that goes without saying," he said and put his arms around her, but she pushed him away.

"George, please. I have to finish," she said.

Dudley looked at his wife of twenty-one years. This was not the first time she had pushed him away. It was becoming more frequent. There was never anything mean about it, just setting a new boundary, and he wasn't sure why. Their sex life had been nearly nonexistent for the past year, and she was usually asleep when he came to bed. But the gentle refusals and the decreased touching were starting to become the norm.

"Oh, don't look so dramatic George. Pop in the movie and fantasize about Jennifer. Let me finish these," Darcy said.

"Speaking of dramatics, did you see Facebook yesterday? Players posted their cast for *Mockingbird*," Dudley said angrily.

"I saw that dear. Congratulations."

"Congratulations? They cast me as the Sherriff. The Sherriff! Bill Rawlings got Atticus."

"Oh, that's a good choice," she said. "I can see Bill doing that."

"What? Rawlings? Not me?"

"Seriously George, you are a very good actor, but the part of Atticus Finch needs something… more," Darcy said.

"What more? What does that mean?"

"Like Gregory Peck in the movie. He had that presence. That inner fire. Or even… ah… what's his name, he just did it on Broadway?"

"Jeff Daniels," Dudley said automatically.

"Yes. Not the *Dumb and Dumber* Jeff Daniels but the *Newsroom* Jeff Daniels. Witty. Confident. Sexy as hell."

"I'm not sexy?"

"You're not Atticus Finch, dear. That's all I'm saying."

"And Bill Rawlings is," Dudley said, a little peeved now.

"Oh, definitely," she said, a little too quickly.

Dudley put *Passengers* into the DVD player and then sat down. She finished drying her hands and sat next to him. "Oh, don't be that way, George. You'll be a great sheriff. Players have been doing some wonderful stuff lately. You were great as Jefferson in *1776!*"

"That was two years ago," George said, exasperated.

"Still," she said. They watched Chris Pratt wander about the empty spaceship, then he reached for her hand. She gently patted it and placed it in his lap, moving to the farther edge of the sofa.

They watched in silence. Then Darcy's phone pinged. She looked down, and said distractedly, "How was work?"

Dudley noticed she was involved in an intense text chat.

"It seems you were right," he said looking at the TV. "Murdoch was there to see me."

"Oh, really dear. That's nice," she said, her eyes glued to her phone.

He looked at her. "Yes. He was not very happy with me. Or Elliott."

She did not respond so Dudley muted the movie and waited for her to respond. She continued to type, a big smile on her face. Finally, she clicked send and looked up, startled.

"What dear?" she said, feigning innocence.

"Did you hear what I said?" he asked.

"Yes, another hard day at the office," she said, patting his hand. "Did Elliott yell at you?"

"No. He was too busy cleaning out his desk."

"What?" she said astonished. "Murdoch fired him?"

"Yes, dear," he said slowly. "Right after he fired me."

She leaped up from the sofa. "Because of that Moskowitz piece? Oh, George how could you have been so stupid."

"Excuse me. I was expecting a little sympathy here."

"Sympathy? You knew Murdoch would blow a gasket," she said, her voice rising now as the consequences filled her mind. "You knew it. You even said it to me while you were writing it. How could you be so stupid, George?"

"There's that word again," he said, calmly.

"Because I can't think of a harsher one!" she yelled. "How about irresponsible? Self-destructive?"

"There's that English major I married."

"STOP IT!" she suddenly screamed. "Not today."

Dudley tried to calm her. "Honey."

"Don't honey me, goddamnit! Don't apologize. Don't do anything!" she said, fury filling her voice. "God. I can't stand it anymore." She pulled out her phone and showed him the display.

"Here. You want to know who I've been chatting with? Bill Rawlings."

"Why? About *To Kill a Mockingbird*?" Dudley said, confused.

"Oh, my God. You are so dense, George," she screamed. "Not about *Mockingbird*."

She took a deep breath and began to pace in front of the TV. "I was going to wait until the holidays were over. I swear I was. I know how important these 'traditions' are to you. But I'm sorry George. It's all too much. And now you're fired? What are we going to do for money? Your buddy stole all our savings, remember?"

"Murdoch gave me a generous severance package," he added, still reeling from the turn of the conversation.

"Oh goody," she said. "And a non-compete too, I bet?"

"How did you know that?"

"Because I'm smart George. I read. I actually have friends, and talk to people, unlike you!"

"I talk to people," he said annoyed. "Hey, what's going on here?"

"I'm leaving you George!" she blurted out. "Do you get it now? I'm tired of it all. We never go out. You're only friends are theater people, and they're not real friends, just show friends."

"I have friends."

"Oh really? Name two? No, just one. Name one friend, George."

He was silent and then said weakly, "Well, there's Bill."

"Try again, George."

"Are you sleeping with him?"

Darcy stared at him, a pang of guilt lodged in her throat, but she pushed it down and said, "I'm going to Meredith's for a few days, George. I need time to think." She walked to the bedroom and shut the door.

Dudley sat unmoving on the sofa. Jennifer Lawrence and Chris Pratt were having drinks at a bar in space. They looked happy. *People in movies always look happy*, he thought.

The dishwasher continued to hum; otherwise, Dudley heard no other sounds. He continued to watch the movie, without watching it. He knew there was something he should be doing, but for the life of him, he couldn't figure it out. *What is it people do in situations like this? What would Cary Grant do?*

"George, did you hear me?"

She was standing behind the sofa, a small suitcase in her hand. "I'm sorry dear, what?"

"I said, please don't call me. I need time." She left without another word.

On the television, Jennifer and Chris were kissing.

Alone in his New York apartment, George Dudley started to cry.

REFLECTIONS ON REPORT #2

Why does he keep asking what I would do? I had five wives. My opinion would be a bit suspect on this subject. Still, I feel for the guy. His kids abandon him, the wife leaves him, and but damn, not getting Atticus Finch. I know what that feels like. I could have been James Bond, but Cubby went with that Scottish kid. Poor George. What's he going to do now?

Chapter 5
Home Again

REPORT #3

"Mom. Mom! Can you hear me? I said I'm at the airport now," George Dudley said into his cell phone. Three days after he lost his job, two days after Darcy left him, and one day after his world turned upside down, he boarded a plane for Orlando, Florida, for a long overdue vacation, and hopefully a chance to get his life back in order.

Darcy was right about one thing though; he really didn't have any close friends. He spent most of the day after Thanksgiving calling, texting, and posting his woes and receiving less sympathy than he expected. Most of the responses were of the 'Yeah, you should have seen that coming' variety. Finally, he called his mother and said he was coming to visit for a while.

"Why did Darcy leave you?" his mother said.

"What? How did you know?"

"Oh, Georgie. You can be so dense sometimes," Elsie Dudley said, chuckling. "Of course, you can stay here. The place is so big and empty. I'll probably forget you're here after a couple of days."

He then called Paul and told him to keep an eye on the apartment while he was away. He tried to console him. "Don't worry son. Your mom and I will work this out. We'll be back together soon."

Paul barked out a laugh. "Really, dad? I don't think so. She called you some pretty nasty things last night."

"Last night? You saw her?"

"Yea. She and Mr. Rawlings came to the show."

"Oh great," Dudley said, shaking his head.

"It was a long time coming, Pops. I'm sorry but maybe the two of you will be happier now."

43

"I thought I was happy," Dudley said.

"Really pop? Happy? You weren't happy. You were a robot. And a bit of a sap," Paul said, not unkindly. "Mom treated you like shit and Elliott was even worse. I would have smacked him years ago."

"I am NOT a sap. That's just how business works. It's not personal. That's just his personality. You learn to deal with it."

"Not personal? Dad, it was all personal," Paul said, then lowering his voice he said confidentially. "But, seriously, dad, I don't think mom wants to get back together. She looked happy last night. Decey thought so too."

"December was there too?" Dudley asked shocked.

"Yea. She and Gabe came late," Paul added. "He's not as big an ass as I thought after you get some drinks in him. Bought a round for the house. Can you believe it? What a guy. Anyway, I'll keep an eye on the house. You take care. Love you."

Dudley ended the call and sat on the hard plastic chair travelers use when waiting for their luggage. He only packed one bag. Not because he thought the trip was going to be short, though secretly he did, but because he packed urgently and just threw in some shorts and golf shirts and underwear. He wore his favorite gray slacks and blue blazer on the plane, but otherwise, he was ill-prepared if this visit lasted more than a week or two. Hopefully, that would give Darcy a chance to come to her senses. But now, after listening to Paul, he doubted it would be as soon as he would have liked.

He rented a sensible Corolla for the week and within forty minutes he was pulling up to his childhood home on Sycamore Place, in the dignified Lake Copeland area, near the center of town. The elegant two-story Spanish-style bungalow had a peach-colored exterior and a classic red tiled roof. Growing up, Dudley never noticed how beautiful it was. He did not notice today either.

He knocked on the heavy red oak door, and when his mother did not immediately answer, he grabbed the door handle and found the door open. "Mother," he cried upon entering, "You left the door open."

"Lucky for you," Elsie Dudley said coming down the spiral wrought iron staircase in the center of the spacious entrance area. "You look like shit Georgie."

"Thanks, mom. That didn't take long."

"Oh, hush. Give your mother a kiss," she said offering her cheek. "Now put your bag down and let's have a long chat and a drink."

"Mom, it's not even noon,"

She stopped and turned to look at him. "Got somewhere else to be? Any pressing appointments? Meeting the Pope later? Then shut up and pour your mother a highball."

"Seven and seven, okay?" Dudley said from the sidebar she had set up in the living room area.

"Better make it a seven and eight. I feel a real pity party coming."

"Jesus Christ, mom. My wife just left me!"

"Don't use the Lord's name in vain, Georgie. I thought I brought you up better than that."

"Sorry."

"Sorry," she said at the same time. "I love you Georgie, but yes I do believe you are sorry."

"Oh, come on, mom, not you too," he moaned.

"Why are you here, Georgie?" she said sweetly, her painted-on eyebrows arching up high on her forehead. "Is it to see your sweet, lonely old mother? Is it to finally take that way overdue vacation? Or maybe it's to check out all the new and wonderful additions over at Mr. Disney's Funland!"

"Mom," he whined, mixing her drink.

"No, dear. You're not here for any of those reasons. No, my blundering, bumbling son, you are here, because you ran away."

"Aw, mom."

"Don't interrupt, dear." She crossed the room and took the glass from Dudley's hands. "You always run away, Georgie. It's who you are. Whenever you feel attacked or rejected, you pack up your toys and leave. You left home when your father wouldn't invest in your publishing idea, you left *Orlando Magazine* when they wouldn't make you an editor and you left Mary when she wouldn't go to New York with you."

He took his own drink, Jack Daniels on the rocks, and turned his back on her so she could not see the tears beginning to well up in his eyes. He moved to the large bay window and looked out at his mother's pride, her colorful daylily garden. The ice in his glass was rattling. He gripped it tighter with both hands to muffle the sound.

"And now here you are again," his mother continued, speaking to his back. "You lost your job, you might lose your wife, and you lost the opportunity to play Atticus Finch in your little theater group's production of *To Kill a Mockingbird*."

Dudley turned to her with surprise on his face. "And by the look of you, that one hurt the most," she laughed. "Sit down dear. And give me your glass. I think you need a double." Dudley did as she asked and sat on the sofa.

"How about we watch a good movie," she said. "I'll order us a nice lunch from Shang Chi's, okay? Sweet and sour chicken still your favorite?" She kissed the top of his head and said, "Don't worry so much dear. There's nothing that Chinese food and a little Cary Grant and Ingrid Bergman can't fix."

The afternoon floated into the evening, and after his third refill, Dudley couldn't figure out if Cary Grant was the good guy pretending to be bad, or the bad guy pretending to be good. But, either way, Ingrid sure looked fine. He finally crawled into his childhood bed around 10:00 pm He closed his eyes and the stress of the past few days receded and he drifted off quickly to a restful sleep. His last thought was of a short, brunette with large green eyes and a wicked smile.

REFLECTIONS ON REPORT #3

So far, his mom is the best part of this story.

Chapter 6
Of All the Gin Joints

REPORT #4

1

The next day George Dudley felt better. Not perfect. He was still unemployed, and his wife still had not talked to him. But he did not feel like a total loser, despite his mother's best efforts.

"I have a hair appointment this afternoon Georgie, but I should be home by four," Elsie said while they ate a couple of Cobb salads for lunch on her backyard patio. It was a beautiful, cool Florida day in late November, and Dudley relaxed comfortably in his green Jets football jersey and a pair of gym shorts. "I thought I'd take you to dinner tonight at Ruth's Chris Steak House. To cheer you up. How does that sound?"

"Sounds great, mom. I love Ruth's, Chris," he said, genuinely touched.

"Who doesn't," she added, then just because she couldn't let a good moment last, she said, "then maybe we'll stop by Dillard's and get you a new sweater and some grown-up slacks."

"I need to make some calls anyway, mom. I'll clean up the dishes, for you."

"See Georgie. You can be sweet if you just put a little effort into it," she kissed his cheek and went inside.

He called his lawyer, Gary Reade, who happened to also be his brother-in-law. "Hi, Gary. It's George."

"The enemy," Gary said, and Dudley knew Darcy had already called him.

"So you know. Good, that'll save some time," Dudley said. "I'm still hopeful Darcy and I can work things out but just in case, I'm probably going to need a lawyer, and you're the only one I know."

47

"I'm flattered George, but my sister would castrate me in my sleep if I even thought about representing you," Gary said deadpan.

"Well, I don't want to upset half of the female population of Manhattan Island Gary, so I was wondering if you could recommend someone?"

"Carl Schumann," he said immediately.

"Well, sure Gary, take your time. Think it over a bit, why don't you."

He laughed and said, "I anticipated your call, George. Darcy said I was the only lawyer you two ever used, so I deduced you'd need council picking counsel."

"Council picking counsel, Gary? Really? That sounds like bad Shakespeare."

"Merchant of Venice," he said, "Act 3 Scene 2."

"No, it's not."

"Should be. Maybe I should be the writer George and you practice law."

"I'm not even a writer right now Gary," Dudley said. Gary Reade was silent for a moment and then said, "Yes, she told me that too. Look, give Carl a call. He's a good guy. A little eccentric, so I think you two will get along. He's been talking of retiring so maybe he can take you on as a pity case."

"I said I was out of work, Gary, not destitute," Dudley said.

"We should probably not talk money, George, especially if I'm going to represent my sister."

"Yeah, I figured. Well, thanks. I'll call him."

George did not call Carl Schumann right away. *Another day or two won't kill me*, he thought. Dudley wanted to hang onto what little scraps of hope he had left. So he checked in with his son, who said he was going over to water the plants today. Then he called Decey, but he had to be satisfied with leaving her a message. Then he realized he had no one else to call. So he did the dishes.

2

Ruth's Chris Steak House parking lot was packed, but Elsie Dudley had called ahead and made reservations. The hostess looked up when she said her name, and said, "Oh, Mrs. Dudley, there's a note here by your name, it says…"

"I know what it says, dearie," Elsie said sharply, cutting her off. "Show us to our table, please. I'm starving. I could eat an entire cow."

The young girl, clearly frustrated, looked down at the note again, then at Dudley, and he could see she wanted to say something. Elsie growled. So instead, she grabbed two menus, and without another word, led them into the semi-dark restaurant.

"Mom?"

"Quiet dear, I need to concentrate," she said. "They make these places so dark I'm always afraid of accidentally sitting on someone."

The hostess seated them in a booth of soft, lush leather. "Mathew will be your server." She took one more look at George and then quickly moved away from the table.

Dudley turned to his mother and said, "Ok, mom. What the hell was that?"

But she did not answer. Instead, she smiled like the cat who ate the canary and looked over his shoulder. Then Dudley heard a voice he thought he would never hear again. "Of all the gin joints, in all the towns, in all in all the world, he walks into mine."

Dudley turned, and standing next to him, was the one that got away. Mary Jordan. His eyes opened wide, and his mouth moved but nothing came out. *She looks exactly the same*, he thought. It had been twenty-two years, but she looked better at forty-two than she did when George Dudley left town.

She still styled her dark brown hair in a pixie cut, though it was a little longer on the left side now. It was easy to see from the way her black evening dress hugged her, that her lithe body was unchanged. Her full lips were curled back into that smirk he loved, and the red lipstick she had applied generously only emphasized the effect. But it was her eyes that he remembered the most.

Wide and curious, as if life was an unending series of glorious surprises.

Dudley blinked and finally croaked out, "Hi, Mary."

"You look at me as if you didn't know me," she said enjoying his discomfort.

"Oh, Jesus, I'm sorry, Mary. It was just a shock seeing you," Dudley said stumbling. Then he said over his shoulder to his mother. "Thanks, mom!"

Mary Jordan laughed and said, "When Elsie called earlier and said you were in town, I thought it would be fun to see you again. You look good George. Just the same," she said and brushed the hair out of his eyes like she had done a thousand times before when they were young and in love.

A young woman approached and said, "Miss Jordan, Andre needs you in the kitchen."

"Okay, thanks, Bethany. Duty calls. It was nice seeing you again, Georgie."

"Me too Mary. This was a wonderful surprise," George said.

She hesitated at the table then impulsively asked, "Hey, how you long you in town for?"

"Not sure. A week or two, maybe. Why?"

"The old gang from *Orlando Magazine* is having a party here Friday night," Mary said. "I'm sure some of your old friends will be here. Byron's getting some kind of award."

"Byron Tucker's still there? My old boss?"

"He's retiring. But… look why don't you come, as my guest," she said. "And if anyone complains, what can they do, I run the joint." Then she flashed that smile. That smile took him all the way back.

"It's a date."

"A date," she said looking at him. "Well, you don't waste much time, do you, tiger?"

"Miss Jordan!" Bethany cried.

"Right. On my way." Then to George, "Be here at 7:30. We'll have a drink and catch up before the craziness begins at 8:00."

"Looking forward to it," he said, and then he extended his right hand toward her, palm down. She started a moment, then remembering, slid her own palm underneath before pulling it away, and rushing off.

"I think she was actually blushing there Georgie," his mother interjected. "Though it's hard to tell for certain in this light."

"You think so?" he said.

"She wasn't wearing a ring either."

"No, she was not."

REFLECTIONS ON REPORT #4

I like this girl. Maybe this little trip was just the ticket for our man Dudley. I might be done in six days instead of six months.

Chapter 7
George and Mary: Catching Up

REPORT #5

He arrived at 7:30 sharp. Bethany, the pretty blonde hostess, greeted him by name and said, "Miss Jordan is waiting for you at the bar, Mr. Dudley."

"Thank you. Bethany, isn't it?" he asked.

"Yes, sir. The bars over there," she said pointing to the far-right wall. "I'll show you. If you'll follow me." She was navigating the tables and chairs. Then she said, "So you're Miss Jordan's old boyfriend?"

"Yes. It was a long time ago."

"Wouldn't know it by the way she's been acting. The ice queen actually cracked a joke yesterday at the staff meeting."

"Ice queen?"

Bethany turned around quickly and said, "Oh, God Mr. Dudley, don't tell her I said that."

"It's fine, Bethany. Your secret is safe with me."

"It's just, she's always so professional. Prim and proper. Everything in its place you know, by the book. I guess that's why she's such a good manager."

"Is she a good manager?" George asked, just making conversation.

"She's the best. Corporate wanted her in Virginia, you know headquarters, to train people, but she said, no, I like it here. I think it's because of her dad. You know about her dad, right?"

"No, how is Mr. Jordan?" George Dudley had fond memories of the old history teacher.

"Alzheimer's," Bethany whispered. "He's at Brookdale. Miss Jordan visits him nearly every day. She's the best. My dad's a shit."

"Are we going the right way, Bethany?" Dudley asked, certain that he had passed this table before.

51

The large bar area dominated the entire right side of the room. Seated on a high stool at the far end was Mary Jordan. She was wearing another black dress, but this one had a serious slit up the side, he could see almost to the top of her thigh. The only accessory was a simple necklace of pearls laying elegantly across her chest. She looked fabulous.

"Here we are," Bethany said, unnecessarily. "Anything else I can do for you, Miss Jordan?"

"Just let me know when Mrs. Andrews gets here," Mary said, not looking at her, her eyes were for George only.

"Well, hello," George said again, and they laughed. "You look great Mary. May I say that?"

"Why not? I worked on this look all afternoon."

"I just meant, if your husband or boyfriend is here…" he started lamely.

"Jesus, same old George. Uses the side door when the front is wide open. No, George," she said waving her left hand in front of his face. "I am an unattached woman. But we can get into all that after we get you a drink." She turned and spoke loudly to the barman. "Ricky? Get me my usual and get my friend here a white Russian. And use the good vodka."

"You remembered," Dudley said, sitting beside her.

"You'd be surprised what I remember Georgie Porgie."

"Oh, God, not that," he said and dramatically laid his head on the bar. When he looked up, his hair had fallen over his eyes.

"You need a haircut," she said, brushing it back.

"I need a lot of things Mary," he confessed.

"Why are you here, George?"

"You invited me."

"You know what I mean. Your mom told me a little, but I'd like to hear it from you."

"So we're jumping right into it are we?" he said, still reluctant to go over his recent failures.

"Okay, then I'll go first," she said, taking a sip from her wine glass. "Let's see after you dumped me…"

"Come on,"

She smiled to reassure him. "It was a very sweet letter, George. I was hurt. I admit. I knew you had big dreams. You always were the grass is greener kind of guy. I was young too, George, and afraid. I'd only lived here my whole life, and you just wanted to go. The funny thing is, I did move a few years later. I left the magazine too, finished my management degree, and got a job at the new Morton's that just opened. Did well, too. They transferred me to their headquarters in Chicago. Met a guy, not like you at all. Corporate type. Good-looking."

"Not like me at all, thank you."

"Stop. Let me finish. I don't think I can say this twice. I stayed in Chicago for four years. Johnny wanted to have children. We tried, but when we discovered I couldn't, well it lasted a little longer but at least it ended amicably. But between me and you, the children were only a part of the problem. I was promoted to lead the national training program. Which essentially made me Johnny's boss. Well, some men can handle that sort of thing, and some can't. It got ugly for a while, and a headhunter was courting me pretty hard and offered some serious cash if I would jump ship and go to Ruth's Chris, who was on an aggressive national growth program at the time."

She waved to Ricky and indicated a refill. "I took the job, did stints in Dallas, San Francisco, and D.C. But then dad got sick. Mom died a few years earlier and he was all alone, so I took the manager job here, to be close to dad. That was just after Christmas last year."

Mary was running her finger around the rim of her wine glass. Dudley watched her and then said softly. "Bethany said your dad has Alzheimer's."

She took a deep breath and forced a smile and said, "Yes. Later stages. Pretty bad. Hardly recognizes me anymore. Had to put him in Brookdale Conway. It's a good place. They take good care of him."

Dudley placed his hand over Mary's and said, "I'm so sorry Mary."

"For which part?" she said laughing. "That was just a highlight reel, Georgie. It wasn't all bad. About the only thing I really hated was the Chicago winters. Won't miss them at all."

"Can't be any worse than New York," Dudley said, smiling.

"Are we still talking about the weather?" she said slyly, looking at him sideways.

And, suddenly, the strain of the past two weeks engulfed him like a drowning man. His chest tightened, his face turned red, and his eyes filled with tears.

"Oh, Georgie," Mary said holding his face. "I'm sorry."

"I failed, Mary. Everything I touched, my entire life. Failure after failure."

"No, George. No. It's bad now. That's obvious. But one thing I learned the hard way…" she took his face in her hands. "One thing I learned is that things change. They really do. No matter how bad things are now, in a week, a month, or maybe a year, things WILL be different."

He smiled weakly, but she continued. "I'm not going to give you any cheap 'one door closes, and one opens up' inspirational crap, but calling yourself a failure, that's got to stop. Right now!" She said the last part forcefully and suddenly kissed him. It was quick and surprised them both, but it helped. He wiped his eyes and picked up his drink and drained it. Ricky was right there with a new one.

"You gotta love bartenders," he joked.

Mary smiled at Ricky and leaned back against the bar. Over George's shoulder, she saw Bethany approaching with a short, middle-aged woman in tow. Her red hair was shoulder-length and cut in the latest style. Everything about her said fashionable, from her oversized black eyeglass frames and her aggressive military style jacket, complete with large brass buttons and a tight bright yellow pencil skirt. Her high-heeled pumps did little to bring her over five feet, but what she lacked in height she made up in sheer personality.

"Jordan," she yelled, before she reached them, "where is my banner? We agreed Mr. Tucker's banner would be hanging over the hostess desk in the entryway." The dynamic woman walked past Dudley without noticing him and stood directly in front of Mary Jordan.

Mary slipped off the stool and stood in front of the lady and said calmly, "The banner had a typo, Amy. So I called my guy over at Signs Today and he's on his way right now with a new one. Okay?"

"Oh. Well, good. Sorry, Mary," she apologized. "I've been planning this fucking thing for six months now, and I am over it. I spent the entire afternoon at the spa at the Marriott. You ever use them? Oh, it's heaven, Mary, Heaven. Ask for Alwena. Tell them I sent you. They worked wonders on me. Went home. Put on my new Dior," she did a pirouette to display the entire outfit, then her fury returned instantly, "Drove directly here and the first God damn thing I see is the—" Mary took hold of Amy's shoulders and said, "Everything is going to be fine, Amy. Byron's going to be very pleased."

Amy lowered her head and took a deep breath. "Right. Right. God, I need a drink."

"Ricky, get Ms. Andrews a Manhattan, please."

"Make it with Jack Daniels, Ricky. And two cherries," Amy demanded.

"And now, my friend, I have a surprise for you," Mary said.

"Oh, for fucks sake, Jordan. You know I don't like surprises."

Still holding onto Amy's shoulders, she turned her toward Dudley. "You're going to like this one. Remember this guy?"

Amy Andrews squinted her eyes and then opened them wide and screamed, "Georgie! Holy shit!" Amy threw her arms around Dudley. "I didn't think you were coming?"

"It's good to see you too Amy," George said.

"George Dudley. Wow. Byron's going to love this. He threw your Moskowitz article at me last week. Like it was my fault. Oh, Georgie. Let me look at you. Wow. He looks like shit, doesn't he Jordan?"

Mary smiled and said, "Nothing a trip to Milano's couldn't fix. And a good haircut."

"What are you doing here, George?" Amy began, then looking at her watch said, "Oh damn. Look I gotta go but, George you staying for the party? I have to check on some things. We'll catch up later, okay?"

"I'll be here. Good seeing you."

"Same here, George," she said and turned to go, then abruptly spun around and said, "Hey. You're a writer." But she did not ask it as a question. It was a statement of fact. An idea had just popped into her head, and she said, "We definitely have to talk. Do NOT leave before we talk, okay George? Promise me," she said intensely.

Dudley held up his right hand and said, "I promise."

"Good. Good," she said and walked briskly away. A moment later she screamed, "I still don't see my banner, Jordan!"

"I need to go to work, George," Mary said placing a hand on his arm. "Feel free to eat and mingle. I put your name on the guest list. I'll find you later." She turned and followed Amy. Andrews into the restaurant. Dudley watched her gracefully navigate the tables, the bustling waiters, and the rapidly growing crowd. Then, abruptly, she turned, looked directly into Dudley's eyes, and said, "I'm really glad you're here, George."

That Andrews woman is a spitfire. Reminds me of Rosalind's character in 'His Girl Friday'. Oh, that was a fun time. Good movie too. I wonder why Dudley left Mary? She seems swell.

Chapter 8
The Return of Archie Leach

REPORT #6

"Ms. Andrews will be with you in a moment, sir. Would you like some coffee or water?" Tiffany Pierce asked him.

"No, I'm fine."

George Dudley was seated in the lobby area of the *Orlando Magazine* offices, a modern building near downtown Orlando. He was still unsure why he agreed to this Saturday morning meeting. The night before, an overly excited Amy Andrews convinced him it would be worth his while to meet with her. He agreed but was starting to have second thoughts.

Just then, Amy came bustling into the reception area. "Good, you're here. Come in George. You too, Tiffany."

Dudley and Tiffany followed her down the hall to her office. "Did you bring it, George?" Amy said immediately.

"Good morning to you too, Amy. Yes, I am fine, thank you."

"I don't have time for comedy George. I have a headache that could register on the Richter scale. Last night I asked you two things. Be here at 9:00 and bring your non-compete from Murdoch." She held out her hand. "Did you bring it?"

Dudley reached into his inside jacket pocket and pulled out the four-page document.

"Give it to Tiffany. Make three copies. Email one to Barry in legal and bring me the rest."

Tiffany left and Amy sat behind her glass desk. "Sit. Sit," she commanded Dudley who was still standing, a little flabbergasted at the speed of things. "And shut your mouth George, you look like a fish."

"You were very mysterious last night Amy. Mind telling me why I am here, instead of in front of my mother's 48-inch TV watching Saturday morning cartoons?"

She looked at him astonished, and said, "I thought I made that clear last night George. I am saving your life."

Dudley chuckled and said, "Well, thank you, Amy. I don't see you for twenty years, and the first thing you do is get me a heart transplant."

"No, George," she said leaning forward, "I'm about to give you a career transplant."

Tiffany came back in, placed the copies on her desk, and said, "Anything else, Ms. Andrews?"

"No thank you, Tiffany. You can go home now. Thanks for coming in. Shut the door."

Dudley watched as the pretty young girl shut the door. "You had her come in on a Saturday to make copies?"

Amy was studying the non-compete documents. "I had her come in on a Saturday morning George, to test her loyalty. An assistant editor position was posted last Wednesday, and I made it clear to the entire office that I was still undecided about who I was going to give it to. Tiffany is in the running."

She turned to the last page, smiled, and looked up. "However, an even better position just opened that I am NOT going to post. And that's where you come in."

"Well, you got me to come in on a Saturday too, so let's hear it," Dudley asked.

"You remember Bob Kennedy, don't you?"

"Of course. He was my first editor here, back when it was called, *What's Happening, Orlando*. Primarily a tourist rag."

"Ten points for Gryffindor. I know the magazine's history, George. I am senior editor," she said.

"Did you know that Bob is still here?"

"No. Didn't know that. Thought he'd be dead by now. He was ancient back then."

"Just turned eighty-one last June. Now he's on a ventilator at Orlando Medical," she said, and Dudley noticed a real sense of concern in her voice.

"Oh, I'm sorry."

"Not your fault. But if you truly are worried about him and his family, I have a way you can help them."

"Okay. I'm still not sure I follow you, but I am intrigued."

"Then let me get to the point." She stood and started pacing between her large glass desk and the wall of glass behind her.

"*Orlando Magazine* is more than just a magazine. We partner with the Orlando Chamber of Commerce. We supply them with x amount of magazines each month and they give us free rent and access to their administrative staff. We consign 33% of the magazine to articles about chamber companies, why businesses should move to Orlando, and ads for select Gold Chamber Members. In return, they give us guidance, influence, and help with side projects we're working on. That's where Bob comes in." She stood with her back to him, "Don't you love this view."

"I'm afraid of heights."

"I forgot how funny you are. But I do remember you being great at interviews. And by what I read out of New York, you still are, even though it's mostly finance and stock market crap."

"And an occasional obituary," he said quietly.

"I've already run my idea by Travis and to be honest he hated the idea. But he'll be gone by the first of the year, so he really doesn't have a say."

"And what is this idea?"

"I'm getting to it. Hold your horses. You got somewhere better to be? Brunch with mommy dearest?" she said.

"She's actually been quite sweet."

"Oh, please Georgie. I know your mother, remember? We go to the same club. We're both on the Art Museum board. She was the chair of the Republican reelect committee here in Orlando for twelve years. I know her."

"Better than me, apparently,"

"Maybe. But I digress," Amy said then began pacing again. "Orlando Publications, the mothership of *Orlando Magazine* is starting a book division. Bob Kennedy was writing our first. This was a commission from our partner, Universal Studios, or to be precise, NBC Universal, because Bob does voice-over work down the street at Universal Orlando. Particularly the Jurassic Park ride."

"Which is one of my favorites."

"Oh, shut up. So the next Jurassic movie, *Jurassic World Dominion*, is set to open in six months and Universal wants to do a book tie-in about its stars, Pratt, and Bryce Howard. But Bob proposed an alternate idea, one with, and please forgive the pun, more Universal appeal. It's called '*The Last Matinee Idol*'."

"Sounds like a movie title," Dudley quipped.

"A movie title about a movie company and its galaxy of stars. Chris Pratt, and subsequently, *Jurassic Park*, will be on the cover and the lead story, but the rest of the book will be about matinee idols: Clark Gable, Tyrone Power, Errol Flynn, Gary Cooper, and Cary Grant. Along with some current idols: George Clooney, Bruce Willis, Ryan Reynolds, Bradley Cooper, and of course, Chris Pratt."

She was behind her desk again and pulled a 200-page manuscript from a desk drawer and dropped it heavily in front of George. "This is Bob's draft so far. He's done all the research on the old-time guys, but he was just setting up the interviews with the new ones when he keeled over last weekend. What I need you to do is interview those actors and finish the book."

George Dudley stared at her. "You want me to do what?"

"Am I speaking too fast, George?" Amy said. "I have a problem and a deadline. I need you to finish the book."

"You mean like a writer, which the four-page document you have been analyzing for the past 15 minutes clearly shows I am not."

"This book needs to come out June first," Barry Tillerman said, entering Amy's office. "And it does not look like Mr. Kennedy will be up to it."

"George, this is Barry Tillerman from legal. Barry, meet George," Amy said.

"But we must put Kennedy's name on it, regardless," Tillerman continued. "That's a condition Universal demanded,"

"All we need you to do is interview the five actors and finish the book."

When George did not answer her, Amy continued. "We'll pay you handsomely. Plus, you'll get to meet movie stars: Bradley Cooper! George Clooney!"

"You're forgetting the IRS," Dudley said. "How am I going to explain this money in my bank account to them?"

"Consulting fee," Barry Tillerman said. "Your non-compete specifically says writing and editing, it says nothing about consultation, even to another publication. As long as it is not in New York."

"But NBCUniversal is headquartered in New York," Dudley said.

"Ah, but Universal Studios, our client, is headquartered in California. A small, but important detail, for our purposes," Tillerman added with a smirk, as if he just hit a winner down the baseline.

"But why do you need me?" George said, looking around at the spacious building. "You must have access to hundreds of writers here?"

"All my regular people are tied up, and I need someone now who can travel and be at the whim of these movie stars," she replied quickly. "Plus, you're an excellent writer, and you interview exceptionally well. And you're probably a little desperate right now. Am I right?"

"No need to get hardball, Amy," George said, standing, stalling for time. It would be great work for the magazine again, and writing a book was always on his bucket list, but actors? Matinee Idols? He had planned a book about money, power, and corruption. Not method acting and close-ups. "What do I tell these people when I show up instead of Bob Kennedy?"

"Tell them you're his assistant," Tillerman said promptly. "He's 81; he got sick, tired, whatever. You're just filling in until he's back on his feet."

"And what about my name? The non-compete says, I, George Dudley, cannot conduct interviews and write books or articles. Your 'consultant' cover may not be enough if my name gets out."

Barry and Amy exchanged a look, and then Barry said, "It may hold up, but just to be safe, we'll get you a new name. A pen name, as it were. People don't know your face outside of New York, so we should be safe."

"Yes. A new name," Amy said liking this idea. "Like John Wayne or Marilyn Monroe."

"Or Cary Grant," Dudley said.

"Too obvious. Plus, Cary Grant is in the book," Barry said.

George walked toward the glass windows and looked out. It was a spectacular view. Trees surrounded a park, swings and fountains, and blue skies that went on for miles. So different from his New York office, which was sandwiched in between other tall buildings. But it wasn't his office anymore. He was kicked out. Fired. His last memory of the place was staring across at the Wells Fargo bank building, holding the Grant and Bergman photo in his hand. Then inspiration hit him.

"Then how about Archie Leach, the name he left behind," Dudley said.

"Oh perfect," Amy said, clapping her hands. "Plus, all the movie people will love it."

"So we're agreed?" Barry said holding out his hand.

"Sure. Why not." He shook Tillerman's hand and then asked, "When do I start?"

"Next Wednesday at Universal in California."

"Wow. So quick. Who's up first?" Dudley asked.

"Bradley Cooper."

"Oh great."

"Jennifer Lawrence might be there, too."

"Oh fuck."

REFLECTIONS ON REPORT #6

Well, isn't that an interesting twist? He's going to write a book about me and Coop and the others. I never liked the term, Matinee Idol. But we're going back to Hollywood. Oh, I can't wait. I have to ask Kay if there is a fast-forward button on this thing.

Chapter 9
George and Mary: Sitting in a Tree

REPORT #7

"She offered you a job?"

The waiters were closing up the restaurant, and Ricky the bartender placed two Stingers in front of Mary and George. "Last call darling."

Mary smiled and said, "Give me the tally receipts before you leave, Ricky. I'll turn off the lights."

"Yes, ma'am," Ricky said and started running the close-out sequence on the register.

"I love these things," Mary said holding the glass up, the amber liquid reflecting in the light. "I always feel like a 40s movie star."

"It's very sweet," Dudley said, surprised. "What's in it?"

"Cognac and White Crème de Menthe," she said, sipping slowly.

"I fly out to LA next week," Dudley said and took a big sip. Then he coughed and nearly spilled the drink all over the bar.

"Slow down there, tiger," Mary said.

"Sorry, it's been a long and strange day."

"Why did you pick Archie Leach?" Mary said. "Why not Marion Morrison?" She was laughing now.

"Very funny."

"Or Norma Jean? Nobody would have guessed that connection."

"You done yet? This is serious," Dudley said.

"What is? You impersonating your own personal idol to interview current movie idols?" Mary said. "Really, George? Why not, John Smith? Or George Smith, less confusing."

"I hate my life," he said suddenly, his eyes downcast, staring at the bar.

"Georgie," she said placing a hand on his arm. "You're going through a bad patch, that's all."

"For the past twenty years?"

"Don't exaggerate," she soothed. "You knew it was risky to write that Moskowitz obit. I'm sorry you lost your job, but you can't be totally surprised. And Darcy leaving you, was that from left field? Had things been rough lately? Did you see any signs?"

"Nobody likes me, Mary," he said, pitifully.

"You don't have any friends. Nobody likes you," Mary said, doing an exceptionally good Gollum voice, from *The Two Towers* movie. "Gollum. Gollum."

He laughed, despite himself. "You could always make me laugh," Dudley said.

"Yes. Yes. Make Master smile. Good. Good," she added.

"You also never knew when to stop," he said, smiling.

She held up her glass, close to her face, caressing it. "My precious."

And they both started laughing. Impulsively, Dudley leaned over and kissed her. She did not move away. She held his face and kissed him back. "I like you just the way you are, goofball."

"I'm a goofball? Who was just doing Andy Serkis for five minutes?" Dudley said, his lips close to hers.

"You know Cary Grant had his problems too," Mary said, pulling away. "What did he have, like six wives?"

"That was Henry VIII. Grant had five," Dudley said, picking up his drink again.

"Hell of a role model."

"I'm 42 years old, Mary. I've spent my life being a good boy. Trying to please others in a pathetic gesture to get them to like me in return. But it didn't work. I'm mocked at work, ignored at the theater and my wife isn't proud of me. Even my kids disrespect me."

"George," Mary started, but he cut her off.

"No, Mary, it's not all self-pity," he said. "Maybe a little but it's also true. I don't like who I've become. Maybe I should chuck it all and change everything."

"Well, don't change too much, Georgie. Except those glasses," she said removing them from his face. "Have you ever thought of contacts? You are not an unattractive man, you know."

"Was there a compliment in there somewhere?"

"Just a word of warning. Take it from a survivor," she said, suddenly serious. "Change is inevitable. And sometimes you do have to fight back, but trying to become someone else? It has disaster movie written all over it."

He smiled then and looked at her. "Why did we break up?"

"We didn't break up, George. You left," Mary said, an edge in her voice.

"It was for a job. A great job. In New York."

"Always somewhere else. What's the name of that Cary Grant movie? *The Grass Is Always Greener*?" Mary said. "That's you, Georgie. Happiness is always over there."

"What is it you want, Mary? What do you want? You want the moon? Just say the word, and I'll throw a lasso around it and pull it down."

She smiled then and came in with her line from the famous scene from *It's a Wonderful Life*. "I'll take it. Then what?"

"And then you'll swallow it see," Dudley said, rising from his stool, getting fully into the scene. "And it'll all dissolve see, and the moonbeams will shoot out of your fingers and toes and the ends of your hair…. Am I talking too much?"

Then Mary stood and threw her arms around his neck. "Yes. Why don't you try kissing her instead of talking her to death?" And she kissed him, hard. For all those missing years. For all those missed kisses. For the hurt he caused her. For the love they lost. For the hope that burned inside her now. "Take me home Georgie," she whispered in his ear. "I need you so goddamn much."

But movies are not real life and happy endings rarely happen. He followed her home. They undressed in the dark, and even though the passion was there, Dudley failed to perform. Mary was kind and said all the right things, 'It Happens, Don't worry it's no big deal' and 'It was just nice to be with you'. But George Dudley was no stranger to failure. These past few weeks were a testament to that fact. But he wanted her so much. It just wasn't fair.

During the long ride home, he cried. It started to rain, and he turned on the windshield wipers, but he did not wipe the tears from his face. He was a failure. This was not a judgment. It was a fact. Experience had taught him so. His work, his wife, his love, his life. So he made a vow to change. Right then and there, alone in his rental car, driving in the rain. "George Dudley was dead; Cary Grant would be my new mantra. I will change," he said out loud, "I can't live this way any longer. I deserve happiness, even if I have to create it." And the rain came down harder.

REFLECTIONS ON REPORT #7

Oh damn.

Chapter 10
The Matinee Idol

REPORT #8

Dudley left Amy Andrews's office Monday morning with Bob Kennedy's draft under his arm. Barry had prepared a contract. They agreed on a weekly salary of two thousand dollars. They also gave him a company American Express card for expenses. Bob had already arranged interviews with George Clooney, Bradley Cooper, Bruce Willis, Ryan Reynolds, and Chris Pratt. Amy gave Dudley a list of contact names and told him his first job was to get in touch with them to confirm arrangements.

After that he would meet with the actors, do the interview, write it up then email it to Amy. His first draft must be complete by April first. That gave him four months.

He called Bradley Cooper's personnel assistant Tyler Woods from Amy's contact list Monday morning to confirm the appointment.

"What happened to Mr. Kennedy?" Woods asked.

"He's just a little under the weather. I'm his assistant, more like a co-author really. He's been my mentor for years," Dudley said, surprised at how easy the lie came to him.

"Well, I guess that will be okay, Mr. Leach. But Mr. Cooper must see a draft before publication. That's still in the agreement, right?"

Dudley had no idea, but he said, "Absolutely. You know between me and you, this project wouldn't have even been green-lit without Bradley's participation."

"Mr. Cooper," Woods corrected him.

"Right. Sorry. So we're all set?"

Tyler Woods took a deep breath and said, "Yes. We'll hold a room for you at the Belvedere for the 27th and 28th. Someone will pick you up at 7 am sharp. Good day, Mr. Leach."

Dudley checked that off his 'to-do' list and then went online to make his airline reservations. He punched in the AmEx numbers of his new card. He held his breath until he received his confirmation number. *Well, the AmEx card is working. That's a good start.*

He shot Amy a quick email updating her on his progress, and settled in to read Kennedy's book, *The Last Matinee Idol.* He hated the title, but he hated Bob's prose even more. The whole thing read like a car owner's manual.

Gary Cooper stood six feet tall. He was a man's man. When shooting *High Noon*, the one most people remember him for, he arrived on set in costume and character each day. He was the consummate professional. Everyone liked him and liked working with him. He was a big star, but he acted like a regular person. This was his appeal. He was approachable. He was just a regular guy.

Dudley put the manuscript down and made an additional line on his to do list, meeting with Amy about a complete rewrite.

The section on Errol Flynn was even worse and full of untruths. 'Flynn invented the swashbuckler. His movie Captain Blood broke box office receipts for 1935 and made Errol Flynn a household name'. Did Kennedy forget about Douglas Fairbanks's 1920 hits *Mark of Zorro*, *Black Pirate*, and *Robin Hood*? And I guess he forgot about a little Clark Gable movie called *Mutiny on the Bounty* that won Best Picture for 1935.

Was Bob being lazy or was he rewriting history to shine a brighter light on his subjects? These things were too easy to google. Why sloppy journalism?

Bob Kennedy was kinder to Cary Grant. The writing was stilted and bland, but at least his facts were true. "Grant bought out his Paramount contract to get away from Gary Cooper's shadow, became one of the first independent stars not owned by a studio, got $50,000 for Topper (That's $500,000 in today's cash), and during a six-year stretch from 1934 to 1940, solidified himself as the most popular leading man in Hollywood." Kennedy got one other thing right, the Cary Grant character was born around the time he started shooting *Philadelphia Story*. He had been using the name for 10 years through 30 movies, but the Katherine Hepburn comedy perfectly showcased his balance of good looks, comic timing, and style. He was the definition of debonair, a role he fashioned for himself by imitating Noel Coward, Douglas Fairbanks, and Cole Porter. By 1940, Cary Grant was the epitome of the Hollywood matinee idol.

Kennedy wisely glossed over Grant's five marriages and concentrated on the who's who of onscreen love affairs: Ingrid Bergman, Myrna Loy, Irene Dunn, Doris Day, Eva Marie Saint, Leslie Caron, Sophia Loren, Debra Kerr, Audrey Hepburn, and Grace Kelly. Kennedy focused on Cary Grant the movie star, with the perfect smile, impeccable tailoring, and witty repartee. The Cary Grant women loved, and men wanted to imitate.

He added two sidebars that exemplified this. The first was a column of headshots from some of Cary's biggest hits: *Philadelphia Story*, *Indiscreet*, *North by Northwest*, *Bishops Wife*, *Affair to Remember*, *Houseboat*, *Notorious*, and *Touch of Mink*. Under each photo was the name of Cary's character in the film. Dexter, Nicky, Johnny, etc. But Kennedy points out, they were not important. As far as the audience was concerned, they were all Cary Grant. This was not a slight to Cary's acting ability. Quite the contrary. It was a compliment to the professional in Cary who knew what audiences wanted. He created Cary Grant, a matinee idol, and he gave it to them, picture after picture. And he played it magnificently.

The other sidebar was a scene from *An Affair to Remember*. Cary and his costar Marie Blight are attending a concert. Seated behind Cary is a gorgeous young blonde, a Marilyn Monroe type. She can't keep her eyes off him and flirts brazenly. And when she says, "I love my seat," it's what every woman in the movie theater was thinking. Cary did not do a thing. He did not have to.

Dudley was impressed with Kennedy's selective use of movie roles for each of his subjects. He did not give an IMDb listing of all their movies. Instead focused on those roles that emphasized the actor's idol status. But by doing so he could not ignore the biggest flaw with his title, matinee idols were not known for their acting ability, mostly their good looks. Cary was a perfect example. Whenever he tried to expand his range (*None but the Lonely Heart*, *Mr. Lucky*, *Crisis*, or *The Howards of Virginia*), audiences stayed away, which was not fair. Cary does a marvelous acting job in those films, especially *Crisis*. But as a professional actor, *To Catch a Thief* was a better choice. All he had to do was smile, walk around, kiss a young and gorgeous Grace Kelly, and climb onto a roof or two. Pure box office magic.

After finishing the book, Dudley realized his problem right away. How was he going to interview five of today's biggest movie stars without insulting them? How was he supposed to write about George Clooney's acting prowess while staying true to the book's theme? Ryan Reynolds and Chris Pratt may be channeling Cary with their choice of roles, but Bradley Cooper stretches all the time. So does Clooney. And does Bruce Willis even qualify? Yes, he is big-box office, but he is more of an action-hero type than a true matinee idol. The only time he came close was with his TV show, *Moonlighting.*

George Dudley wrote down a dozen questions he planned to use as the base for his interviews. From experience, he knew there would be deviations from the script, but a solid starting point would help him. Because he was nervous. He didn't admit this to Amy. "Interviewing George Clooney? Bruce Willis? My big screen heroes? Who am I kidding?"

REFLECTIONS ON REPORT #8

A matinee idol? Really? That's all I've become? That's my legacy? A nice smile and I always get the girl? Oh, you better rewrite that crap, Georgie. I was an actor, first and foremost. Do you think it was easy being Cary Grant for forty years? Now that was an acting job.

Chapter 11
On Set with Bradley Cooper

REPORT #9

"Would you like another iced coffee, Mr. Leach?" Tyler Woods said to Dudley.

"No thanks, Tyler. Three is my limit," Dudley said laughing.

"Oh, sorry, I forgot I already gave you one."

"It's fine," Dudley said. Then asked. "But do you know how much longer they're going to be? It must be lunchtime now."

Tyler Woods had placed Dudley in a director's chair when they arrived on set at 7:30. It was a great spot to watch everything going on during the shoot. He was about ten feet behind Bradley Cooper and the main camera.

"Mr. Cooper is a perfectionist, Mr. Leach. They'll be done when he's got the shot," Woods said a bit testy, before walking away.

"Tyler wait, where's the bathroom?" Dudley asked, but Woods had already moved behind the set. It was a large interior of a library/drawing room. The type you would find in some-turn-of-the-century English Manor. An impressive pair of oak doors were off to the right of the room. A thick circular rug was in the center. To the right of the door was an elegant writing desk, and to the left, a very comfortable-looking sofa dominated the center of the room. A coffee table was situated in front of it and a pair of tall lamps flanked the sofa. To the far left was a glass patio door, through which could be seen a lush green garden. The patio door was slightly ajar, and a fan must have been set up out of sight because the sheer curtains were swaying gently.

Dudley looked around for someone else to ask, but everyone was busy. He had been sitting for almost four hours. He stood up, cautiously, then stopped. Cooper had called action and the three actors went through the scene again. A beautiful blond was on the sofa. She was leaning over the coffee table, a champagne bottle in her right hand. She was in the act of filling her glass when an older man came in through the big doors to her left. He stood in the doorway looking around. "Where is he, Yvette? I know he is here. I heard you two talking!"

The woman glanced quickly at the open patio door to her right just as a hand appeared, trying in vain to close it.

"Cut!" Cooper yelled out. "You're late again Jimmy. Damn it. Your hand needs to be there BEFORE Sandy speaks. Reset. Back to position one. Speed. Lights up. Ready? Slate it."

A young woman stepped in front of the camera, "*Saving Sandy.* Scene six. Take nine." Then she clicked the slate board and moved behind Cooper as he said, "Action."

Dudley realized immediately that he had started moving too late. He had tried to get off the set during the stop in action. He saw an exit sign between two large light stands behind the patio door. But, just as Bradley Cooper yelled 'lights up', Dudley was looking directly into the light fixture. He was temporarily blinded when the powerful LED fill hit him full in the face. He stifled a scream and reached out; his right hand took hold of the light stand; and he tried to move straight ahead past it. But his loss of vision messed up his sense of direction, and instead, he blundered straight into Jimmy Miller, the actor who was trying to get back into position behind the patio door.

Dudley let go of the light stand and whispered 'sorry' and tried to step around Miller, but he failed to see the collection of electrical cables on the floor in front of him. The toe of his left foot hit the cables and he stumbled to his right. Miller had already started his action, reaching for the patio door, just as Dudley grabbed him from behind to stop him from falling. Miller continued to move forward, and Dudley hung on to his jacket as the pair of them crashed through the patio door.

Miller fell to his knees, but Dudley somehow kept his feet under him and stumbled into the room. Luis Zapados, the older actor who had just entered the room saw Jimmy Miller fall to the floor. Luis halted his line delivery and stared, bewildered. Sandy, the actress on the sofa, screamed when Miller exploded through the door. She managed to turn her head in time to see another man come rushing at her. Sandy raised her hands to protect herself, but the stranger stopped suddenly. He was caught in the curtains. They wrapped him up and he spun around. He tried to extract himself but only served to tie up his hips and legs completely in the material.

The back of his legs bumped into the sofa, and he flipped over and fell onto his back. Sandy jumped up, still clutching the champagne bottle, but in her hurry to get out of Dudley's way, her high heel hit the edge of the carpet and she lost her balance and started to fall backward. Still on his back, Dudley reached out to catch hold of her to help, but he missed Sandy's hand and found the bottle's neck instead. He tugged hard, saving Sandy, but the exertion threw him to the floor. He landed hard.

Dudley awkwardly stood up, still holding the champagne bottle in his hand. He smiled at Sandy and bowed. "I believe this is yours, madam."

Sandy Thompson laughed and returned the bow, taking the bottle. Dudley backed away, forgetting the curtain was still tightly gripping his ankles, and started to fall, again. He windmilled his arms and began taking tiny, rapid steps. He twirled and twisted his body to free itself from the gauzy material, which resisted but finally fell away.

When Dudley finally stopped moving, his knees were flexed, and his arms were stretched out like an Olympic gymnast nailing the perfect vault. "Ha," he said.

"Now that's what I call an entrance," Luis said, clapping.

"All I was trying to do was find the bathroom," he whispered to the actor.

Luis Zapados laughed and gestured behind him. Dudley thanked him and exited through the large doors.

"Kevin," Bradley Cooper asked cautiously. "Please tell me you got that."

"I got it, Bradley," the cameraman said. "It was like watching Buster Keaton. When did you hire that guy?"

"Five minutes from now. Tyler!"

"Yessir?" Tyler Woods appeared at Bradley Cooper's side.

"Who was that?"

"Archie Leach. The reporter guy for your lunch interview."

"Go get him and take him to my trailer, now," Cooper said. "Archie Leach. That's funny. I don't think Cary Grant could have done that better. Send that to my laptop, will you Keven." Then he stood up and shouted to the crew, "Take lunch, everyone. We'll give this one more try in an hour."

Woods found Dudley outside the men's room and hurriedly dragged him to Bradley Cooper's trailer. Cooper was rewatching the footage on his laptop.

"I am so sorry, Mr. Cooper," Dudley said as soon as he entered.

"Wait. Watch this." He was replaying the moment Dudley took hold of the bottle and saved Sandy. "You did that in one take. Without rehearsal. All instinct. Are you an acrobat, Leach?"

"No, sir. I'm a writer."

He had pressed play and was watching Dudley twist around, trying to get his legs free of the curtain.

"How did you not fall down?"

"I almost did a couple of times. Look, Mr. Cooper, I am so sorry about that."

"Sorry?" Cooper said. "That was the best thing we shot all day. How did you do that?"

"I don't know," Dudley said nervously. "Please don't ask me to do it again."

Cooper laughed. "Sit down Archie. Hungry? Here, I got you a turkey sandwich."

"Thanks. I'm starving." He took a seat across from Cooper at a small table. "I hope I didn't mess up your movie."

"Mess it up? I'm trying to figure out how I can work it into the movie. It was brilliant. I haven't seen that kind of physical comedy since… well I don't know when."

"I was just looking for the bathroom."

Cooper stared at him and then broke out laughing. "You're killing me, Archie. Oh, love your name by the way. Your parents must have been Cary Grant fans."

"Well, my mom does have a weird sense of humor," Dudley said.

Cooper watched him, sipping his drink. "What are your plans tonight?"

"Oh, I don't know. Watching a movie in my room I guess."

"I have to cut our meeting short," he said standing up. "I got to finish this shot and one more before I'm finished today. But I'm throwing a little party tonight at the house for Jen. Why don't you come? We'll grab a couple of minutes of quiet time there. What do you say?"

Dudley choked and said, "Yes. Sure."

"Great. Tyler will arrange for someone to pick you up. Say, eight-ish?"

"I'll rearrange my schedule. Thank you," Dudley said.

Cooper looked at him and laughed again as he left the trailer.

Dudley looked up at Tyler Woods and asked, "What just happened?"

"Welcome to the big time Mr. Leach. I hope you brought a tux."

REFLECTIONS ON REPORT #9

I had no idea George had that in him. That reminded me of when we were shooting the restaurant scene in Bringing Up Baby. Kate was hilarious. Did the whole scene in one take. I kept messing up the timing with the hat bit, but she was a trouper. Never said a word. I think we did ten takes. Gosh, that was fun. Maybe George and I are a little bit alike already.

Chapter 12
Spielberg and Jennifer Lawrence

REPORT #10

"Nice tux," Cooper said, greeting George Dudley at his front door.

"Yes, sorry about that, Mr. Cooper. The Hotel Belvedere didn't have my exact size," Dudley said, holding out his arms. The jacket sleeves rode up his arms. "I'm a 42 Long you see and all they had was a Regular."

"Better than nothing," Cooper added with a smile. "If you don't salute anyone, I think you'll get away with it."

"Aye aye, sir," Dudley said, saluting.

"Find Woods," Cooper said. "He can show you around. We'll meet in my den in an hour. Okay?"

With that, Bradley Cooper moved toward a stunning, tall dark-haired woman who Dudley would later discover was Cooper's girlfriend, Irina Shayk. Dudley walked in the opposite direction and took a glass of champagne from a waiter carrying a tray of them. He drank it too fast and was looking for a place to put down the glass when he bumped into a short, round man wearing a red checkered vest and a purple beret.

"Oh sorry," Dudley said. "I didn't…"

"…see me," the short man said sarcastically. "I haven't heard THAT one before."

"No seriously. I just got here and I…, well, actually I'm a bit overwhelmed."

"Ah, a virgin," the man said. "HENRI! Come now!" he yelled. "Sorry, dear boy. I'm being rude. Introductions. I am the famous Albert Poots, but everyone in the States calls me the Colonel." He bowed and added, "Howdyado." He said it fast as if it were one word.

"I'm Geor… I mean Archie Leach," Dudley stammered. "Nice to meet you."

The Colonel looked at Dudley sideways and said, "Really? Your name is Archie Leach?"

"Yep. Archie Leach. That's me," Dudley said, looking around for an exit.

A tall, slim, elegant-looking woman came up behind the Colonel. "And what do we have here, Colonel?"

"Henri Darling, meet Archie Leach."

The tall woman with the Prince Valiant haircut said, "No, it's not."

"That's what it said."

"Really? Archie Leach? From Bristol?"

"Orlando, actually," Dudley said, and the two bizarre strangers broke out into laughter.

"Oh, I love this Archie Leach," the woman cried, then sticking out her hand she grabbed Dudley's with a strong grip, "Henri Harrison. Howdyado?"

"I'm a bit out of my element, Miss Harrison," Dudley stammered, trying to pull his hand away.

"Call me Henri, everybody does. Now Leach, what's your game? Friend of the help? Gate crasher?"

"No, no, I was invited by Mr. Cooper."

"Mr. Cooper, eh," Henri said. "Sounds suspicious, don't you think Colonel."

"I would say so, Henri. No one who's anyone calls Bradley MISTER Cooper. I'm voting for gate crasher."

"Not so fast Colonel. Not so fast," Henri said circling Dudley. "Not enough evidence yet. We need to dig a little deeper. Notice the ill-fitting tux. The 10-year-old eyeglasses. The unshined shoes."

"Like I said Henri, gate crasher."

"But he came in through the front door and William didn't toss him," Henri added quickly gesturing toward the two bodyguards near the front entrance.

"Which one is William?" the Colonel asked.

"I think they both are. Easier to remember. But back to the case, Colonel. The case of the mysterious, Mr. Leach."

"But there's nothing mysterious, Miss… ah Henri, I was…" Dudley began but Henri Harrison cut him off.

"Yip. Yip. Yip," Henri said holding up a commanding hand. "Try not to speak."

"This is a famous game of ours," the Colonel said. "We pride ourselves on figuring out who someone is with the barest of clues."

"You're a guest at the… The Belvedere Hotel," Henri said.

"Well, that's right," Dudley said, smiling, "you see I…"

"Quiet. You arrived last night. You are from the other coast. You've been recently fired. Your wife left you and your real name is NOT Archie Leach."

"Oh, my God," Dudley stammered. "How did you… Do you know my mother? Did she call you?"

"No. But she's not too wild about you crashing on her couch after all these years, I can tell you that."

"I need to sit down," Dudley said and slid onto a large gray couch.

"Would you like a drink, Archie? How about some champagne?" the Colonel offered.

"I really don't think I…"

"Say no more. Coming right up," and he scampered away toward the bar.

Meanwhile, Henri, still staring at Dudley sat next to him on the sofa. She crossed her legs, brushing an invisible piece of lint off her tight black slacks. "There's a Belvedere label on the inside of your jacket. You already told me you're from Orlando. Bradley told me you were the new guy working on that Universal book, so I figured you must have recently left your other job. And I just guessed your wife left you, because, well, you look sad."

"Oh," was all Dudley could say.

"Don't tell Albert. He thinks I'm like Sherlock Holmes or something. So what's your real name?"

"George Dudley," and as soon as he said it, he placed his hands on his mouth. "Oh fuck. No one's supposed to know that."

"Don't worry sweetie," Henri said placing a comforting hand on Dudley's leg. "I am the queen of secrets. You are Arche Leach until you tell me otherwise." Then she winked at him. "I'll have to tell the Colonel, though. We have NO secrets. That's why we are such good partners. But he is the sole of discretion. I'd trust him with my life," she said suddenly serious. "As a matter of fact, I have. On more than one occasion."

"What are you guys? Private investigators?"

"Worst. Talent agents. *My Fair Agents*. Heard of it?" Henri asked.

"I'm sorry, no."

"No need to apologize. Only A-listers and Producers need to know who we are. Of course, all we have now are a handful of B-listers, but Oprah likes us, and Bradley lets us send him people to audition."

"Here you go old boy," the Colonel said, sitting down. "And a G and T for you, my dear."

"Thanks, C. The Colonel here headed up one of the biggest UK agencies from 1990 to 2011."

"2012, but let's not quibble."

"And we've been together since what, five years now?" Henri said, thinking.

"Five years, six months, and a smattering of days," the Colonel added. "You watch *The Journey* on FX?"

"I can't say I do," Dudley said.

"No one does. Anyway, Jimmy Miller is one of our rising stars. He'll hit it big one day. Got a call back for a Superman remake last year. Just a matter of time. Just a matter of time. Good attitude that boy. And good-looking too."

"Oh, there you are Mr. Leach," Tyler Woods said. "Hello, Henri. Albert."

"The boy wonder," Henri Harrison said, with a sneer.

"Private York returns from the front," the Colonel said, jumping up and saluting.

Woods ignored them and grabbed Dudley's arm. "Come Leach. Bradley asked me to show you the place."

"A private tour of the palace," the Colonel said to Henri. "Maybe he is somebody."

"It was very nice meeting you," Dudley said as Tyler Woods dragged him away. "Come Leach. I'll introduce you to some 'important' people."

"Were we just insulted, Henri?" the Colonel said, feigning shock.

"It's hard to tell with those types, Colonel," Henri Harrison said, lighting a cigarette. "You can never trust what comes out of their mouths."

"Jesus Leach. Of all the people to sit with," Woods admonished him, as soon as they were in the next room.

"I found them very charming," Dudley said.

"Everyone is charming, Leach. It's Hollywood. But there are people to meet, then there are 'people' to meet, if you know what I mean."

"No," Dudley said. "But I'm sure you'll explain it to me."

"Oh, don't be dull. Wait, there's Spielberg. We'll say hello then find Jennifer," Woods said excitedly. "Have you ever met Jennifer Lawrence?"

"Jennifer Lawrence?" Dudley gasped. "She's here?"

"HA!" Woods laughed, a single honk. "You are a riot, Leach."

They approached Steven Spielberg who was patiently listening to two young movie enthusiasts.

Dudley couldn't tell if they were writers or directors, but they threw around the jargon like they were reciting from textbooks. "Just wait until I introduce you," Woods said. "He's a bit touchy. Even at parties."

"No, it's the sequencing, Lionel. The shot sequences, and of course the cuts," the shorter one said, reaching out to touch Spielberg's arm.

"It's the pacing, Wally," Lionel, the taller one cut in. "The building of the tension. Small scenes, added on top of each other, with the obligatory action scene, but all the while the character conflicts dominate."

"Yes, yes character conflict, obviously Lionel, but the subjective use of angle and dolly shots, when you least expect them," Wally said reaching out again, but this time Spielberg quickly turned away and jostled Dudley who had just taken a large sip of champagne. The bump startled him, and he spit out the champagne onto Spielberg's shirt.

"Oh, my God," Wally (or maybe Lionel) cried out.

"I am so sorry, Mr. Spielberg," Dudley said.

"Damn it, Leach," Woods said horrified. He stepped forward and tried to wipe Spielberg's shirt with his handkerchief. "Sorry, Mr. Spielberg. This is Archie Leach, he's a reporter or something. He's here to interview Bradley."

"Archie Leach," Spielberg said, grabbing Woods's handkerchief from him and finishing the cleanup job on his shirt. "That's a great name to have in this town."

Everyone laughed, like a bad laugh track from an 80s TV comedy. Except for Dudley. "Well, my mother liked it."

Spielberg studied Dudley for a moment then grabbed his arm and thrust him between himself and Lionel and Wally. "Help me out here, Archie. These two were trying to tell me why my movies are always so successful. The tall one said it was the fascinating characters. The short one said it was the editing. What do you think?"

The room became very quiet. Dudley felt that every single person was looking at him. He swallowed, blinked, and cleaned his glasses with a paper napkin. He coughed, stalling for time. He had no idea what to say. He hated being put on the spot like this. He embarrassed himself on set this morning. His too-small tux made him feel uncomfortable. Now these movie people were all looking at him. *I was just supposed to ask Bradley some questions.*

"Well, Mr. Leach?" the shorter one said belligerently. "Please. Dazzle us with your insight." Something sparked in Dudley then. He could always spot a bully, whether in gym clothes or a tuxedo. He turned his back on the little man and said. "It's neither of those things, Mr. Spielberg. Your movies are successful because you always use the same production crew for all your movies. Set designer, costumer, editor, light designer, even casting; pretty much everything. So there's a consistency already built in." Everyone stared, mouths open, and Spielberg smiled.

Then George leaned in closer and whispered, "And good writing of course."

"Exactly!" Spielberg shouted. "I love this guy. Someone get him another drink." Three people, including the tall one, ran off in different directions.

Spielberg grabbed Dudley's hand. "Archie Leach. I will remember you. Have Woods get you my contact info." Then to Woods, "The real ones, Tyler."

"Yes, sir," Woods said, hardly able to speak.

"Very nice meeting you," Spielberg said.

"Same here. Sorry about your shirt," Dudley said before Woods dragged him away.

"He's very nice," Dudley said when they started up the central stairway.

"You spill your drink on Spielberg's shirt and he gives you his private number, I'm speechless."

"Where are we going now?" Dudley asked.

"Bradley wanted me to introduce you to Jennifer," Tyler Woods said.

Dudley pulled away from Tyler. "No. I'm not ready for that."

"You have to. This party is for her," Woods said. "Sort of a holiday tradition, I think. Anywho, they are great friends. They did four movies together, you know." Tyler was behind Dudley now, pushing him up the stairs.

"But look, is it really necessary I meet her? I mean…"

"What? You don't like Jennifer? Everybody loves her." Tyler continued to guide Dudley down the hallway.

"Yes, I know, that's exactly the problem," Dudley said, quickly turning to face him. But at the exact same moment, Tyler pushed him through a pair of saloon doors that opened into a small sitting room. He bumped rear ends with Jennifer Lawrence. The large glass of red wine she was holding went flying into the air.

"Oh shit," she said. Dudley turned and found himself face to face with his fantasy girl.

"Oh my," was all he could get out before he ducked and tried to get past her, but in his haste, he did not see the large wine spill on the floor and his shiny new black shoes lost all traction and he fell backward again. Reaching out for something to break his fall, he grabbed Jennifer Lawrence's dress and pulled her down on top of him; her butt landed hard on his crotch.

"Fuck," Dudley said.

Tyler Woods covered his face with his hands and cried, "Oh, God, not again." The other guests held their breath, not knowing what was going to happen next. And George Dudley wished he were anywhere else in the world, but right here, right now.

Jennifer Lawrence looked up at her friends, then slowly turned her head to catch George's eye beneath her. "Okay," she replied, "but go easy back there, big boy. We just met."

No one spoke. Then everyone broke into great gasps of laughter. Dudley placed his hands over his face. Jennifer rolled off him and there was a crunching sound.

"Oh. What was that?" she said.

"My glasses," Dudley cried.

"Oh, sorry," she said, sitting up and holding the two pieces in her hand. She examined them carefully. "You know, with a little tape I think we can fix you right up, mister?"

"Dud… Leach," Dudley said, just catching himself.

Jennifer stood and helped Dudley up. "Well, Mr. Dud-Leach, let's see if we can find some tape."

"Tyler, get some towels and clean that wine up before someone else has a sexual encounter."

"Yes, ma'am," Tyler Woods said, heading into the kitchen.

"Yes, ma'am," she mocked. "He always makes me feel sixty years old." She stood in front of Dudley and placed a hand on her left hip and thrust it out, her right leg nearly fully exposed through the slit in her red evening gown. The effect was very sexy. "Do I look sixty years old to you Mr. Dud-Leach?"

Dudley, who was nearly blind without his glasses, chose at that moment to lean toward her and squint.

"Oh, that's right big boy. Take a good look," Jennifer said, pushing out her chest and doing her best Mae West voice. "Why don't you come up and see me sometime."

"The line is actually, '*Why don't you come up sometime and see me?*'" Dudley said, correcting her. "It's a common mistake."

Jennifer Lawrence stared at Dudley, annoyed, and thrust the two pieces of his glass into his hands. "Well, Mr. Dud-Leach. You can forget about seconds," and left the room.

"Nice going Archie," Tyler Woods said. "Come on. Bradley is ready for you now."

Woods led Dudley down the hall and into a small den. A desk and two chairs dominated the room. The walls were covered with framed posters of vintage movies (*Casablanca*, *Double Indemnity*, and *Captain Blood*) and bookshelves, an eclectic mix of popular fiction, classics, spiritual, and history.

Bradley Cooper was seated behind the desk and pulled out a roll of tape. "Give me your glasses, Leach. You're going to look like the classic high school nerd when you get these back on, but at least you'll be able to see."

"Wouldn't be the first time," Dudley mumbled.

"What was that?" Cooper asked.

"Oh, nothing. Please apologize to Ms. Lawrence for me, will you? I am so embarrassed."

"Don't worry about it. She probably won't even remember it," he said, taping the two pieces together. "There. Good as new." He handed them back to George. "So shoot. What's your first question?"

Dudley slid his broken glasses back on his face and adjusted the uncomfortable fit. "Thanks, Bradley. Better than nothing." He pulled a small notebook from his jacket, squinted then said, "Do you consider yourself a matinee idol?" Cooper looked at him and laughed.

"What?" Dudley asked.

"Seriously. That's your first question?"

"Well... yes. I mean the book is about..."

"I know what the books about, Archie," Cooper said still laughing. "But seriously, you going to ask all the other guys that? You gonna ask Clooney? He'll throw you out a window. And Bruce will just punch you in the mouth.

Reynolds might answer you though now that I think about it. You're going to have trouble shutting him up."

"Okay, how about this? Who was your favorite matinee idol growing up?"

Bradley Cooper looked at Dudley, smiled then, and looking at his watch said, "You know what, I really have to do this thing with Jennifer now, why don't you email over your questions to Tyler, and I'll see what I can do."

"But you invited me."

"Yes. Well, that bit this morning was classic. But this isn't working Mr. Leach," he said standing. "Thanks for coming. Tyler will take you back to the hotel when you're ready."

REFLECTIONS ON REPORT #10

I can't put my finger on it but that pair, Henri and the Colonel remind me of someone. I need to keep a watch on those two. But that Jennifer Lawrence; feisty. She's like a young Jean Arthur. George likes her too, poor sod. Things didn't go well with that Cooper boy. I could have helped with that, but 'No interference'. Stupid rules.

Chapter 13
My Fair Gentleman

Dudley found his way back to the living room. He was looking for Tyler Woods. He was tired and disappointed and just wanted to go back to his hotel room and get into bed. He was not sure what he was going to tell Amy. "Hi, Amy. I threw champagne at Steven Spielberg. I knocked down Jennifer Lawrence, and oh, by the way, Bradley Cooper thinks I'm an idiot. Great first day."

As he stepped out of Bradley's den, he was immediately surrounded by Henri and the Colonel. "My, my, my, have you been busy," Henri said.

"We leave you alone for ten minutes and you got Jennifer Lawrence pregnant and Spielberg's private number," the Colonel said. "What's next? Joy riding with Van Diesel through Starbucks?"

"What? Jennifer Lawrence isn't pregnant. We didn't have sex. She just fell on top of me. Oh shit, what a lousy night, I just want to go home."

"But it's early. Here, have a drink," the Colonel said, handing him a glass of dark liquor.

"What is this?" Dudley asked.

"Well, after your evening, we decided you needed an alcoholic upgrade. Enjoy."

Dudley took a large swig and coughed. "Slowly dear boy," the Colonel said. "That's Remy Martin. You're supposed to sip and savor, not gulp."

"Now you tell me. Wow, has a bit of a kick, doesn't it?"

"Yes, but mixing with all the champagne you've drunk probably isn't such a good idea either. Let's sit." Dudley tried, but failed, slipping off the edge of the sofa and ending up on the floor; again. "Just where I belong."

"No, no, no dear boy." The Colonel and Henri picked him up and plopped him onto the couch.

"No, leave me. I'm a disaster. I can't even do a simple interview."

"Oh, self-pity," Henri said. "Can't have that, can we Colonel?"

"I usually deal with money, you know. CEO's. CFO's. Financial advisors. Those sorts of people. I don't know how to talk to movie stars. How did Amy think I could pull this off? I should get home. Where's… oh, what's his name?" Dudley mumbled.

"Woods? He left right after Jennifer gave you a lap dance," the Colonel said.

"She did not…," he started to protest but then gave up. "Someone call me a cab." Albert and Henri exchanged a look and then shook their heads.

"No," Albert said, "too easy."

Dudley tried to get up too fast and then sat back down. "Oh, my head. I don't feel too good. I don't usually drink this much. I hardly drink at all, you know."

"Teetotaler?" the Colonel sneered.

"Coke Zero actually, my wife is the drinker," Dudley said.

"You're married?" the Colonel said, suddenly curious.

"For now," Henri added. "She left him."

George started to cry. "She doesn't love me anymore. I think she's sleeping with Atticus Finch."

"Oh, this just keeps getting better and better," the Colonel said smiling broadly.

"It will be so simple, Amy said. Just ask them a few questions, write it up, and bingo-bango we have a book. Easy as a Sunday morning!" Dudley rolled off the couch again.

"Just leave him there, Albert. He looks comfortable," Henri said.

"Pitiful, but comfortable," the Colonel said, patting George on the head.

"Archie Leach. That was a good one," Dudley slurred. "The man who would be Cary Grant. I knocked down Jennifer Lawrence. I ruined Bradley Cooper's movie. I spat on Steven Spielberg. And this is just my first day!" Dudley removed his glasses and rubbed his eyes.

"Doesn't exactly fit in does he, our Archie Leach," Henri said, and cocked her head to one side, appraising the man on the floor with a gleam in her eye.

"He is rather handsome without those ugly spectacles." Her left foot was bouncing fast, up, and down.

"Oh no," the Colonel said. "I know that look."

"I mean it's too perfect, Albert. His name is Arche Leach, for heaven's sake. It's destiny. We have to help him."

"But why Henri?"

"The challenge, dear boy. The challenge."

"Yes, I admit I like the boy but the last one didn't exactly turn out that well," the Colonel said.

"She didn't listen to me," Henri said. "All she wanted to do was dance all night. Get the car, Albert."

"So we're doing this," the Colonel said, resigned.

"Yes. We're going to turn our Archie Leach into the new Cary Grant."

The next morning, George Dudley woke to a painful headache and mass confusion. *Where am I?* he thought. He was lying on a four-poster king-sized bed, covered with pillows and a deep blue down comforter. The room was spacious but definitely not his hotel room. The furnishings were all antiques, the wallpaper was powder blue with yellow daisies, and there were too many small glass and porcelain figurines on the dresser and the shelves. *Looks like the set for Glass Menagerie*, he thought. *Maybe I'm dreaming.* He pulled the covers over his face. His door was suddenly opened, and the smell of freshly brewed coffee made him sit up again.

"Wasn't sure if you were a coffee or a tea man," Albert Poots said entering with a tray. "So I brought both. I brought Advil too. How are you feeling?"

"Bit of a headache. Um… where am I?" Dudley asked.

"1222 Mulholland Drive."

"This is not the Belvedere?" Dudley asked.

"No, we checked you out before we brought you here. This is Henri's house."

Albert Poots pulled open the curtains and bright sunlight flooded the room. "Oh no. Is it morning already? What time is it? I have a 9:00 am flight home."

"You missed it. It's 9:31, precisely," the Colonel said, handing him the Advil bottle.

"Four should do it."

"Fuck. I missed my plane."

"Anxious to get back to mommy?" the Colonel asked.

Dudley looked at him, or at least where he thought he was. "Where are my glasses?"

"Henri is fixing them."

George sat up and pain shot through his head. He squinted toward where Albert's voice came from. "Where's the tray?"

"On the end table. To your right."

George reached out carefully and found the edge of the table. He moved close and saw the coffee mug. He popped the Advil and took a sip. Then another.

"Your suitcase is next to the foot of the bed. Get dressed and meet us downstairs for breakfast and we will all have a nice chat. Okay? The bathroom is to your left." He walked to the door, turned, and said, "You know George, I believe this is the beginning of a beautiful friendship."

"The actual line is, 'Louis', I think this is the beginning of a beautiful friendship."

"Is it? Potato-potato. I like mine better," the Colonel said. "See you downstairs. Uva made pancakes!"

The coffee and Advil helped the headache, and after he showered and dressed, he almost felt normal. He searched inside his suitcase for his cell phone and was relieved it was charged, so he called his mother.

"Jesus, Mary, and Joseph, what time is it, Georgie?" she said.

"It's 9:30 here, mom. I'm still in California. I missed my plane I'll call you when I make new reservations."

"No rush, Georgie dear. It's not like you have to be somewhere. Are you having fun at least?"

"I got Spielberg's number and I think I slept with Jennifer Lawrence," he said. "Oh, and Bradley Cooper threw me out."

"Sounds like you're having a great time," his mother mumbled, half awake. "Call me later, I'm going back to sleep." She hung up.

He dressed then groped his way down the hall and found the kitchen, more by scent than vision. He located a stool and sat at the island kitchen counter. A tall, ghostly image spoke to him from the corner. "Good morning. You want coffee?" It was Uva the housekeeper, dressed all in a white, collared shirt; pleated linen pants; and a long, linen overcoat.

"Do you have orange juice?" Dudley stuttered.

"Of course. This is California." She poured him a glass and placed it directly in front of him and said, "You are handsome."

"Um… thank you."

"The girls usually bring home the ugly ones," she said touching his hair, which was still a little wet and slicked back. "You are almost attractive."

He pulled away and squeaked, "Where's Henri?"

Uva examined him for a moment longer before returning to the refrigerator. "Out. The other one is by the pool. One egg or two?"

"Two, thank you. Scrambled."

"I will bring to you when ready," she said and turned her back to him.

Dudley slid from the stool and groped his way through the patio doors. Albert Poots was reading a newspaper and sipping from a Disneyland coffee mug. George Dudley groped around for a moment then finally found a metal lounge chair. He sat down and sipped his orange juice.

The Colonel folded his paper and placed it on the table. He was wearing a colorful kimono with a large dragon pattern sewn into it. He had on a large floppy hat and pulled his sunglasses down and peered at George. "Feeling refreshed, Georgie?"

"I should have never told Henri my name."

"Henri didn't tell me. I looked at your driver's license, while you slept," the Colonel said.

"You what?"

"Oh, don't get all indignant. Yes, we did sort of kidnap you, but you are a stranger. A cute lost bunny type of stranger, but a stranger nevertheless." the Colonel said, smiling. "You can't be too careful nowadays. There are lots of crazies out there."

"Fair enough. But please don't tell anyone, I could get into a lot of trouble," Dudley pleaded.

"You mean with Rupert Murdoch?"

"What? How did you…"

"We googled you, dear boy," the Colonel said, patting his hand. "Relax. You are even more intriguing now than you were last night. The nom-de-plum, the awkward social skills, the disasters that seem to follow in your wake."

"Oh, just kill me now," Dudley said, his head in his hands.

"Don't worry Georgie. Your secret or secrets are safe with me," the Colonel said. "I never hurt a friend. I am very loyal that way."

"But we just met."

"I am an excellent judge of character and I believe in fate. We were meant to meet."

Uva came out and placed a plate of food in front of Dudley. "I made toast and bacon. You like the bacon?"

"Um, no actually…"

The Colonel reached over and snatched the bacon from the plate. "Waste not, want not. Uva, let Henri know we are out here when she returns."

"Ya Colonel," she said with a brisk salute and reentered the kitchen.

"I love the way she says Co-lo-nel. I feel like a Nazi," Albert Poots whispered. "Or at least that guy on the old Hogan's Heroes TV show."

"Werner Klemperer. 1965 to 1971. He was nominated for a Tony in 1987 for his role in Cabaret."

The Colonel stared then started clapping. "That's marvelous George. You should be on Jeopardy."

Dudley ignored the compliment and started eating. He didn't realize how hungry he was.

Between mouthfuls, he asked, "You mentioned some sort of plan?"

"A grand plan," Henri Harrison said, sweeping onto the patio. She was dressed in a charcoal gray Alexander McQueen double-breasted suiting blazer, cut very low in the front. She removed her oversized sunglasses and stood behind the Colonel with her hands on his shoulders, staring directly at George Dudley. "The Master plan, my friend."

"Do you have my glasses?" Dudley asked.

"Look, Colonel," Henri Harrison said, pointing at Dudley's face. "A simple device of removing his glasses and it's like Clark Kent transforming into Superman."

"Yes, I did notice that when he came down. A remarkable difference."

"It's almost too easy. Contact lenses, a workout regimen, tanning booth, yoga for the posture, you can handle the wit and I'll handle the voice… it's almost too easy," Henri said, her voice rising in excitement. She slid into an open chair opposite Dudley and crossed her long legs.

"He'll need a new wardrobe," the Colonel said seriously.

"Oh, that goes without saying," Henri returned.

"Could be pricey."

"You know I can't see you, but I can hear you," Dudley added annoyed.

"Do you have an expense account, dear boy?" Albert Poots asked.

"Yes. They gave me an AmEx card for…"

"Well, that solves that," Henri said cutting him off and leaning in closer. "Here are your glasses…, Archie."

Dudley put them on and said, "You know that's not my real name Henri. I had to pick a pen name. Because of the non-compete."

"Yes, but I'm curious why of all the names in the world you chose THAT one?"

Dudley could hear Uva in the kitchen loading the dishwasher and humming *Climb Every Mountain* from *Sound of Music*. Albert Poots sipped his drink and Henri Harrison reached over and gently removed the glasses from Dudley's face. She pulled a linen napkin from her jacket and began cleaning the lenses. "Why Archie Leach, Mr. Dudley?"

"Because…" and a lump appeared in Dudley's throat interrupting his words.

"It's alright," Henri whispered. "Words have power. Especially deep truths. Why did you want to be Archie Leach?" she asked again.

"I didn't," George Dudley said softly.

"You didn't?" the Colonel said leaning in.

"No. I wanted to be Cary Grant," Dudley said, covering his face with his hands.

"I'm sorry," Henri asked, and there was real tenderness in her voice. "What did you say?"

Dudley wiped his eyes and then looked directly at Henri Harrison. "I want to be Cary Grant," he said forcefully. "I've always wanted to be Cary Grant. And this seemed like the best opportunity for me to try it out."

"Get our boy a napkin, Albert," Henri said.

"Are you unhappy, George?" The Colonel asked.

Dudley nodded.

"Have you been unhappy for a while?" Henri asked.

Dudley nodded again.

"And you truly believe that if you were Cary Grant, you would be happy?" the Colonel asked, gently.

"All women want him, and all men want to be him," Dudley recited.

"Yes, that's the myth isn't it," Henri said. "That's the character the original Archie Leach created. Your problem is you tried to do it on your own."

"What?" Dudley asked, putting his glasses back on.

Henri stood and started to pace between Dudley and the inground pool. "You thought just by adopting the name, the rest would come. I admit it was clever and a good first step, but the real Archie Leach had the entire Hollywood PR department working for him, developing this image. The studios chose pictures that cast him as the leading man, with women fawning all over him. Mae West did more in creating Cary Grant than Archie Leach ever did. She was the reigning sex symbol of her time, and she chose him. Powerful stuff."

"I don't understand, Henri. What does Cary Grant's early career have to do with me?" Dudley asked.

"Why everything, dear boy. That Archie Leach had the Hollywood studio machine helping him to create the Cary Grant we all know and envy today. But you don't have the Hollywood machine to help you. You have something better. Your Archie Leach has us," the Colonel said, placing his arms around Dudley's shoulders and kissing his cheek.

"Your next interview is in five weeks with George Clooney. The Oprah Winfrey party." Henri paced and planned. She was a big-picture type of person. See all the players. Find the weakness and make your move. Sun Tzu is at his finest.

"Wait. How do you know that?" Dudley protested.

"Please, George. Stop asking ridiculous questions. We looked through your stuff," the Colonel smiled.

"We would need to stick to a rigorous schedule," Henri continued. "Morning runs and hours in the gym to get that body into shape. A tanning booth for that all-weather healthy glow. Elocution in the afternoon, and basic etiquette classes. You'll have to stay here of course."

"Of course," the Colonel parroted.

"But…" George tried to protest.

"He'll need contact lenses. Make an appointment with LeMue, Albert. He does mine. We'll need some press too. Not too much. Too bad we don't have a photo of that Jennifer Lawrence incident."

"Oh, but we do," the Colonel said, thrilled to be able to surprise Ms. Henri. "Someone posted it on Instagram, last night."

"Lovely. Let's get that out there with something like *Who's Archie Leach?* ask Jennifer Lawrence. She knows him up close and personal. Are you writing all this down, Albert?" Henri said.

"Every word," he said, not writing a word. He winked at Dudley. "Isn't this exciting?"

"What's going on?" Dudley asked the Colonel.

"Your dream is about to come true, George Dudley. Henri and I are going to turn your Archie Leach into Cary Grant."

"You are? How?" Dudley said unbelieving.

"How, my dear boy?" the Colonel said throwing his arm around Henri Harrison's shoulder. "Haven't you ever seen *My Fair Lady*?"

REFLECTIONS ON REPORT #11

Damn, Damn, Damn, Damn, Damn. He has help!

Chapter 14
Tut, Tut, Tut

"He has help," Cary said, storming into Clarence's office.

"I'm sorry, Mr. Odbody, I told him this was your reading hour," Kay Kendall said, following Cary into the room.

Clarence put down the Jackie Collins novel he was reading and looked up. "Tut, tut, tut, Miss Kendall. It's alright. I need to take a break anyway. This Jackie Collins is no Mark Twain, but I can't seem to put it down." He removed his reading glasses and placed the novel into a desk drawer.

Cary Grant walked directly up to Clarence Odbody's desk and placed both of his hands on it.

"Clarence, there are people down there helping him become me."

"I know Cary," he said calmly.

"You know? Well, there's your problem right there. Case solved," he said, and he began to pace in front of Clarence's desk. Back and forth. "Hit them with a lightning bolt or something."

"Oh, tut, tut, tut. We don't do that anymore," he said laughing to himself. "Would be nice to see though."

"I can give you a list of people to hit if you want to practice," Kay Kendall said, sitting down.

"That won't be necessary, Miss Kendall," Clarence said. Then to Cary, "Of course, we knew he had help. Read the files. There is a whole industry of people helping others change who they are. Psychiatrists, dietitians, personal trainers, and my favorite life coaches. Now that sounds like a fun job. Didn't have that when I was walking around down there."

"But…" Cary started, but then he threw himself into the chair.

"Tut, tut, tut dear boy. There's nothing to be upset about. You're doing fine. Just keep filing your reports," Clarence said, holding up another manila folder. "I've passed your reports onto Saint Peter, he thinks you are a natural. Though I did have to edit a few things. You should have caught that, Miss Kendall."

"Those were the best parts," she countered.

His phone rang. "There we go. Another angel got their wings!"

Kay stood and grabbed Cary by the arm. "I think that's our cue to leave."

Once outside she said, "He was right about one thing. Your reports are incredibly good. You're a talented storyteller. I can't wait for the next report."

Cary looked around, distracted. "Thank you. You're very kind."

"What's the matter?"

"This is not what I expected," Cary said, his voice barely above a whisper. "I thought I'd sit there, watch him go through his boring little day, write it up and that would be it. I didn't realize I would start to care. I like George Dudley."

"Yea. That can happen. I should have warned you," Kay said, placing a hand on his shoulder.

"Especially on the longer ones."

"I want to help him," he said earnestly. Then he dropped his voice and said, "One time I actually did."

Kay stopped and instantly grabbed his arm. "You did what, exactly?"

"It was when he was in the elevator at work that first day, with those two rude girls. I got so angry I reached out to grab Miss Jamison, I wanted to give her a shake, you know. But all I got was the zipper on the back of her skirt," Cary said, ashamed. "When she got off the elevator, her skirt fell to the floor."

"I don't remember reading anything about that." There was an edge to her voice.

"I didn't put it in the report," Cary said.

"Cary. We talked about this."

"I know. I know," he apologized, "But they made me so mad."

Kay took hold of his shoulders, her face inches from his. "You must promise me you will never, ever do that again. Promise me. Now!"

"Okay. Ouch. You're stronger than you look," he said rubbing his arms.

"I should tell Clarence. This was a mistake," she said.

"No. Please Kay," he pleaded. "I'm sorry. I won't do it again. I promise." And then he used his famous smile on her, and she melted a little and playfully punched his arm.

"Oh, I knew you were going to be trouble."

"What? Little old me?" and they laughed together, but Kay was not convinced. She decided to keep a close eye on Mr. Cary Grant from now on.

"Now if you don't mind, I'm going home. I need some rest. Dudley has a big day planned tomorrow."

"Good night Cary," she said, kissing his cheek. "And please, stay out of trouble."

He held up a hand, cocked his head to the side, and said, "Scout's honor."

She shook her head and turned away. "Trouble with a capital 'T'."

Chapter 15
I Think He's Got It

"Hello, Mary. I hope it's not too early to call," Dudley said into his cell phone.

"No. I just got home," Mary Jordan said. "It's good to hear from you. Your mother said you're still out in Los Angeles. How long have you been out there? A month now?"

"About that long. Yes," he said. "Decided to stay out here a while. Staying with some new friends."

"I didn't know you knew anyone out there?"

"Met them at Bradley's party."

"Bradley's party," Mary mocked him. "You're sounding like a Hollywood jerk already."

"I think there's something in the water out here. Makes you talk that way."

"Who are these new friends," Mary asked.

"Henri and Albert. They're helping me."

"With the writing?"

"Well, no. With other stuff," Dudley said vaguely.

"You're being very mysterious George. Do you have a cold? Your voice sounds funny."

"Funny?" he asked.

"Yes. Kind of nasal. Almost British," she laughed.

Dudley blushed. He'd been working on his Cary Grant voice that afternoon. He and the Colonel had watched *My Girl Friday*—they picked a different Cary Grant movie each day—and he would recite the lines with Cary. When the movie ended, the Colonel gave him a rare compliment. "I think you've got it, by George."

He ignored her observation and said, "Did mom give you the Christmas present?"

"It was lovely George, but you didn't have to do that," Mary said, smiling.

"I miss you," he said suddenly.

"Really? Then why didn't you come right back after the interview?"

Silence. "Um. Well, you see…" he began.

"Well, it was nice seeing you again," she said, cutting him off. Mary was happy he called, but now she couldn't tell if he was interested in seeing her again or not.

"I liked seeing you too. It was fun," he said. Then he remembered his performance. "Well, most of it."

"Oh, George, I don't care about that. You had a lot on your mind, and I pushed too hard. I just liked being with you again."

"Me too." Then he said impulsively, "Say what are you doing for Valentine's Day?"

"That's a month away."

"Put it on your calendar," Dudley said. "I'll be back February 12th, after the Clooney meeting. I want to see you."

"Okay. It's a date."

"That's great," and he meant it. It felt so comfortable being with her again. "Okay, I must go for my run now. I'll call you soon. Bye," he said ending the call. Mary smiled and then thought, *Going for a run? George Dudley is exercising?*

Dudley changed into his sweats and running shoes and was pounding down the beach by 7:00 am He was up to three miles now but feeling better than he had in years. The first few weeks were torture, but like most exercises, once you got into the routine, it seemed the body craved attention. He felt he could be up to five miles by week's end.

His contacts arrived the day before and after a few tries, he was able to slide them onto his eyes without too much trouble. They were surprisingly comfortable, but he still found himself unconsciously reaching for the glasses on his face. Running without his glasses bouncing up and down on his nose and fogging up was a definite improvement.

After he showered, he met Henri for breakfast. One hard-boiled egg, fruit, and orange juice. Then an hour of voice lessons in his study. They started with piano scales for fifteen minutes, up and down the register. "Good for breath control," Henri told him. "Also, relaxes the jaw and loosens up the lips. An excellent exercise."

He was at the gym by noon and made use of their tanning booth three times a week. Afternoons were with the Colonel. They would usually have lunch together at a different Hollywood restaurant. They would observe people and he would practice his accent. "It isn't necessary to speak the Queen's English," Albert Poots said. "You must sound like you were born there and now you're trying to hide it."

"That sounds easy," Dudley said sarcastically.

"Easier than you might think. American actors have been trying to pull off British accents forever, with very few successes. So the bar is already low. Just give the impression of the accent. A hint. Chose a small selection of words and let them do the work for you. For example, say Hello."

"Hello," Dudley said.

"Now emphasize the second part. Let your voice go up. Hel-LO. Like that."

"Hel-LO," Dudley repeated.

"Perfect," the Colonel said. "And always look people in the eye. Almost challenging. Movie actors learn this trick of turning their heads while maintaining eye contact. It's a curious thing. Makes the other person uncomfortable. Use it mostly on men. With women, simply stare at them and give a hint of a smile. Mysterious. What is he thinking? That's the reaction you want, with a deep sexual undertone. You don't talk about sex, but everyone is thinking about it. Understand?"

"Yes. I think I do," Dudley said.

"Good, because Henri was able to reschedule your Bradley Cooper interview. You are meeting him tonight for dinner. Jennifer Lawrence will be there."

"Oh no, Albert. I'm not ready for that!"

"Yes, you are. Just keep two things in mind the whole time you are there. One—You are more important than them. And two—Say as little as possible. Got it? Good, let's go shopping."

They went first to Anton's in Beverly Hills. "I called ahead. Anton has the exact shirt Cary wore in *North by Northwest*."

"Won't it be a little dusty?" Dudley quipped.

"That's good," the Colonel said, laughing. "Always remember, Cary was a first-class comedian."

The shirts fit perfectly. "Now a suit or two to match," the Colonel said. "And since we are in Beverly Hills, let's go to Greg Chapman's."

They were met at the door by a tall, elegant young woman. "My name is Audrey, Mr. Leach. I will be helping you today. Mr. Poots said you are looking for two suits. A dark navy and a light gray, yes? A classic cut, single-breasted."

"Think Saville Row, darling," the Colonel added.

"I always do, Mr. Poots." She led Dudley into a changing room. Two suits hung there. "I see you brought your own shirts. Oh, Anton's. Excellent. I added a few silk ties for you to choose from. Try it on and let's get a first look."

Dudley unlaced the black leather oxford shoes he bought earlier and slipped on the navy-blue suit first. He chose a metallic silver colored tie. The effect was stunning. "Oh my, Mr. Leach. You look like you just walked off a movie set."

"I believe that was what we were going for," the Colonel said. "Tell me truthfully, Audrey, does he look as good to you as he does to me?"

Dudley turned to face them, his right hand in his pants pocket, the Noel Coward pose he'd been practicing. The saleswoman lost her professional demeanor for just a moment, then took a deep breath, and said in her best professional voice, "This is a very good look for you, Mr. Leach."

He suddenly took two steps toward her, looked her in the eye, cocked his head ever so slightly, and said, "Why Audrey, that's so kind of you." Then he reached out, took her hand gently in his, all the while maintaining eye contact, and kissed the back of her hand. "Thank you, my dear. You've been extremely helpful."

Albert Poots, who was as shocked as Audrey was, saw the young girl blush. "We'll take it."

Back in the car, the Colonel asked, "What was that?"

"I don't really know. I've never done anything like that before," Dudley said staring straight ahead, lost in the reverie of the moment. "It was impulsive as if someone else was controlling me."

"The Ghost of Cary Grant," the Colonel whispered and felt a chill run through his body. "Well, my boy, I do believe you are on your way."

Greg Chapman's? Anton's? I do not like this at all. That Colonel fellow has done his homework. George did look good, though. That girl certainly thought so. He even sounded a little like me. Damn. This might actually work.

Chapter 16
Bradley Cooper—Take Two

REPORT #13

"Well, there you are," Tyler Woods said rudely, standing up as George Dudley approached the booth. Jennifer Lawrence and Bradley Cooper were already seated, a couple of beer bottles in front of them. They had agreed to meet at CASA VEGA's at 6:00 pm. It was now close to six fifteen.

"We said specifically 6:00 pm," Tyler continued harshly.

"So sorry I am late," Dudley said sincerely pointing at his watch. "They had a little problem fitting the band on my new watch. I asked them to switch the metal band for a leather one." His eyes never left Jennifer Lawrence. He tilted his head and smiled apologetically. "Kind of ironic isn't it," he said.

"What's that?" Tyler Woods said, crossing his arms. The look he gave Dudley would wither trees.

Dudley turned his full gaze on Woods and said simply, "That I am late because of a watch." Then he added, "Would you be a dear boy and go pay the Uber driver? I didn't bring any cash."

"But they take credit cards," Woods said.

"Oh, do they?" Dudley said, but he had already pulled Tyler Woods up and taken his seat. He found a napkin, pulled it onto his lap, and ignoring Woods said to Jennifer Lawrence, "And I hope you have forgiven me, Ms. Lawrence." He held out his right hand, "For not only being tardy but for my horrendous manners the other day at Bradley's home."

She took his hand and mumbled, "It's okay." He surprised her by placing his left hand on top of hers. "No. It's not okay. I've always admired you personally and professionally, and I ruined your evening." Then he quickly turned to Cooper and added. "And you too, Bradley. May I call you Bradley?

I insulted a guest in your home. I hope you can forgive me, too." He smiled then. "Friends?"

"Of course," Jennifer said, a little breathless.

"No problem," Cooper added. "Forgotten."

"Wonderful. So how's the shoot going?"

"It's a struggle," Cooper said seriously. "I might have to replace Jimmy 'No Talent' Miller. The guy is killing me. Take after take after take."

"I told you, Bradley," Jennifer added. "He was the same on *Winter's Bone*."

"My favorite movie," Dudley said.

"What?" Jennifer said.

"Of yours. My favorite movie of yours. Most people I'm sure say *The Hunger Games* or *Silver Linings*, but for me, it will always be *Winter's Bone*. I didn't even know who you were then, but a friend said, watch this movie, and there you were. I thought, Oh, my God! Who is this girl? She steals every scene. You can't NOT look at her. And she is talented too. A star was born, right Bradley?"

Cooper laughed. "I thought the same thing. I told you that Jen."

"You were nominated for *Winter's Bone*, weren't you?"

"My first. You never forget your first," she said, waving her hands like a princess in a carriage.

"Who won that year?" Cooper asked.

Jennifer started to speak but Dudley beat her to it. "Natalie Portman. *Black Swan*. A little over the top for my taste. I love Natalie, but you were robbed. New kid syndrome, I guess."

"Exactly," Jennifer agreed. "They never give it to first-timers. Especially young first-timers." Then she added, using a deep, authority figure voice, "Must wait your turn dear. Earn your stripes. Don't be too eager. There will be other roles'. What bullshit!" she said, banging her beer bottle onto the table.

"I think you struck a nerve there Archie," Cooper said.

"And what's with that name? Archie Leach?" Jennifer said loudly. "Seriously? Maybe I should change my name to Norma Jean."

"I was born the same year *Charade* came out," Dudley lied. "My mother was a big Cary Grant fan. She thought it was funny. My Father not so much. He left us soon after."

"Oh, I'm so sorry," Jennifer said, reaching for his hand.

"I'm just kidding. My Father loved it too," Dudley said, laughing.

She slapped his hand playfully, "Oh, he got me, Bradley. He's good. Maybe you should replace Jimmy with him?"

"Well, your pratfall bit is still the best piece in the film so far," Cooper said, seriously. "So sure, why not. Wanna be in a picture, Archie?"

"Well, I'm flattered, but…"

"Haha, did you see his face?" Cooper laughed.

"I think he was composing his academy award acceptance speech already," Jennifer Lawrence laughed.

"Okay, you got me," Dudley said. Then he reached inside his suit jacket and pulled out a small notebook. "Now, can we get the interview out of the way?"

"You look different," Jennifer said, leaning closer.

"I got contact lenses," Dudley said, demurely.

"No," Cooper jumped in. "No, it's more than that. Look at that suit. Is that Saville Row?"

"Um… Greg Chapman, actually."

"It's a nice suit," Jennifer purred, touching the jacket's lapel. "It suits you." And she laughed again. "Get it? Suits you? C'mon guys, these are the jokes here."

"Looking sharp, Leach," Cooper acknowledged and toasted him. "Okay, fire away. And I hope your questions are better than last time."

Dudley looked at him, tilted his head, and said simply. "Why you?"

"What?"

"Of all the actors in the world, why did fate choose you for movie stardom?"

Lawrence leaned back and drained her beer. "Now that's a question you don't get every day."

"Actually, no one has ever asked me that before," Cooper said with real emotion. "And yet I think about it all the time. Why me? Who the fuck am I?"

"Yes, that is the question," Dudley said and waited.

"Actors aren't matinee idols. That's not how we think. That's a PR term. And a derogatory one nowadays. I like good actors. Real emotions. Comic timing. Cross genres—western, space, rom-com, and action. I don't want to be pigeonholed and neither did those guys. Yes, I read up on them too."

"Who were your favorites, growing up?"

"Cary Grant," Cooper said.

"I had you more of an Errol Flynn type," Dudley said.

"Really? Why?" Cooper said, leaning forward.

"Grant always had that cocky, detached persona. Assured and witty but detached, you know. Like he was watching you react to what he was doing and saying."

"Yes, I can see that," Cooper said.

"You're not like that at all. Your sincerity is right out there. That's why even when you play jerks, you can pull it off. Just like Errol Flynn. *Wedding Crashers*, the first *Hangover*, even *Silver Linings*. These are not likable guys, and yet… you make it work."

"Thank you. I worked hard on those pictures."

"And Tyrone Power. You remind me a lot of him," Dudley added.

"Maybe I am a matinee idol," Cooper admitted.

"Maybe. Once, but I think you've outgrown it. A matinee Idol would never direct a picture in which he kills himself in the end."

"That may be the nicest thing you've said all night Archie," Cooper said, and there were tears in his eyes.

"*A Star is Born* was a brilliant picture. It was my choice for Best Picture."

"You have a vote?"

"I'm a writer. A documentary I worked on got nominated," Dudley said.

"Cool. Thank you, Archie," Cooper said and looked at his watch. "Let's keep going. I thought we'd be out of here by 6:30, but this might be fun. What's next?"

REFLECTIONS ON REPORT #13

That was unexpected. Yes, George was a bit rude to that assistant boy, but his confidence with Lawrence and Cooper, was, engaging. Likable. Yes, that's the word. I liked this version of George Dudley. A little bit of me and a little bit of him. I think the boy's upstairs wouldn't complain about that. That's growth, and change for the better. Yes, this is a good development. I can't wait to tell Kay.

Chapter 17
Happy Birthday, Oprah Winfrey

REPORT #14

George Clooney's Los Angeles mansion was proving difficult to find for the young Uber driver. "I apologize most profusely, sir," the driver said. "I have been here many, many times and never am I lost." He smacked his GPS monitor and cursed it in Hindi.

"It's no trouble at all, dear boy," the Colonel said from the back seat of the elegant Hyundai Equus. "We still have half a bottle of Cabernet to finish."

"Wait, I recognize that rock. Yes, we turn left here," the driver said definitively.

"Turning on your lights might help, don't you think," Dudley said nervously from the front.

"Ah, yes," the driver said, turning the lights on. "Sorry. They are supposed to turn on automatically."

"Take your time," Henri said leaning back into the lush leather seat. "I love this car. It's almost better than a limo."

"It is top of the line, sir… er madam," he said, quickly glancing away.

Henri leaned forward and whispered into the young Indian boy's ear, "Just get us there in one piece deary, and I'll give you a big tip."

Fearing for his life, the diver moved away from Henri and lost control of the large Hyundai automobile for a moment. The car's right wheels found the gravel on the side of the pavement, barely avoiding the tall trees flanking the two-lane roadway He corrected, with a deft turning of the wheel, and found the smooth road again.

"Careful there, old boy," the Colonel said testily. "I almost spilled my drink."

After the next bend in the road, Dudley pointed ahead. "There's a sign. It says CASA CLOONEY. This must be the place." Just past the sign, a line of cars had slowed, and just past them, Dudley could see the top of the massive Clooney home. "It's all lit up like Christmas."

"That was last month, George… I mean Archie," the Colonel said, correcting himself.

"Yes, Archie Leach's coming out party," Henri said from the back. "How do you feel?"

"Like a debutante in a penguin suit," Dudley said. A stream of guests, all elegantly dressed, were making their way up the front stairs of the Clooney mansion. The driver followed the other cars and then stopped. A college-aged boy in a white tuxedo jacket opened Dudley's door.

"I just texted Billy Bates," the Colonel said. "He said he would meet you in the library, Archie."

"I hope they provide a map," Dudley said, getting out of the car. "This place is huge. It's bigger than my high school."

"Don't forget to tip the man, Henri. You promised," the Colonel said after they all exited the car.

"Here you are my Slumdog friend," Henri said, handing him a hundred-dollar bill. "One Benjamin Franklin." The driver stared at the bill in shock, but before he could say anything, Henri quickly leaned in his window and kissed him on the cheek. "Five-star rating."

"Now remember Archie," the Colonel said taking his arm as they moved up the stairs, "ask questions, but try to avoid answering questions. If you do, make them short and vague. Funny and self-deprecating work best."

"I remember Albert," Dudley said. He knew he should feel nervous, but instead, he felt strangely at home.

"When you find yourself in a group ignore the men and always, always, always talk to the ladies," Henri said into his other ear. "And compliment…"

"Their shoes," Dudley said, cutting him off. "I know Henri. Manolo Blahnik, Gianvito Rossi, Jimmy Choo… I remember." He stopped at the top of the stairs and turned to his creators. He was thinner now, but muscular. His Giorgio Armani tuxedo fit so well that he could model it for a magazine ad. He placed his right hand in his pants pocket, cocked his head, and simply said, "Mom, dad, I'm ready." Then he turned and walked into the Clooney Castle, confident and ready for anything.

"By George, I think he's got it," the Colonel said.

"Oh, shut up Albert," Henri said.

George Dudley found Billy Bates in the library talking with George Clooney and his wife Amal. He stopped in the doorway and watched them. Clooney and Bates were arguing about a famous actor's drinking problems on set. Amal, uninterested, noticed Dudley first. She smiled and waved a welcoming hand, but then her smile froze. He was staring at her.

Not flirtatious, just admiringly. Then he looked down at her shoes, and for just the briefest of moments Amal thought she was barefoot. But then she looked down, saw indeed she was wearing black high-heeled shoes, and looked back up at the strange man. She shrugged her shoulders. Dudley pointed and mouthed silently *Manolo*. Amal shook her head amused and mouthed, *Rossi*.

Dudley bowed his appreciation. Amal laughed out loud. "Oh, sorry, George."

George Clooney looked to his wife and then noticed Dudley. "Can I help you?"

Dudley crossed the floor and extended his hand. "Archie Leach, Mr. Clooney. Sorry to disturb you. I was told I'd find Billy Bates in here."

"And so you have," Bates said cheerfully. "This is the writer fellow I told you about, George."

"Oh right," Clooney said, and for no reason he could put his finger on, he was suddenly uneasy. He reached out and shook Dudley's outstretched hand and said, "Nice to meet you, Leach." Then he looked at his Omega wristwatch and said, "Let's meet back here in half an hour, okay?"

Dudley flashed his own watch, a Rolex Oyster Royal, and said, "30 minutes. Got it." Then looking directly at Amal Clooney said, "Looking forward to it."

Amal stepped closer. "That's a beautiful watch, Mr. Leach."

"Archie this is my wife…" Clooney started.

"No introduction necessary," he said, taking her hand and kissing the back of it. "A pleasure, Mrs. Clooney."

"Call me Amal, please."

"Amal it is," he said, still holding her hand. "You have a lovely home, Amal," Dudley smiled, his eyes only for her.

"Yes, we like it," Clooney said stiffly, extracting Amal's hand. Then he pointed to the door and said, "Billy will give you the grand tour. See you soon."

"Right this way Mr. Leach," Billy Bates said, escorting Dudley out the door.

"Nice to meet you, Mr. Leach," Amal said to his back.

Dudley turned and said, "Archie, please." Then he smiled once more, as if they shared more than just an admiration for footwear, bowed slightly, and followed Billy out. As soon as he was out of the room he thought, *Oh, My God, did I just flirt with George Clooney's wife, right in front of him? That was incredible. That shoe bit worked great. I can't wait to tell Henri.*

His mind was lost in thought. Dudley didn't notice that Billy had stopped at the bottom of the main staircase. Billy took his arm and squeezed hard. "We just met Leach, so let me give you a piece of advice, Mr. Clooney is very jealous of his wife."

"As well he should be," Dudley said, winking.

Billy Bates gripped Dudley's arm harder and added, "Remember you are a guest in this house, and…"

Dudley pried Billy's fingers off his arm, and in one swift movement, ended up behind him, holding onto the arm. Billy Bates cried out in pain. "Oww!"

"You don't have to tell me the rules of the house Bates," Dudley said and shoved him up the stairs. "Now be a good boy and show me around."

Billy Bates looked around nervously to make sure no one noticed the altercation. "Now see here, Leach," he started to say, but Dudley moved in close, his face inches from Bates's ear. "And if you ever touch me like that again, I'll give you a knuckle sandwich, hear me?" 'Rule number one might be to compliment ladies' shoes, but rule number two is, take no shit from cocky bullies'.

Dudley released Bates who backed away, bumping into the curving stairway banister. Billy Bates started to protest when Dudley began laughing. "C'mon, Billy. That was my best Humphrey Bogart. *Maltese Falcon?*"

Bates could only stare. A moment ago, he could have sworn this maniac was about to throttle him. And he wasn't too sure if 'knuckle sandwich' was a line from *The Maltese Falcon*. "Oh, yes, Good one," he said wiping his mouth and neck with a handkerchief. "I didn't know you did impersonation. You just surprised me, is all."

"No worries, dear boy," Dudley said, clapping him on the shoulder. "Now show me around this palatial bungalow."

Bates nodded genially, but he watched this newcomer much more warily for the rest of the tour. They started at the top where the bedrooms were, but most of the doors were locked. To their left, they heard music. "The staff having their own party?" Dudley joked.

"That must be Ms. Winfrey's private guest room. We should go back down."

"Wait a minute Billy," Dudley said. "I just remembered. Did someone say this was Oprah Winfrey's birthday party?"

"That's right Archie. But you weren't invited to the party, just the interview. Let's go," he said impatiently. Dudley started turning the knobs on the closed doors around him. "What are you doing?" Bates said in alarm.

"I need to find an envelope and a slip of paper," Dudley demanded. He tried another locked door. "Are any of these opened?"

"Stop that, please. We have to go back down."

Dudley turned to him and said, "Please. It's important."

"You are very odd, Mr. Leach," Bates said, but Dudley's sincerity touched him, so he opened a door to his right. "This is Ms. Amal's sitting room. There's a desk in here."

Dudley entered and found the desk. A stack of Thank You Notes and Envelopes were in a small box. Dudley took one of the note cards, quickly wrote something that Bates tried vainly to see, and placed it in the envelope. Then he wrote a large 'O' on the envelope, sealed it, and placed it in his pocket. "Ok ready."

"You are very weird Leach," Bates said and led him down the hall to a large receiving room, attached to one of the guest bedrooms. Ten people were comfortably sitting on sofas and dancing around a small table filled with food, wine bottles, and glasses.

"I think we found the party," Dudley said upon entering. He stood in the doorway and posed, as Albert taught him, surveying the guests. He paid particular attention to the ladies. The effect was amazing. Two of the women on the sofa openly stared and one girl stopped dancing and waved. But before anything else could happen, Bates blundered past him, raised his arms, and announced, "The party will start downstairs in fifteen minutes everyone."

"The parties already started, honey," a young woman said pushing her way toward Bates. She wore a short dark green mini dress that exposed much of her cleavage, which she aggressively pushed toward his face. "Grab a drink baby and relax."

"That's enough, Kelli," a well-known voice called out. Oprah Winfrey entered from the guest bedroom wearing an elegant light blue Christian Dior evening gown. Stedman Graham was behind her, resplendent in a white tuxedo jacket.

"Sorry about that, Billy. Everything ready?" she said crossing the room.

"Just waiting for the band to set up Ms. Winfrey; fifteen minutes, tops," Bates said.

Oprah looked past him and said, "Who's your friend Billy?"

Dudley knew a cue when he heard one and walked directly up to Oprah Winfrey. He was feeling very confident. So far, all of Albert and Henri's training had paid off. He was starting to feel in control of this new persona. But just as he was about to say 'Hel-LO' he heard an even more famous voice to his right, *'Is that Barack Obama?'* Dudley twisted his head to get a better look through the crowd, just as Kelli handed him a glass of champagne. He bumped into her, and his slick new shoes slipped on the spilled champagne. He landed hard on his butt. Somehow, he managed to keep hold of the empty glass.

The small group watched, mouths opened, when Dudley suddenly held up the empty glass and said, "Refill, please." They all started laughing and Oprah and Stedman reached down to help him up.

"That was brilliant," Oprah Winfrey said. "Best laugh I had all day. Are you alright?"

"Nothing broken but my pride, Ms. Winfrey," Dudley said.

"Call me Oprah," she said extending her hand.

"I'm Archie Leach," he said shaking her hand. "Nice to meet you too, Mr. Graham."

Stedman Graham shook Dudley's hand and said, "Are you an acrobat, Mr. Leach?"

"No. Nothing so interesting. I'm simply here to interview Mr. Clooney for my book."

"Oh, a writer too," Oprah said loudly. "I love writers. What's your latest? Have I heard of it? You must send it to me."

"I mostly write nonfiction. Nothing you would have heard about," he said desperate to change the subject. "But Billy here tells me it's your birthday."

"Yes. Yes. One hundred and one today," she said, garnering more laughter from her friends.

"I have a present for you," he said reaching into his pocket.

"You do," she said. "Why Mr. Leach. This is so sudden."

"My mother said you should never attend a birthday party without a gift." He handed her the small envelope.

Oprah looked at it curiously and then said to Stedman. "Big things come in small packages?"

Undeterred, Dudley said, "What do you give someone who has everything? The answer is a surprise."

She turned back to him, eyeing him carefully, and took the envelope. She turned it over and weighed it in her hand. "What do you think Graham?"

Then Graham Steadman, always the most perceptive man in the room, said. "Open it dear and be surprised."

She opened the flap and took out the note card. Unfolded it so no one else could see, and let out a small, surprised gasp. She showed the paper to Steadman, who simply bowed to George. "Excellent gift, Mr. Leach."

Oprah took a step toward Dudley, tears in her eyes, and whispered, "I am not easily surprised anymore, Archie Leach. But this might be one of the sweetest presents I ever got." And she kissed his cheek before turning away, grabbing Steadman's arm, and leaving the room. Steadman glanced back as they left and winked.

"What the fuck just happened?" Billy Bates gasped. "What did you give her?"

"The only thing I had with me. My heart."

REFLECTIONS ON REPORT #14

Okay, I admit. That got me. I like this, George Dudley.

Chapter 18
The Heir Apparent

REPORT #15

"Obviously, when I was first starting out, I took it as a great compliment," Clooney said. They were back in the library on the ground floor, far removed from the guests and the noise.

"I mean, when the Hollywood Reporter calls you the Heir Apparent to Cary Grant, it's a little overwhelming. Those are some pretty big shoes to fill," George Clooney said humbly.

"That was right after *Out of Sight* came out," Dudley added.

"Yes. I did *Batman* and *Peacemaker* around the same time, but people weren't really taking my acting seriously. They were fixated on how I looked."

"Is that why you did *Three Kings*?"

"Yes. And *O Brother, Where Art Thou*. Those weren't films the studios wanted me to do. I was getting pigeonholed, and I didn't like it. What people forget is I'm an actor first and a movie star second."

Dudley smiled. "Did you know that's exactly what Gary Cooper said in 1941, just before he did *Meet John Doe*?"

"No, I didn't. Really?"

"He was one of Paramount's biggest stars in the 1930s. But he got sick of wearing Cowboy hats and turbans," Dudley said. "Plus, he got to work with Capra, one of his favorite directors."

Clooney looked at Dudley and nodded. "You really know your stuff, Archie."

"I read a lot."

"Well, this has been less painful than I expected," Clooney said, laughing and standing up.

"Thank you. I look forward to reading the book."

"My pleasure," Dudley said, extending his hand.

Clooney shook the hand but held it and looked at Dudley. "Have you ever thought about acting? You have a good look. Nice voice too, familiar."

"I think I'll stick to writing," Dudley said smiling.

"How come I never heard of you before?"

Dudley changed the subject. "I'm glad I had the chance to meet Graham Steadman. There's something real special about that man."

"I feel the same way. You know we are on the Foundation Board together in Chicago."

"I did not know that," George said.

"Well, enjoy the party. I've got to go mingle now. Make sure no one's run off with the china."

"Or your wife."

"Excuse me?"

"She's an incredibly attractive woman. Reminds me of a young Sophia Loren. Or Monica Bellucci."

"I'll let her know," Clooney said icily. "You know the way out?" Clooney said and left the room.

What was that? George thought. *Why did I do that? I thought he was going to punch me. It was exciting, Like, someone else was talking. Like…*

"Cary Grant," a voice from the doorway said.

"Excuse me?" Dudley said, turning to the voice. It was the girl from Oprah Winfrey's party. *What was her name?*

"I've been trying to figure out who you remind me of since I knocked you down earlier," the girl in the green dress said. "Then when I saw you with George Clooney, it just sort of clicked. Cary Grant. You know that guy from those old black and white films."

"He did do some in color you know."

"I only know the old ones, from the 1940s. I took a class at UCLA last year—'classic cinema and the screwball comedy'. What a great title for a class. Like *Sex and the Novel.* I mean you just got to take it, right?"

"And you think I look like Cary Grant?"

She scrunched up her eyes and scrutinized him closely. "A little. But it's more the way you are. You know what I mean?"

"He did a lot more films, better films in the 50s and 60s. *To Catch a Thief, Indiscreet, North by Northwest.* How about *An Affair to Remember*? Everyone knows that one." He looked up at the ceiling and used his falsetto voice. "I was looking up. It was the nearest thing to heaven." She looked at him and shrugged her shoulders.

"The Empire State Building scene?" he prompted. "They were supposed to meet at midnight?"

Then recognition filled her face and she gushed, "Yes! Yes, I like that movie. With Tom Hanks and Meg Ryan. Aah, it made me cry. Was Cary Grant in it too?"

Dudley shook his head. "That's *You Got Mail*, not… oh never mind." Her eyes were very green.

And big. "You're lucky you're so cute."

"Right back at ya' buster."

"Must be the tuxedo," Dudley said approaching her.

"It is a nice tuxedo. Drink?" she said and held out a glass of champagne.

"If you promise not to spill it on me again."

"You bumped into me, remember? While you were gawking at Obama," she said smiling.

He took the offered glass and said, "It really was him? Is he still here?"

"You are so funny Mr. Leach," the young lady laughed. "One minute you are cool and charming, the next minute you're a dorkasaurus."

"Is that a real word?"

"It is now," she said, standing very close to him. She held out her hand. "Kelli Lee."

He took her hand and kissed the back of it. "Archie Leach."

She squinted at him. "I know that name. Archie Leach," she repeated. "Where did I hear it before?"

"Maybe it was a class you took."

"You're funny."

He moved closer to her, his free hand sliding around her body to the small of her back. "You're sexy," he said softly, leaning in.

She turned her face up toward his. "We should make a baby. It would be like… Julia Roberts."

"Or Emma Stone."

"Or Sofia Vegara."

"Or Elizabeth Banks."

"Are you good at keeping secrets, Miss Lee?" His hand moved down further, and he pulled her toward him.

"You're just going to have to trust me," Kelli Lee said, kissing his neck.

His mouth found hers. His hand slipped under her short dress and grabbed her bottom. His fingers found her cleft through her silk panties. She moaned and kicked the door closed.

REFLECTIONS ON REPORT #15

I should probably edit that out. The closest we ever got to showing sex in my day was a cutaway to fireworks. But no, this is George now. This is him living out his fantasy. My job is to observe. Isn't this what he wanted? Isn't this what he thought would happen? Hoped would happen?

I wonder if he would be shocked to know my real life was not like that at all. The truth is Cary Grant ruined most of my marriages. Women constantly came up to me in public, throwing themselves at me, whether my wife was there or not. What wife could put up with that? I take full responsibility. I had no one else to blame but myself. Maybe someone should tell George Dudley that being Cary Grant is not parties and sex and tuxedos 24 hours a day.

And that business with that Clooney's wife. I never did anything like that. At least I don't think so. Not consciously anyway.

This is going to end badly.

Chapter 19
Reporting In

"He's me!" Cary cried.

"Try to relax, Cary. Breath," Kay Kendall said. They were in her condo. He rushed over after his last session in the peer review, banged on her door, and threw himself on her couch as soon as he entered.

"I watched him, Kay. He's got everything down. The Fairbanks smile, the Noel Coward pose, the walk. He even sounds like me. It was like looking in a mirror."

"Let me get you a drink. You like Stingers, right?"

"NO! No Stingers! No champagne. No tuxedos. He's even wearing my shirt!" Cary raved. Kay didn't understand what he was talking about, so she gave him a can of Diet Coke. He took a large swig and started to cough. "What the hell is this? You trying to kill me?"

"Too late dear," and they both laughed.

"You are too good to me, Kay. Thank you," he said taking her hand. "It was just a bit too much, you know? It was one thing watching Dudley bumble around for the past few months, but when he started to truly inhabit… me, it was very unsettling."

Kay sat down next to him and asked, "How was he though? Any good?"

"Good? Let me tell you a story. No one knows this. It's not even in any of those books about me."

"You've read them?" she asked, surprised.

"Of course, I read them. Now listen. When I was shooting *Gunga Din* with Douglas Fairbanks, Jr., I got to meet his father. The original matinee idol."

"I thought that was Valentino?" Kay said.

"Valentino was electric onscreen, but off-screen, he had nothing on Fairbanks," Cary said. "Go ask him yourself. Oh, wait, he's downstairs, isn't he?" Kay nodded.

"Anyway, we were having dinner one night, Jr., Slim, Tonga, and I, when the room suddenly went silent. We were wondering what just happened. We looked around and there was Douglas Fairbanks, dressed to the nines, just standing in the doorway. He was smiling that big toothy grin of his."

"He did have a great smile," Kay added.

"And he was just, looking around the room. Nothing else. And not for anyone in particular, he was just taking it all in, for five, maybe ten seconds. Then he took a drag on his cigarette, waved to us, and walked casually to our table, the smile never leaving his face."

Cary stood and walked to the balcony window and looked out into the night sky. "Later, after many, many drinks, I asked him, 'What was that entrance all about?'"

"It's the only way to enter a room of strangers, Cary," he said. "If you want to get their attention that is. And let's face it, we make our living getting people's attention."

"Well, it worked. You had every eye on you."

"Of course," he said, blowing smoke into the night air. Then he lowered his voice and said, "You want to know how to do it?"

"Yes. Please."

Then Douglas Fairbanks, the sexiest man alive gave me the secret, which I used in every movie I was in after that. "First, you must act like you don't have a care in the world. You must assume you are the most interesting man in the room. You are confident and fearless. And you must always keep in your head, wherever you are, you are the star of the moment, everyone else is an extra in your movie. Understand?"

That was the perfect analogy for me.

"When you enter, be relaxed, a secret smile on your face, and wait. Then, let your eyes take it the entire room until you find the most beautiful woman in the place, walk up to her and make sure the first thing out of your mouth is a compliment; her hair, her clothes, her eyes, whatever. Then touch her, lightly, not aggressively. You can shake her hand or just caress her arm. Then go to your seat or the bar and relax like nothing unusual just happened. I waited for more and asked, 'Is that it?'"

"What more is there? Trust me, after that, they will come to you. Especially the woman. And, if not her, another."

And, as if he had planned it, a lovely dark-haired senorita brushed past me and extended her hand toward Douglas Fairbanks and introduced herself. I made a timely retreat and rejoined my friends. But I never forgot the lesson.

"You did it in *Philadelphia Story* and the *Bishops Wife*, too," Kay said.

"And our boy down there has perfected it," Cary Grant said, with a hint of pride in his voice.

"But that's good right?" Kay asked.

"No, Kay. That is definitely not good. Because there's always been a dark side to 'being Cary Grant'," he said and emphasized it with air quotes. "Being the Alpha male means you sometimes have to fight the other male lions. It's something most biographers miss. They like to concentrate on female conquests. They overlook the violence," he confessed.

"Violence?" Kay said surprised.

"Haven't you ever noticed in many of my films there's a bit of a brute there? *My Girl Friday. Mr. Lucky. None But the Lonely Heart.* Even some of the later pictures. *Catch a Thief, North by Northwest.* Even *Charade*, and I was fifty-nine when I did that one."

"So what does that have to do with George Dudley?"

"He's becoming more aggressive too. Confrontational."

"But Cary," Kay smiled. "That's why women wanted you. Just ask Miss Kelli Lee."

"Yes. That was a little hard to watch," he said modestly. "I don't like this new George Dudley."

"Don't be so hard on yourself, Cary," she said and kissed his cheek. "The peer review is an amazing device, but people aren't supposed to know everything about another person. That's God's job. Our job is to get through the day the best we can, without hurting anyone else."

"But that's what Dudley is doing now. I worry for him."

"Now that is something your biographers missed. Cary Grant is a big softy," she said, holding him in her arms.

"I am a big softy. Just ask my daughter Jennifer," he said, and his eyes teared up at her memory.

"She knew the real me, better than anyone."

"I'd like to get to know the real you," she said, lacing her arms around his neck.

"You're wonderful. You know that?" he said kissing her. "Where have you been all my life? Alive and dead."

"I was busy… with Rex," she said, looking away.

"Oh, yes. Him. I was surprised they let him in," Cary said.

"*My Fair Lady* is Sant Peter's favorite movie. He has Rex and Audrey do *The Rain in Spain* song at least once a year."

"Well, maybe we could sing *If I Loved You*, that old Rogers and Hammerstein tune."

"Why don't we whisper sweet nothings and get into bed," she said, her voice low and husky. She kissed him again.

"You always know just the right thing to say."

Chapter 20
The Afterglow

REPORT #16

The Colonel was leaning against the Black Noir Equus, anxiously surveying the crowd leaving the party. He was tired, he was bored, but more importantly, his feet hurt. He wanted to go home and take a long bath. Then he saw George Dudley coming down the stairs, holding hands with a slim Asian girl. "Where have you been?" the Colonel asked. "Your Clooney meeting was over a half hour ago?"

Dudley ignored the question and said, "Albert, this is Kelli Lee. Kelli, this is my friend Albert."

Kelli stuck out her hand. "Charmed, I'm sure."

"Well, aren't you the precious tart," Albert said, spinning her around. "Sexy little ensemble you have on. Emphasis on the little," he said smirking. "Getting a nice updraft there?" he whispered to her.

"Oh, how rude," she said and clutched at Dudley's arm.

"Rude but true. My legacy. Hurry up you two, before Henri molests our Uber driver," he said and opened the rear door.

"I smell sex in the air," Henri said from the front seat as soon as Dudley and Kelli got in.

"We were wondering where you got off too, and now we know," Albert said, laughing at his own joke.

"It was a very productive evening," Dudley said, his arm around Kelli. She smiled and caressed his leg.

"Really?" Henri said, turning in his seat. "Then maybe you can explain your scuff up with Billy Bates."

"Oh, that," Dudley said dismissively. "He got a little aggressive and I put him in his place. That's all."

121

"That's all? That's all?" Henri said, her voice rising. "We gave you yoga lessons Georgie, NOT boxing lessons."

"Hey, watch that," Dudley said. They discussed not using his real name during their lessons.

"You have been banned from Casa Clooney; you know that right?"

"But why?"

"Did you or did you not flirt with Amal Clooney?" Henri continued. Kelli pouted and removed her hand from his leg.

"Maybe," Dudley said, and his hand went to adjust his glasses before he realized they were not there. "I was caught up in the moment, you know. I was working the look we practiced, and I complimented her shoes and suddenly there was this electricity, like sexual tension. It was intoxicating. I couldn't help myself."

"We created a monster," Albert said.

"I hear the Oprah meeting was a success though. What did you give her? She couldn't stop talking about it," Henri asked.

Dudley looked out the window, annoyed at being attacked for doing exactly what they trained him to do. "It's a secret. Between Oprah and me."

"It's Oprah and I, dear."

"Oh, fuck off Albert," Dudley said harshly. "And you too Henri. It was great tonight. It all worked. I felt in total control the whole time like I was watching myself giving a performance. I was the poster boy for Suave and debonair. And if you should need any more evidence, just say Hel-LO to our lovely guest here," he said gesturing to Kelli.

Henri was silent for a moment and lit a cigarette. "We'll talk more tomorrow. When cooler heads will prevail."

"Yea," the Colonel added. "What he said."

Kelli whispered to Dudley. "Did I do something wrong?"

"You, my dear, are the only civil thing in the car," Dudley said, kissing her cheek.

Albert rolled down his window and said, "I think I'm going to hurl."

Henri said nothing. He smoked and watched the night slide by her window. They drove home in silence and Dudley did not even say goodnight when he and Kelli went up the stairs and into his room.

Albert watched them ascend the stairs and then said to Henri, "He's right you know. He was the buzz of the party. Instagram is blowing up about him."

"I should have anticipated this, Albert," Henri said taking a Coke Zero from the refrigerator.

"Don't be so hard on yourself darling. Even you can't anticipate everything," he said and opened the patio door. They sat and enjoyed the clear night air. "Not too much smog tonight," Albert said.

Henri nodded, but her thoughts were miles away. A tune from a Rodgers and Hammerstein musical kept playing in her head. "How do you solve a problem like Maria."

Upstairs in Dudley's room, Kelli said. "I don't think your friends like me."

"They don't like anyone but themselves baby," Dudley said, hanging up his tuxedo with impeccable care.

"The thin one is a little scary. Did she call you, George?"

Dudley looked at her. She was sitting in the middle of the bed, the covers tangled around her middle, her breasts exposed, firm, and appealing. Dudley had a moment of doubt. *What am I doing? This girl is way too young and way too out of my league.* But the sex did happen. And she was in his bedroom. The encounter in Clooney's study was unreal. Dudley didn't even think, he just reacted; his pants were around his ankles before he knew what was happening. When it was over, Dudley felt like he was emerging from a dream. But it wasn't a dream, it was real. This beautiful, sexy girl wanted him.

No, he thought, *she wants Cary Grant. But isn't that me now? Am I not the new Cary Grant?*

"What are you doing, sweetie? I lost you for a moment there," Kelli Lee said.

Dudley smiled and crawled into bed. "I'm not lost. I know exactly where I am."

REFLECTIONS ON REPORT #16

You didn't create a monster, Albert. I did.

Chapter 21
The Morning After

REPORT #17

1

The next morning, George Dudley dragged his suitcase down the stairs and placed it by the front door. He hung his garment bag, with his two new suits and the tuxedo, on the coat rack.

"Going somewhere." The Colonel was standing behind him.

"It's time, I think," George said.

"Mommy's gonna love your new roommate," he said.

Dudley did not want to play this game. "Look, I really appreciate all you and—"

"Really?" the Colonel cut him off. "You don't seem very appreciative right now. Sneaking off without a hello or a goodbye."

"I wasn't sneaking," he said, even though he knew he was.

"C'mon Archie," Kelli yelled from the driveway. "The cab is here!"

Dudley looked at Albert Poots and stuck out his hand. "I'll call you."

The Colonel ignored the hand and rushed into Dudley's arms and gave him a crushing hug.

"You better. I'm going to miss you," he said, and he was having trouble holding back the tears.

"Where's Henri? I should say goodbye."

"No. She's in her room. Sulking," Albert Poots said, wiping away the tears. "You go, you big lug. We had some fun, but it's time for you to leave the nest," he said and pushed Dudley out the door. "Au revoir. *Think of me, think of me fondly*," he sang. Then he said seriously, "But be careful, George," before closing the door.

Dudley stood on the porch, suitcase and garment bag in hand. The cab driver beeped his horn, but Dudley hesitated.

"Archie. Come on. I have to get to work," Kelli Lee called. She was standing by the open cab door. Dudley smiled. Took a deep breath and said, "I'm coming dear."

They arrived at Kelli's place at 9 am. He checked his messages on his phone. Amy, Paul, and December left messages. Nothing from Darcy. *I guess I'll have to call that lawyer after all*, he thought. Two months had passed without a word. December said her mother appeared happy, so maybe it was time.

He made coffee and called Amy Andrews.

"Jesus fucking Christ on a pogo stick. What the fuck happened at Clooney's?"

"Good morning to you too," Dudley said calmly.

"Don't good morning me. I just got an ear full of shit from Billy Bates. He hinted at a lawsuit. Did you assault him? Did you flirt with Amal Clooney? Are you fucking nuts?"

"Maybe. Yes and no," Dudley said. "The guy got physical. I got more physical. Bates's a nothing, Amy. Don't worry about him."

"A nothing? He's Clooney's assistant. He's our main contact!" Amy screamed.

"The interview went well. I'll email over my notes later," Dudley said, changing the subject.

He could hear Amy breathing, hard. In and out. In and out. "Did you really flirt with Amal Clooney? With Clooney right there?"

"I just complimented her on her shoes, that's all."

"Her shoes?" Amy said. George could almost hear her shaking her head through the phone.

"I met Oprah too. And Graham Stedman. Very nice people."

Amy was silent for a moment then said. "I need to see you, George."

"And I need to see 'you', Amy," Dudley returned smoothly. "I'll be back on Valentine's Day. How about we meet the day before? Say, eleven-ish?"

"We need to talk about your expenses, George."

Dudley laughed and said, "I'll send the pages this afternoon. I think you'll like them. Bye now," he said and hung up before she could reply.

He called Carl Schuman next and made an appointment to see him in New York before he returned to Orlando. Then he texted Paul and Decey and informed them he would be in New York in a couple of weeks.

He turned on his laptop and wrote up his notes from the George Clooney interview. He had another cup of coffee and reviewed what he had written and made a few changes. Then he pulled up the Bob Kennedy draft of The Last Matinee Idol and started rewriting it. He blazed through it. He was in the zone.

The words flew. The phrases came easy, and by lunchtime, he had a very workable first draft. He changed the tone of the book and made it freer flowing. He intertwined the stories of the actors, moving away from the history lesson feel of Kennedy's book. He even questioned the term, Matinee Idol, and soon a story of real men, not untouchable movie stars, was starting to materialize. He knew exactly where he wanted the next interviews to go, and the final chapters were taking form in his imagination.

He was absorbed in his writing when the phone rang.

"Oh, hello, mother," Dudley said.

"I saw a picture of you today on the internet," Elsie Dudley said without preamble. "What happened to your glasses?"

"Contact lenses," he said.

"You look nice. Did you get a haircut too?" Elsie said. "Looks… stylish." Dudley shrugged and lit a cigarette and said, "When in LA."

"Are you smoking?" she asked. "When did you start smoking?"

"Bad habit I know, but goes nicely with coffee, don't you think? Or brandy," he said.

"Well, stop it. They'll kill you."

"Yes, ma'am," he said, putting it out.

"Been going to the beach too? You have a tan."

"Been working out too, mom. Yoga. Eating better, you know, the whole lifestyle change thing."

"Was that really Oprah Winfrey in that picture I saw?" she said, and she could not hide the admiration in her tone.

"Are you on Instagram now, Mom?" he laughed.

"December told me. She sent me a photo," Elsie said. "What was that about?"

"A birthday present," he said smiling, remembering the moment fondly.

There was silence on the line for a moment then Elsie asked. "Did you give her your heart?"

Dudley smiled broadly but said nothing.

"So, you did pay attention when I was telling you those stories," she said proudly.

"I made her cry, mom. In a good way."

"What's going on with you, George?" she asked, and he could hear real concern in her voice.

"Mid-life crisis?" he said.

"All right mister, who are you and what have you done with my son?"

2

When George Dudley returned from dinner there was a party going on. All the windows were ablaze with light. The bass from the stereo was pounding so hard, Dudley felt it in his teeth.

A young man and woman were sitting on the front porch drinking beers. "Hello, Pops. Lost?" the boy with the blond dreadlocks said, and his female friend laughed.

Dudley stopped and considered the boy. He had known punks like this growing up. Cocky. Superior. A smart ass. The old Dudley would have smiled, apologized, and tried to make friends with this Neanderthal. But that Dudley was dead. Archie Leach did not suffer fools. And Cary Grant didn't either.

"Lost? You kiss your mother with that mouth, asshole?" Dudley said aggressively.

The smile dropped from his beer-addled face, and the boy stood up, balling his hands into fists.

"Hey, who you calling—"

But Dudley was already moving forward and shoved the boy back down, hard. He let out a 'oof' as the breath and fight left him. Then Dudley turned to the girl, whose mouth was open, forming a perfect circle. Dudley snapped his fingers in her face, and said loudly, "Hey! Sweetheart. Is Kelli inside?"

The girl merely pointed and said, "Yeah."

Dudley stared at her, then quoted Hobson from that *Arthur* movie he liked. "Yes, my dear. You obviously have a wonderful economy with words. I look forward to your next syllable with eager anticipation."

127

"Huh?"

"Exactly," Dudley said. Then to the boy, "Stay." He pushed open the screen door and entered the home.

"Archie!" Kelli Lee yelled and threw herself onto Dudley, wrapping her legs around him. She kissed him and he could taste and smell the marijuana. "I missed you so much," she cried and hugged his neck with crushing force for a girl so petite.

"It's only been twelve hours, Kelli," Dudley said.

"Twelve hours?" she complained. "Felt like twelve days, twelve months, twelve…"

"I got it dear, now hop down and get me a beer," he said holding onto her hips and helping her down.

"Did you miss me?" she said childlike.

"Like a garden misses the sun," he said. She stared at him in confusion, her pretty, dark eyebrows lowering. So he added, "Yes, dear! Every single moment."

"Yes! He loves me!" She grabbed his hand and dragged him through the living room. It was crowded with young people talking and drinking and smoking, "We have Bud Light or Corona," she said, opening the refrigerator.

"Corona, please."

"I remember you," a husky voice said behind him. He turned to find a very tall dark-skinned woman with a short, styled afro and giant hoop earrings looking at him. She had a hand on her hip and was wagging a finger in Dudley's face. "You were at the Oprah party. You fell on your ass," she said, then laughed a huge braying laugh.

"Guilty as charged," Dudley said, bowing.

"You gave something to Miss. Winfrey," she said and moved close to him. "What was it?"

"A gentleman never reveals his secrets," he said and raised a finger to his lips.

She acted like he didn't even speak and continued, "I think it was your phone number."

"Well, your imagination has gotten the better of you, young lady," he said.

"Um huh," the sexy girl said, not believing him in the least.

"Archie," Kelli put her arms around the girl, "this is my best friend in all the world; the sexy, Brandi Morgan. The best dancer on the west coast."

Dudley reached out and took Brandi Morgan's hand and kissed it. "Charmed, Ms. Morgan."

"You talk funny," Brand asked. "You from England or something?"

"Something like that," George said. Inside he smiled. He couldn't wait to tell Albert his voice lessons were working.

"Get this guy," a tall, shirtless boy said. He was standing next to Brandi, his arm draped over her shoulder. Dudley assumed he was the boyfriend.

Brandi elbowed him hard in the stomach. "This guy's got class, dickwad. Like Denzel. Which is something you could use a little bit more of!"

The young man was shocked at Brandi's sudden attack, and his glare at Dudley was not friendly.

"Let's go upstairs, baby," Kelli said taking George's arm again. "Get us a little *pri-va-cy*," she said, over annunciating each syllable. The young man made a point of hitting Dudley with his shoulder as they passed by. Dudley decided to let it pass. *No sense breaking any of Kelli's furniture for this jerk*, he thought.

The stairs were crowded, but eventually, they made it to Kelli's room. It was not empty. "Get off my bed, Clarice." A big girl with long dark hair was on lying on Kelli's bed. A boy was helping her take her pants off.

When Clarice didn't immediately move, Kelli Lee pushed her off the bed. "Now. Get out."

"You too Junior." Dudley took hold of the boy and guided him out the door. Clarice followed, buttoning her pants.

"People are so rude," Kelli said, readjusting the pink and white comforter on her queen-sized bed. "I told them, no sex in my room."

"You have a lot of interesting friends," Dudley said.

"I guess. You do as many shows as I do, you meet a lot of people."

"What kind of shows?" Dudley asked.

She looked at him sharply, hands on hips. "Not that kind, bucko. I'm not a stripper, I'm a dancer slash model. Do pretty well too. Enough to pay my third of the rent here," she said. "But what I really want to be is an actress. I've done some extra work and had a few lines too."

She sat on the bed, her mini skirt riding high on her upper things. "You could do movies, Archie. You're good-looking enough."

"You know, you're the second person who told me that," Dudley said looking around the small bedroom.

"Oh really? Who was the other?"

"Bradley Cooper," he said simply.

Kelli jumped off the bed and hit him with both hands in the chest, knocking him into the door.

"SHUT UP!" she screamed. "You know Bradley Cooper?"

"Ow, Kelli, that hurt," he said holding his chest.

"Shut up, you baby. You really know Bradley Cooper? You're not saying that to sleep with me."

"I've already slept with you Kelli, but yes, I met him twice. Just before Christmas and a few weeks ago. I interviewed him."

"Interviewed him?" she said not understanding. "I thought you were a writer?"

"I am a writer. I'm writing a book about actors," he said sitting on the bed.

"You don't write movies?" she said, still not quite grasping what he said.

"No," Dudley laughed. "I guess I am the only writer in Hollywood who does not write movies."

"Well, that's weird," she said disappointed. She lay down on the bed next to him. "But you really do know Bradley Cooper? Can you introduce me?"

"I don't see why not. Next time he has a party, I'll take you," Dudley said.

She screamed again and crawled on top of him. "Oh, Archie. You are the best."

Her top was nearly off when she noticed the music had stopped. She looked up, curious. "Who turned off the music?"

Then they heard yelling and screaming coming from downstairs. Kelli jumped off the bed and threw open the door.

"Fucking pigs!"

"Get the hell out of here!"

"Leave us alone. Stop hassling us!"

Kelli made her way halfway down the steps. Dudley was right behind her. A Police Officer was standing in the doorway. A female officer was standing by the now silent stereo.

"Everyone. Please calm down," the imposing policeman said. He was an older man, his gray hair showing under his cap. He had his hands up, trying to calm the unruly crowd. "We've received numerous complaints about your music. All we want is for you to turn it down."

"I'll turn you down," a male voice screamed.

"We just need to speak to the owner of the house, then we'll be on our way," the older man said again, surveying the room.

"Well, you found her copper," Kelli said walking up to him. "And she is telling you to get the fuck out! I know my rights."

"And your name is?" the officer said looking down at Kelli, a notebook in his hand.

"I ain't telling you nothing without a warrant," she screamed. And her friends took up the line.

"Yea! Where's your warrant?"

"I watch *Law and Order*."

"This is harassment. Someone video this."

The female officer came up to Kelli and touched her arm, "Can we discuss this outside, miss?"

"Oh. Police brutality!" Kelli yelled dramatically. "She assaulted me. I got witnesses." The older officer shook his head and gestured to his partner to wait outside.

"Oh, you think you're going to abuse me and then run away? In my own home? I'll sue you…," but Dudley was suddenly there and spun her around to face him. His face was inches from hers.

"What are you doing Kelli?"

"That cop assaulted…"

He shook her, "Kelli, get a grip. You're making things worse."

Her anger flared again, and she was about to turn it on him when Dudley shook her again. "You have two choices, fight these guys and go to jail, or go outside with me and it will all be over in ten minutes. Are you listening to me? Do you trust me?" He was so close she could smell the beer on his breath, but he finally got through to her and she nodded.

Dudley looked up and making eye contact with the older officer jerked his head toward the door. Sergeant Mike Mulligan nodded, and they went outside. Dudley, still holding onto Kelli, followed. But just before he left, he turned and stared at the group in the living room and said with as much authority as he could muster, "Do not touch that stereo. I'm warning you." He made eye contact with as many as he could then went outside, Kelli in tow.

Sergeant Mulligan was standing in the middle of the front lawn, his legs spread apart holding his notebook open. He began speaking before Dudley and

Kelli were off the porch. "We're going to need the names of everyone inside. If indeed this young lady is the owner, I will need proof…"

Dudley stepped up to him. "What's your name, Sergeant?"

"Please step back, sir."

"What are you going to do? Arrest twenty kids because their music was too loud?" Dudley said.

"Disturbing the peace…"

Dudley turned his back on him and went back to the porch and sat on the steps. "Here's what we're going to do. Write this down. My name is Archibald Leach. This young lady rents this place. I am giving you my personal guarantee that we will not disturb the peace for the rest of the night."

"Listen here, Mr. Leach," Sergeant Mulligan said taking a step toward him. Dudley interrupted him again.

Dudley quickly stood up. "When I was talking to Mayor Garcetti at the George Clooney party last week," Dudley said, "I complimented him on how low the crime rate had dropped recently. And his wife Amy, a lovely lady, great dresser by the way, was so impressed she took a selfie; me and her and Oprah Winfrey. Would you like me to forward it to you?"

The two men stared at each other. Officer Mulligan was used to dealing with men who thought they had all the answers, but to Dudley, this was brand new territory. He was going on instinct. He had succumbed to the Cary Grant persona fully and was just along for the ride, come what may.

But before the confrontation could escalate any further, Officer Kassandra Lopez looked at her Sergeant and said, "We have an active 414 over on MLK, Sergeant. Should we take it? Everything seems to be quiet here now."

Sergeant Mulligan was still watching Dudley, not wanting to give in when Kelli stood up and said, "I'm sorry I lost my temper officer. I'll make sure we keep it down. Promise." Sergeant Mulligan nodded and said, "But I'm still going to need your contact info for my report."

"Here's my card," Dudley said, crossing to the policeman. "Thanks for coming by. You're a credit to the force. Let's go, baby." He placed his arm around Kelli's waist, turned her around, and stepped back onto the porch.

Officer Lopez was watching them. Sergeant Mulligan was too. "I hate Hollywood."

The party broke up soon after, and Dudley and Kelli were soon back in her bed. Her shirt was off, and he was giving her a back rub. "You were fantastic."

"I'm sorry I got a little rough with you," he said massaging her back. "I didn't want us to spend the night in jail."

"I appreciate that," she murmured.

"But that apology was a nice piece of acting, by the way," Dudley complimented her. "You almost sounded sincere."

She laughed and said, "We make a good team, don't we?"

Dudley stopped massaging her. He thought Kelli was sexy and gorgeous, and he loved her body, but the thought of a long-term relationship with her never crossed his mind before now.

"What's the matter, sweetie?" she mumbled.

"Nothing apparently. Nothing at all," he said and started kissing her naked back.

REFLECTIONS ON REPORT #17

Yeah, I know this guy. This is not Cary Grant, George. This is the original Archie Leach, the Bristol, England tuff. You would have recognized him if you popped in 'None but the Lonely Heart' when you and Albert were conducting your Cary Grant movie retrospective. Maybe it would have given you pause. Well, too late now. You're in it boy, with both feet.

Chapter 22
New York State of Mind

REPORT #18

1

"I'll be back in time. I swear."

Dudley and Kelli Lee were at the airport. He was booked on the United 10:30 direct flight to La Guardia. His son was picking him up and they planned to go directly to his apartment in Manhattan. Darcy was living with Bill Rawlings now, so the place would be empty. He had an appointment with his lawyer, Carl Schuman the next day, and dinner plans at Decey and Gabriel's home tomorrow evening. He was looking forward to seeing his children again, and even the prospect of sitting down with Schuman didn't bother him. It was time. No more looking back.

A meeting with Darcy and her brother Gary was set for the following day. Divorce negotiations were finalized. The only thing left was his signature. *Twenty years*, Dudley thought when he read over the final paperwork, *reduced to thirteen pages of legal bullshit.*

"Why do you have to go?" Kelli said, hanging on to him at the terminal entrance.

"I'll only be gone four days baby. A couple of days in New York then a couple in Orlando. I'll be back here at 9:07 pm, Valentine's Day. I have my tickets right here," he said patting his jacket pocket. "I'll be back darling, I promise."

She kissed him one more time, started to cry then got back in the yellow cab. She waved at him through the rear window, and he blew her a kiss. *I'm going to miss her*, he thought. *Life is truly weird.* Then he thought of Mary. He wondered for the hundredth time what he was going to tell her.

134

The flight arrived on time and his son met him in the baggage claim area of La Guardia airport.

"You look good, pop. L.A. agrees with you."

Dudley slipped on his Ray-Bans and said, "You have no idea, son."

They found a cab and the familiar Manhattan skyline was soon scrolling past his window. The sun was setting over the Hudson River and her final rays were flashing between the tall buildings. "I love this city."

"I always thought you hated it," Paul said.

Dudley turned to him. "Hated it? Why would you say that?"

"You always seemed a little… sad."

Dudley smiled. "That had nothing to do with New York son. That was me. I spent my entire life thinking the way to get people to like me was to be helpful, easygoing, and nonconfrontational. I didn't even like competing because I didn't want the other guy to be upset. Isn't that stupid?"

Paul Dudley looked at his father. He was not used to him talking about himself, especially his feelings. "No, dad, I think it's what makes you a nice guy."

"Yeah, but they always finish last, don't they?" Dudley said, and Paul noticed a change in his father's voice, a hardness.

"It's better than being an asshole," Paul said laughing, trying to lighten the mood again.

"That's true, but it doesn't hurt to kick ass every once in a while," he said coldly. He turned and looked his son directly in the eye. "Does it?"

Paul opened the apartment door and Dudley went directly to his old bedroom. He threw the suitcase onto the bed cover and suddenly stopped. The scent of his soon-to-be ex-wife came rolling up from the comforter. He closed his eyes, and nearly fell over. The last time he lay in this bed, he made love to Darcy. And it saddened him that he could not remember the details. He assumed that was a natural consequence of a long-term relationship, but it still saddened him.

"You want to grab something to eat?" Paul said coming in behind him.

Dudley wiped his eyes and said, "No. It's been a long day. I'm going to crash. How about we have lunch the day after tomorrow at Monte's on McDougal after I see your mother?"

"Okay, pop. Love you. See you then," his son said before leaving.

"Love you too, son," Dudley said automatically. He pushed the suitcase to the floor and lay down on the bed, fully clothed. He was asleep in seconds.

2

He woke to the noise of the city. His windows were closed, but still, it seeped through. The garbage trucks growling, the delivery van's rock music, the incessant honking, all of it had been a part of his morning routine for two decades. New Yorkers say they don't notice it, you get used to it. But it's a lie. It's one of the main reasons people move out of the city. And when you've been away, especially to somewhere quiet and serene, it seems worse than you remember.

But breakfast in New York was a treat. The smell of the bakeries, the taste of the pastries, the bagels, and the waffles. "Oh, my God, Clinton Street," he said out loud. He showered, dressed, and was on the subway heading south in fifteen minutes. *No better way to start the day, than waffles at Clinton's Bakery*, he thought, and he smiled his first smile of the day. *Well, isn't that something, I even smile more now.*

He checked his watch. 9:15. Carl Schuman's offices were only a ten-minute walk from Clinton's, so he relaxed and enjoyed his breakfast. He ordered the blueberry waffles and sent a private apology to Albert Poots for diverting from his strict diet. He made a mental note to call them when he got back to Los Angeles. He wasn't happy about the way he left, and he owed them more than a swift goodbye.

Dudley was glad he packed a jacket. The temperature was in the high fifties, but the wind chill made him shiver during his brisk walk to his lawyer's. He found the address and told the receptionist he had an appointment. She buzzed Schuman and he came out immediately. He was taller than Dudley and about twice his age. He was dressed in a fine light gray tweed suit, with a vest and a pocket watch and a vintage wooden walking cane. Dudley liked him instantly.

"George Dudley, I presume," Schuman said, his voice deep and sonorous.

"Mr. Schuman. Nice to finally meet you face to face," Dudley said shaking his hand.

"Same here. Right this way. I assume you had a chance to look over the latest draft of the Final Judgement of Dissolution?" Schuman said easily.

"Like reading the US Constitution," Dudley replied. "I only understood half of it, but it sure sounded important."

"A sense of humor," Schuman said smiling. "Good. You're going to need one to get through this process."

Dudley sat next to Schuman at his large conference table. Schuman moved some papers and folders around, found the one he was looking for, and slid it across the laminated surface to Dudley. "Do you have any questions, young man?"

"No."

Carl Schuman smiled. He had settled hundreds of divorce proceedings over the years, and he had seen it all. The tantrums, the screaming, the incredulity, and the tears. Dudley however, mystified him. He just sat there. He didn't even bother looking at the papers. Schuman's staff worked many days getting them prepared. He expected some type of reaction, not apathy.

"The terms are acceptable?" Schuman prodded.

"Yes."

"Does the alimony seem fair?"

"Yes."

"Hmm," Schuman added. "What about the apartment?"

"Sell it."

"You don't want to keep it?"

"No."

Schuman blinked and then laughed softly. "Very well then. Just sign next to the yellow tabs I attached." Dudley did so. "That's right. There, there, initial that one, that's good, and… one more. Perfect," Schuman said. "All done. The rest we sign in front of the judge."

Dudley stood up. "Thank you very much, Mr. Schuman. Quick and painless."

"Yes. Very quick," he said looking at his watch. "Well, I'll send these over to Gary and the County Clerk this morning, and I'll see you tomorrow at the courthouse, but I don't anticipate any complications."

"The only way to live," Dudley said, holding out his hand. "See you then. Nice offices by the way. Love the paintings. Original Remington's?"

"No, just very good prints. But thanks for noticing. No one usually does," he said impressed.

Dudley smiled, waved a cheery goodbye, and stepped back into the New York cold. He checked his watch again and decided to hit the Strand Bookstore before heading back uptown. *Maybe there's a new Stephen King or Ken Follett. Damn, those guys are prolific*, he thought. *Where do all those ideas come from?*

3

He decided to take an Uber to December's house in Manhasset. He did not want the hassle of taking two subway lines, a train, and a cab. The house was a huge two-story traditional colonial. A covered entryway was flanked by two large windows with black shutters on each side and a row of four large windows above. The stone was a pleasant mixture of horizontal gray, black, and white bricks. The lawn was a thick Kentucky bluegrass, so immaculate that Dudley was afraid to step on it.

He followed the curving walkway to the large red front door and pushed the doorbell. A moment later it was opened by a short woman, dressed all in white and a dirty apron. "Can I help you?" she said in accented English.

"Hello. I'm Archie… I mean, George. I'm Decey's dad." The woman looked at Dudley confused.

Dudley tried again. "Oh, I'm sorry. Mrs. December Stanton. I'm her father," Dudley said smiling.

The woman looked like she might close the door in his face. Dudley checked the street number plate beside the door frame. "I believe I have the right house. Though they all do look alike from out here, don't you think?" he asked laughing.

"It's all right, Rosa," December said coming up behind the housekeeper. "This is mi padre," she said, reverting to Spanish. Rosa gave Dudley a suspicious look then said, "Very good Miss Stanton."

"Please check on the duck, Rosa," December Stanton said dismissing her. "I don't want it burned again." Rosa moved back inside the house, and December embraced her dad. "Welcome to my home, daddy."

"It's absolutely lovely, honey," he said. Then he stepped into the sun-drenched grand two-story foyer with a *Gone with the Wind*—styled staircase leading up to an open second-floor hallway.

"Oh, my God. This is huge! Like Grand Central."

"I know," Decey said, a little embarrassed. "We usually have to print out maps for first-timers."

Dudley laughed. "I'm a little early."

"It's okay, dad," Decey said. "Gabe is on his way and dinner, if Rosa doesn't destroy it, should be ready by six. Let me show you around."

He took her shoulders in his hands. She looked up, surprised. Their eyes met and he said, "I am so proud of you, December June."

Her eyes filled with tears, and she hugged him again, this time much fiercer. "Oh, daddy, I've been waiting so long to hear you say that."

"You are my shining star, pumpkin. But I do have to ask you a serious question."

She pulled back and looked into his eyes with apprehension. "What, daddy?"

"Beaumont? Really?"

She laughed and said, "Come on you doofus. We'll start upstairs. Sorry, the elevator is out."

"What a dump," Dudley said using his best Betty Davis voice.

As it turned out, Rosa did not burn the duck. Dinner was splendid. Dudley ate things he didn't recognize and other things he couldn't even pronounce, but he complimented Rosa so much she cracked a smile.

After the meal was finished, Gabriel said, "Let me show you the library, sir. I have a nice selection of brandies."

"You two go ahead, dad," Decey said. "I'll help Rosa clean up."

"Lead the way, son."

The library was just off the main foyer on the ground floor. The walls were covered with shelves of books stacked up to the ceiling. Dudley perused the titles and pulled out a copy of *The Old Man and the Sea* by Ernest Hemmingway. "I read this in high school. The first time," he said, admiring the flawless binding and the gold embossed lettering on the cover. He opened it and heard that distinct crack when you open a book for the first time. He saw the handwriting on the title page. "Holy shit. This is a signed first!"

Gabriel was pouring Cognac into two snifter glasses. "Oh, that. My uncle Thomas gave me that for graduation. Said I should broaden my mind or something."

Dudley looked at Gabe and shook his head. "Well, your uncle was right. You should read this." He carefully replaced the book which he knew would easily sell for $2,500 at auction. He took the offered brandy and sat in one of the brown leather recliners.

"Who's got time to read," Gabriel said. "Unless you're talking the Journal. Amazon was up 10 points today. Did you know that? My dad always says, not everyone suffers in a slow economy."

"Just the poor," Dudley said, staring at him.

"Oh, yeah, well there's that. But they got their welfare and their unemployment."

"Are there no prisons? Are there no workhouses?" Dudley said loudly, standing dramatically and waving his arms. He loved playing Ebenezer Scrooge every year with the Riverside Players. "You really should read more, Gabe. Besides the journal." He sat down again and sipped his drink. "This is good brandy. No, Remy Martin, of course, but good."

Gabriel Stanton had not spent much time with George Dudley during his six-month courtship of December Dudley. Mostly they went to the club or his parents' place. When they were together, her father always struck him as a bit of a loser. A jokester. A middle-class nobody. But this guy sitting across from him was someone else.

"How was L.A.? Decey said you met Oprah?" Gabe did not believe it. Decey had shown him earlier the photo on Instagram, but he knew what Photoshop could do nowadays.

"Yes. She's very sweet. Pretty too," Dudley added. "TV doesn't do her justice. Stedman's a good man. Smart. You know he has a master's degree in Education?"

"I didn't know that," Gabe said feebly.

"Clooney told me they sit on a board together. Some nonprofit in Chicago, I think," Dudley added conversationally. "His wife is nice too."

"Who? Stedman's?"

"No," Dudley laughed. "Clooney. Amal Clooney. Nice looking woman, you know what I mean?" and winked.

"You met George Clooney, too?" Gabriel said, and this time there was real awe.

"So what are my two boys talking about?" December said, entering the library. "Football?"

Later, after Dudley's Uber had picked him up, Gabriel walked back into his library. He pulled down the copy of *The Old Man and the Sea*. He sat in his leather chair and opened it to chapter one.

"Honey? Are you coming to bed?" December asked.

"In a minute."

REFLECTIONS ON REPORT #18

That's one of my favorite books, too. I like George with his children. He's a good dad. I liked being a dad too. Maybe more than being Cary Grant. Good stuff, eh Jennifer?

Chapter 23
Till Death Do We Part. Or Whatever

REPORT #19

1

Darcy Dudley and Gary Reade arrived exactly at 9:00 am Kara Lightly, Judge Gambol's secretary, directed them to his conference room. "Would you like any coffee or water?"

"Water is fine."

"Make that two."

She pulled two EVIANs from a small refrigerator and placed them on coasters in front of them.

"The judge is running a little late, but I expect him any minute now," she said and left the room.

"He's late. George is late! The most important day in my life and everyone is late!" she said, smacking the table with the flat of her hand.

"I thought the birth of your children was…"

"Oh, shut up Gary," she screeched.

"Just relax D. This will all be over before you know it," Gary said patting her hand. He tapped the folder in front of him. "Georgie agreed to everything. We just sign, say 'I do' to the judge, and ipso facto, freedom is yours."

"I don't understand any of this," Darcy said, standing up. She began walking around the room.

"George says I can keep the apartment, or sell it, whatever. He didn't fight me on the alimony, or the kids." She was counting off the list on her fingers. "Why doesn't he care? Does he hate me so much?"

"I don't hate you, Darcy." Dudley was standing in the doorway. He was wearing his new dark blue suit from Greg Chapman's with a silver tie. His hair was perfectly combed, his shoes were shined and there was a white pocket square in his jacket. He had his hand in his pocket and his head tilted to one side regarding his wife, but it was his smile she noticed first. It was big and bright and white, like a movie star.

She inhaled involuntarily. This was not the George Dudley she knew. She suddenly felt the need to sit. She had the ridiculous thought that she might swoon. *Does anyone swoon anymore?* she thought. *And where are his glasses?*

"You look lovely Darcy, as always. Are those new shoes? Jimmy Choo, right?" he said stepping toward her.

She did sit down. Hard. Gary had to reach out to steady her. "You all right D?" Gary said.

"I'm… I was just surprised, that's all," she said and took a sip of the Evian.

Dudley crossed to her and took her hand and kissed it tenderly. "It's good to see you again. Not wild about the circumstances but, c'est la vie."

"Yes," was all she could say. She was having trouble controlling her breathing. *When did he buy that suit? He looks great. Is he working out?*

He touched her hair. "New haircut too. Very becoming. Hello, Gary. Thanks for all your help with this," he said reaching out and shaking his hand. Then he looked at his Rolex and said, "Hm, Schuman's late too." Gary and Darcy only got a brief look at the expensive timepiece before Dudley pulled out the chair next to Darcy and sat down.

Gary started to protest but Dudley waved him off and said, "I saw Decey last night. She seems happy. Gabe's a bit of a pompous prick, but she loves him, so what can you do right?"

Kara Lightly entered again and announced, "The judge will be here in a moment."

"Kara, will you be a dear and get me a coffee? Two sugars, one cream," Dudley said not looking at her.

"Oh, certainly Mr. Dudley. Right away, sir," she said and started to courtesy but stopped herself. "Oh, and you were right about the lenses. I just gave them a good soaking and the pain went right away. You're a genius."

He turned to her then and said, "You're very welcome, dear. Now run along," She smiled at him, giggled, then closed the door.

"What was that about?" Darcy asked.

"What Darce?" he said absently.

"That," she said pointing to where Kara Lightly had been standing a moment ago. "The lenses, the '*right away sir*', and did she courtesy?"

"Oh, that. She was rubbing her eyes when I arrived. I noticed a bottle of Opti-Free on her desk and told her she needed to clean her contact lenses. No big deal."

He had taken her hand again. "You look good… I mean different," she said, still uncomfortable.

"I joined a gym out there," he said and shrugged.

Then her eyes grew wider. "Contact lenses! You got contacts!"

He leaned in closer to her, holding her hand with both of his. "I missed you."

But before she could respond the door opened and Judge Gambol came in. He noticed George and Darcy at the far end of the table, holding hands, and said, "Well, I thought I was doing a divorce in this room not a wedding."

Judge Gambol was a large man with a big white beard. He enjoyed playing Santa Claus for his grandchildren during the holidays, and his cherubic personality was ever-present.

"We are, your honor," Gary said formally, standing up. "I'm Gary Reade with Miller and Bing, and…"

"I know who you are. Sit down Reade," Judge Gambol said then appraised George and Darcy again. "You two look cozy. Do I sense reconciliation in the air?"

Dudley stood up and shook Judge Gambol's hand, "George Dudley your honor. No. I don't think so. I just haven't seen Darcy in some time, and well, doesn't she look swell?" Spoken by anyone else in any other circumstances the line would have sounded corny, but Dudley delivered it with such charm and sincerity, accompanied by that 100-watt smile, Darcy couldn't help herself but break down and cry.

"Oh, George," she sobbed and laid her head on the table.

Dudley looked at her, then at the judge and then he shrugged his shoulders.

"Well," Judge Gambol began. "Just when you think you've seen everything. You better sit down, Mr. Dudley," and he pointed to the opposite side of the table. "Over there. You seem to have an adverse effect on this woman."

Dudley sat down as Carl Schuman arrived. "Sorry, I was late your honor," he apologized immediately.

"No problem, Carl. We were just getting started. Though you did miss some good stuff so far. Yes, indeed," he said chuckling to himself. "Let's get started."

"Wait!" Darcy cried.

"Here we go," Judge Gambol said.

"I need to speak to George. Alone," she said standing.

"Now wait a minute, D," Gary protested.

"This is highly unusual, Mrs. Dudley," Carl Schuman agreed.

"But I'll allow it. Kara?" Judge Gambol called out.

"Yes, sir."

"Take Mr. and Mrs. Dudley down to my office, please." Then he said to Darcy, "Five minutes young lady. I'm already running behind, and this was supposed to be one of the easy ones."

They followed Kara Lightly down the hall to Judge Gambol's private office. Once they were alone, Darcy whirled on Dudley and said, "Who the fuck are you and what have you done with my husband?" She was holding his arms, marveling at his strong biceps.

"You killed him remember?" George said, moving away from her. "Sorry, Darce, but it's true. You and Murdoch, Elliott, and Bill Rawlings."

She took a step back, surprised by his sudden vehemence. *This really wasn't the man she married.* But then she recovered and said, "Well, if you think I'm going to apologize, you're wrong."

He took a deep breath and sat in Judge Gambol's leather chair. "Apologize? Hell Darcy, I have you to thank for all this. Something's been happening to me. For some time now. And I guess I just need a push off the edge to get some perspective. I didn't like what I saw."

He stared out of the window. Not really looking at anything. Then he said, "I read this book once, can't remember the title, but it was something like. When everything sucks, change everything. When I was in New York, I didn't realize everything sucked. I just tried to survive another day. Then another, and another. I didn't even realize how unhappy I was until I got fired and you left me."

"George," Darcy said, but he waved her off and stood again. "So, with a little help from my new LA friends, I changed. I looked at where I was and where I wanted to be, and I made a plan, I became a new man. George Dudley 2.0."

"You can't just change, George," she said.

"Oh, but you can, sweetheart," he replied, and his eyes turned hard. "You just need a great deal of motivation and some talented help. Trust me on this." He smiled and moved closer to her.

"I know I have been a disappointment to you these past few years, 'Darce'. I don't blame you for leaving. But what's done is done, and now we move on." He kissed her then. Short and sweet. It was a kiss full of gratitude and memories. He held her face in his hands and said softly, "Now let's go make you a free woman."

Suddenly, she threw herself at him. His back hit the door, and she had her arms around him and was kissing him passionately. He detached himself, slowly but forcefully, and said quietly, "Enough now."

"Get yourself together. I'll meet you back there." George Dudley opened the door and returned to the conference room alone. Gary looked past him, wondering where his sister was. He rose and was about to ask, but Darcy came in then. Gary, Schuman, and the judge watched her carefully, looking for clues as to what just happened. And, more importantly, what might happen next? But Dudley dispelled all ideas by pulling out his Mont Blanc pen from his inner jacket pocket and asked Judge Gambol, "So where do I sign?"

2

"Mom did what?" Paul asked.

"I think she had a change of heart," Dudley said, scanning the menu. Monte's was busy and they had to shout to be heard.

"Change of heart? She wanted you back? Seriously?" Paul said sipping on his draft beer.

"Yeah. Bit of a shocker there. But cool heads prevailed, and she is now Darcy Reade again," he said, raising his glass.

"You seem happy about it. A couple months ago you were the walking dead," he scoffed.

"Well, my son, there is one thing in this world you can always count on."

"Taxes? Death?" Paul said.

"Okay, three things, smart ass," he said smiling. "But the answer is 'change'. Things will eventually change. Sometimes it just happens, and sometimes you make it happen."

Paul Dudley knew from the moment he picked up his father from the airport two days ago that something was up. The whole LA look, the strong opinions, the aggressiveness. It was such a contrast to the defeated man whose wife left him. "You've gotten quite philosophical in your old age, haven't you, dad?"

Dudley simply raised his glass in acknowledgment.

"You are different. Decey saw it too. And it's not just the contacts or the tan, you act like you don't give a fuck about anything."

"That's not true," Dudley replied seriously. "I care about you and your sister."

"Dad, you haven't cared about us since we moved out. Oh, you help when you can and you ask the right questions, but you only care about yourself. You always have. You're so worried about how other people see you, that you never let them see you."

"Now who's playing Freud?" Dudley said.

"When's the last time you came to one of my gigs? How many times have you been to Decey's house? When was the last time you took mom on a vacation? None, one, and never."

"That's not fair. I was working," Dudley said.

"How many shows have you done in the past four years, Pops? Six? Seven? Your priorities are all screwed up man."

"Here we go." Alice, their pretty blonde server held a tray of food in her hands. "Triple cheese calzone for you, and a chicken alfredo for the handsome gentlemen." She placed the plates in front of them and then touched Dudley's shoulder. "Will there be anything else?" and even Paul could hear the suggestive undertones in her question.

"We're good Alice. Thanks," Dudley said.

Paul Dudley laughed and flicked his hand contemptuously. "This new you dad is all flash no substance. The suit, the hair, the tan it's all cosmetic. It looks good, I'll admit that, but at what cost?"

"I don't know yet son. I'm still figuring that out."

"Are you at least happier now?"

"There are benefits, I won't deny it," Dudley said.

Paul laughed. "Is that it, dad? Is that what this mid-life crisis shit is all about? Banging babes?"

"Actually, I do have a girlfriend now."

"Yea, grandma told me about that. Your old flame before mom, right?" Paul said.

"No. Someone I met in Los Angeles." George pulled up a photo of Kelli on his cell phone.

"Hot. What is she, sixteen?" Paul laughed.

"She's twenty-nine. I think."

"Actress?"

"Actress slash model," Dudley said.

"I rest my case."

3

Later that afternoon, back in the apartment, Dudley boxed up the few belongings he and Darcy agreed he would take. His favorite books. A handful of DVDs. *Five boxes*, he thought, when he was finished. *Twenty years and all I have to show for it is five boxes.*

He laid a stack of framed photos on the dining room table and started to remove them, one by one, out of the frames. He sipped his wine and let the memories come with each image; dressed as a clown for December's fifth birthday party, Paul swinging a baseball bat, the whole family eating crabs with Elsie, December's first holy communion. A close-up of George and Darcy slow dancing at their wedding.

He drank the last of the Merlot and felt a wave of nausea creep up his throat. "I will not throw up," he said to no one and started to laugh. "Talking to yourself now, George?" And tears welled up in his eyes. "NO!" he yelled. "No. This was my choice," he said out loud.

He took a shower then went outside and sat on the balcony overlooking the city. *What would Cary do?* he thought, and then he remembered the scene from his favorite Cary Grant movie, *Holiday*. Every time Cary's character started to feel anxious or worried, he would jump up, snap his fingers and wave his worries away. George tried it. And it worked. He suddenly felt better, and he knew exactly what he wanted to do.

The cab dropped him off in front of the Riverside Players Theater at 7:45. It was the opening night performance of *To Kill a Mockingbird*, and the lobby was full. He was able to get a ticket due to a last-minute cancellation. Front

148

row, center. Not his favorite place to watch a show, but beggars cannot be choosers, as the saying goes.

The Riverside Players were technically a community theater. The actors were not paid for their efforts, but the consistent quality of the productions, especially since Tyrone (Call me Ty) Middleton III took over the General Manager duties, had been elevated to near Off-Broadway levels.

But more importantly to Ty were the financial benefits of these successes; season subscriptions doubled, and four new show sponsors signed up: two banks, a grocery chain, and an airline. His fund-raising efforts allowed the theater to repair the fly system, acquire a state-of-the-art light board and expand the lobby, notably the women's bathrooms, the bane of every theater building.

This brought a more affluent crowd to the company, used to dress up when going to a show.

Dudley was delighted for the opportunity to wear his Armani tuxedo again.

The patrons were heading to their seats as Dudley entered the lobby. As was his custom now, he stopped and surveyed the room before moving further in. He noticed two mature women, elegantly dressed in long evening gowns and fabulous furs near the concessions area. But as he started toward them, he heard his name called out.

"Stop the presses Ladies and Germs, the prodigal son has returned." Ty Middleton III's voice boomed, and all heads turned as he quickly ran up to Dudley and lifted him off the floor in a bear hug. "I almost didn't recognize you, George. You look fabulous," Ty bellowed.

"You don't look half bad yourself Ty," Dudley said as soon his feet touched the ground again.

"Staying out of prison I see."

"Those rumors were slanderous lies, my friend."

"I know. I wrote the article about it for the Times," Dudley said. "I hear the shows selling well."

"Of course. My marketing campaign was brilliant," he said bowing. "And the actors ain't too bad either," he laughed. "I was sorry to hear we had to replace you, but Thomas stepped up nicely."

"I'm sure he did," Dudley said.

"But look at you. Hollywood seems to agree with you. You look like something out of a 1940s rom-com."

"Exactly the look I was going for. It only cost me $3,000," he said. He never liked Ty's insincere bullshit, but he knew money was the only way to shut him up. He displayed his Rolex Oyster Royal and said, "Sorry to rush off, Ty. Hope you still start on time." Ty Middleton watched him go and silently fumed. *Arrogant shit*, he thought, *but damn he looked good. Maybe I can get him to star in Arsenic and Old Lace next season?*

The curtain did rise on time and Dudley spent the next few minutes admiring the set. The designers did a splendid job of recreating rural Alabama in 1933. He knew the story well, so he wasn't paying much attention to the actors until he heard a familiar voice, Bill Rawlings. He was dressed in the same light gray weathered suit that Gregory Peck wore in the famous movie.

And, as the scene progressed, Dudley realized that Bill had decided to forego any acting inspiration on his own and instead tried mightily to channel his limited impersonation of Peck's movie performance. It was a bad choice. Rawlings spent more time reciting the lines exactly as Peck said them than listening and talking to the characters on stage with him.

Dudley had seen it before. Many amateur actors do it. Especially when attempting signature roles of great actors. He was guilty of it himself when he played the lead in *12 Angry Men* and did a passable Henry Fonda imitation.

But the audience was much more forgiving and gave Bill and the rest of the cast a standing ovation when the curtain came down. George lingered in the lobby and waited as the actors came out to say hello and hug friends and family. Dudley recognized Lawrence Gilmore the director standing off by himself by the box office door. He strolled over. "Wonderful show."

Gilmore nodded absently, ignoring him. The day had been long putting the final stamp on next year's season, and all Gilmore wanted now was to get to the cast party and grope Katie Cummins. Dudley remained next to him, smiling and waiting. Finally, he said, "Oh, Dudley. Didn't recognize you."

"I've been getting a lot of that lately."

Gilmore leaned closer and whispered, "You would have made a much better sheriff."

Dudley leaned back and said in the same tone, "I would have made a much better Atticus."

Gilmore opened his eyes wide, shocked. "I thought Bill did a fine job."

"Bullshit Larry," Dudley said aggressively. "How could you let him do that? Was that his idea or yours?"

Gilmore stared at him. "I don't know what—"

Dudley cut him off. "Oh, please Larry." Then he did a dead-on impersonation of Gregory Peck. "Well, you see Scout, a Mockingbird is one of nature's true treasures. No one should ever kill one. Blah, blah, blah." Gilmore's eyes widened even more. "I was very disappointed."

"He wouldn't stop," Gilmore confessed. "No matter what notes I gave him. He insisted on saying every line like Gregory Peck."

"One more reason why we should turn equity, so you could have fired his ass. Oh, there's Katie," Dudley said noticing one of the actresses entering the lobby. "Good seeing you, Larry."

He patted Gilmore's arm and crossed the lobby to stand directly behind Katie Cummings, resident ingénue and the prettiest girl in the company. Her long dark hair was a tangled mess after being constrained for two hours under her character's wig, and she absently touched it while a small group of admirers surrounded her. Her other hand held the front of her silk robe closed. She threw it on hastily after removing her costume, not wasting the time to tie the belt. Her lithe frame was still obvious through the thin material and many, including Dudley, wondered what she wore underneath, if anything.

"You were fantastic Katie," an elderly woman told her. "I almost didn't recognize you up there. So much different than your *Sabrina* from last season."

"Oh, yes. You were wonderful in *Sabrina*," her friend said.

"Beautiful," her husband agreed. "Those dresses in Sabrina were spectacular. This show, not so much," he chuckled.

"Well, each character is a challenge," Katie said.

"I thought you were brilliant, Miss Cummings," Dudley said from behind her. She turned and was about to offer her standard, humble thank you, when she recognized Dudley. She threw her arms around his neck and her robe flew open to the appreciation of the nearby gawkers.

"Oh, Georgie. I thought that was you in the front," she said, then pulling back to examine him closely, she added, "But I wasn't sure. Where are your glasses? Did you finally get some contact lenses?"

"Yes, ma'am," he said.

"And look at this tux," she said fondling the material. "Very sexy."

Dudley blushed. His Cary Grant persona was helpful when dealing with egocentric men like Ty and Gilmore, but he had had a secret crush on Katie

Cummings for many years, and her sudden attention was shaking his practiced composure.

"Oh, well, thanks Katie," he said and unconsciously pushed up his nonexistent glasses.

Katie pulled back and laughed at him, shaking her head, her hair bouncing around her pretty face. "Oh, same old Georgie. You can dress him up, right?" Then she turned, pulling her robe closed, and greeted another well-wisher.

"Hiya, George," Bill Rawlings said.

Dudley turned slowly, still stinging from his aborted moment with Katie, and looked directly into the face of the man who stole his dream wife and his dream role. Inside, Dudley felt a physical change happen. His pulse quickened, his back straightened, blood rushed to his face and just like flicking a switch, the 100-watt smile returned.

"Mr. Billy Rawlings," Dudley said loudly, grabbing Rawlings's hand with both of his. "How are you, old friend?" he said, putting special emphasis on the last two words.

"Oh, good you know, tough show," he said, smiling.

"Yes. How did you ever learn all those lines?" Dudley said, repeating the most popular question from fawning patrons.

"Right. Good one. Really good cast though. Don't you think?"

"I thought Thomas stole the show."

"Okay, Georgie, I know you wanted Atticus, but you know, that's how these things work out sometimes. No hard feelings, I hope old boy," he grinned.

"Of course, of course," Dudley said, spreading his arms out wide. "Think nothing of it. But I do have one thing I'd like to say about your performance. You really looked like you were having fun up there."

Rawlings's face fell. They had been friends for many years, and they had developed a code when reviewing shows. When you hated it and could not think of one good thing to say, the go-to response was, 'You really looked like you were having fun up there'. It was the ultimate insult. The high that Rawlings was riding on from the standing ovation came crashing down and he felt his face flush.

"Okay, George, I thought we could deal with this like adults," Rawlings said, and he placed his hand on George's arm to lead him somewhere more private. But Dudley surprised him by grabbing Rawlings hand and twisting hard. "Hey. That hurt."

Dudley moved closer to Rawlings, "Listen to me you pompous asshole. You suck as a friend, and you suck as an actor. If you ever touch me again, I'll break your fucking fingers."

Rawlings gasped but before he could reply, Dudley released him and smiled again. "Oh, and one more thing," he said leaning in conspiratorially, "Darcy farts in the bed. But you probably know that already, don't you?" He patted him good-naturedly on the arm and said with finality, "Good luck to you, old boy."

He had his hand on the exit door when Katie Cummings came running up behind him. "Oh, Georgie. You're not leaving, are you? There's a cast party."

She was adorable. And in a flash, he remembered all those late-night rehearsals when he wanted to kiss her, those cast parties where he wanted to touch her, and those lonely moments in his own bed when he wished she was there. But he never said anything. He never acted on his desire. He was the good guy. The safe guy. The invisible guy.

But not today, because George Dudley hadn't gone to the theater tonight, Cary Grant did. He suddenly took her in a strong embrace, and her robe slipped, exposing the white panties and bra underneath. His right hand took hold of her shapely bottom, and his lips found hers. Katie's arms hung limply at her side as Dudley kissed her, long and hard.

When he released her, she gasped loudly, "Oh, Georgie." He smiled his best smile, saluted the crowd, and left the theater.

REFLECTIONS ON REPORT #19

Sorry, Clarence, but I enjoyed that immensely. I couldn't have done it any better myself.

Chapter 24
It's Valentine's Day... Again

REPORT #20

1

Dudley took an early flight out of La Guardia to Orlando and was sipping a Starbucks Caramel Frappuccino when Amy Andrews came off the elevator at 10:30.

"You're early," she said, surprised.

"Came right from the airport," he said, indicating his suitcase on the floor next to him. "And I come bearing gifts," he said, handing her a Starbucks cup.

She sipped it and said, "A Grande Caffe Mocha," she said. "My favorite."

Dudley looked over to the reception desk and winked at Tiffany. She winked back. Amy noticed the exchange and said, "Oh, I see. A conspiracy," she smirked and continued to her office. "C'mon, George."

"You can leave your bag here, Mr. Dudley," Tiffany volunteered. "I'll keep an eye on it."

"Thank you, Tiffany. Thanks for the tip."

"Sit down, George," Amy commanded when they entered her office. She sat behind her glass desk and started leafing through a manila folder. Dudley, however, casually walked past her desk and stood behind her, looking out the window. "You do have a wonderful view here Amy."

"I know. Now these expenses…"

He began massaging her shoulders, "Oh, tense," he noticed.

Amy began to move away from him. She did not like being touched. Dudley forced her back down. "Relax. I won't bite." He dug his fingers in hard, just like Rodney at LA Fitness did when they had their daily sessions. "It's these muscles right… here."

"Ow," Amy cried.

"Felt that, right? The upper trapezius is the most important muscle group related to stress because it moves and stabilizes the scapula. Been having trouble sleeping? Raising your arms?"

Amy closed her eyes and moaned. "Yes. How did you know?"

"Common causes of stress and scapular inflammation," Dudley said. "But this should open up things. Try raising your right arm now. Better?"

She did so. "Why yes. I haven't been able to do that all week," she said astonished.

"You should find a good masseuse. Weekly sessions will clear this up easily," he said then patting her shoulders gently, he said. "Did you read my rewrite?"

Amy took a deep breath and opened her eyes. Dudley was sitting casually across from her, one leg crossed over the other. His head was angled to one side, and he smiled directly at Amy Andrews.

"You look different, George."

"You look stressed Amy."

"I am," she admitted, dropping her eyes.

"I guess I should have asked first before I rewrote the thing, but honestly, Bob has lost his touch, if he ever had any." He lit a cigarette and puffed gracefully.

"You can't smoke in here," she said automatically.

"Can't I?" he asked and took a deep drag.

She blinked and pushed an empty Starbucks cup toward him. He leaned forward and flicked his cigarette ash into it. "The rewrite?"

"Yes. It's good. In fact, it's incredibly good. Universal loves it."

"I'm so glad," he said and suddenly stood up.

"Wait," she said and held up the folder. "We have to talk about these expenses."

"No, what I have to do is sleep. I took a very early flight to see you," he said walking to the door. "Email me any questions. Otherwise, I have Bruce Willis all set up for March first, then I'll be back on the fifteenth for the Players Championship and Ryan's charity event. Were you invited?"

"Um, no," Amy said, shaking her head. Things were moving fast. *What was happening here?*

"Get those massages," he said, opening her door. "Love the shoes by the way. Manolo?"

"Um, yes."

"Sexy. Bye now," Dudley said and closed the door behind him.

What the fuck was that? Then she raised her right arm over her head again. Smiled. Sipped her caffè mocha and looked out her window. "It is a lovely view," she said to the empty room.

"Mom! I'm back!"

"I'm in the kitchen," Elsie Dudley yelled. He found her and sat at the kitchen table.

"I'm having tomato soup and grilled cheese. Want some?"

"Please. I'm starving."

She placed a bowl in front of him and said, "I saw Mary this morning at Whole Foods. She said you're taking her to Kadence tonight. How'd you get a reservation?"

"I told them I was Bradley Cooper, and I was only in town for the day," he said, blowing on the hot soup.

She laughed out loud. "You didn't? What are they going to say when he doesn't show up?"

"I made the reservation for four. I'll just say he's running late. He is a movie star, after all."

"Mary is very excited," she said and then added, smiling, "She's also looking forward to seeing you."

"Very funny, Mrs. Dudley."

"She really likes you, George. She talked my ear off. How's George doing in Los Angeles? How's the book coming? Is he happy out there? Do you think he'll move back here after the divorce?"

Dudley kept his head down and ate silently.

"What's the matter, Georgie?" His mother said, perceptive as ever.

"I'm sort of seeing someone now."

Elsie Dudley put down her spoon and stared at her son. Then she banged the table hard. Dudley dropped his spoon and red soup splashed onto his white shirt.

"What the hell, mom!"

"Don't you dare mess this up again, George Alexander Dudley," Elsie said standing. "She is one of the most wonderful girls I ever met in my life. You were a fool to leave her the first time and you'd be the biggest horses-ass alive if you blow it this time."

"Mom. It just happened. I met this actress in LA, Kelli…"

"I don't want to know her name. I don't want you to speak her name. I thought you had changed. I thought you had grown up."

When he didn't respond, she changed the subject. "How was New York?"

"Darcy wanted me back," he said casually.

"What?"

"I said no, of course. We signed the papers."

She took a deep breath and pulled her chair next to Dudley. She took his hands in hers and said, "I don't know what game you're playing here Georgie, with the suits and the tan and the attitude, but you're messing with people's lives. You better think real hard about what you want."

When Dudley didn't reply, she stood and kissed the top of his head. "I love you son, but I don't know if I like this new you." She took a paper towel and wiped up the spilled soup. Dudley stood, picked up his suitcase, and went to his bedroom. He laid down on the bed, fully dressed, and slept fitfully.

He had the dream again. The kids were splashing in the pool and Dudley watched and waited. No one looked at him. No one asked him to join in. No one even acknowledged him. He turned to go. But this time he stopped. Bent to pick up a rock and he hurled it at the side of the pool. It made a small hole and water started to pour out. The children started to scream as he woke up.

2

"Konnici wa. I am Mariko. Welcome to Kadence," the kimono-wearing hostess said when Dudley and Mary Jordan arrived at 4:00 pm. "Reservation for four. Cooper," Dudley said to the stunning black-haired Japanese woman.

"Ah, yes," she said excitedly. Then looking over Dudley's shoulder, disappointment etched on her face, she asked, "Is Mr. Cooper not with you?"

"He's running late, dear," Dudley said easily, consulting his Rolex. "You can seat us. He'll be here in a minute." He smiled and the young woman hesitated, but then said, "Right this way, sir."

Dudley smiled at Mary Jordan and winked. She shook her head. She was not happy when he told her about his deception. But she really wanted to eat here, so she played along.

Mariko seated them at the L-shaped sushi bar. One of the chefs looked up then and questioned Mariko in Japanese. She bowed and said to Dudley, "Mr. Lalicon asked if you wanted to start now, or wait for your friends." Four of the other six stools at the bar were already taken with early diners.

"I think we should start. I don't want to be rude to your other guests," Dudley said politely.

"When Mr. Cooper and Jennifer Lawrence arrive, just bring them over."

Mariko's eyes grew wider. "Jennifer Lawrence is coming too? Oh, hai," she said bowing and ran back to the podium.

"You are so bad," Mary said, but secretly she was pleased. Kadence was the hottest restaurant in Orlando. Reservations opened at 8:00 am on the first day of the month and were sold out within minutes. The experience was unlike any other place she had eaten before in her twenty years in the business. Only ten diners were served at a time. They all ate together at the sushi table. There were no other guests and no menus. The chef served whatever was the best and freshest ingredients he had bought that day. It was called Omakase. Dudley did not quite get the idea.

When a colorful tray of sashimi was laid in front of him, he raised a tentative hand and asked, "Sorry. This looks lovely but can you make sweet and sour chicken?" Mary hit him and groaned.

The chef merely bowed and ignored him.

"What?" he asked Mary.

"You don't get to choose doofus. It's Omakase, the chef's choice. You get what he gives you. Take it or leave it. Didn't you know that when you called?"

"I just picked the most romantic place I could find," he laughed. "I had no idea."

"Well, have some more sake and consider it an adventure." Then she whispered, "I'll buy you a whopper later if you're still hungry."

Dudley smiled gratefully, but Chef Lalicon stared at them. *I think his hearing is as good as his cooking*, Dudley thought and smiled sheepishly.

He swept away Dudley's sashimi and placed a slice of seared salmon on a bed of white rice in front of him.

"That's more like it," Dudley said, jumping off his stool and bowing. The other diners laughed, and Chef Lalicon didn't throw any sharp utensils at him, so he figured he'd passed some sort of test.

"Never a dull moment," Mary said.

By the time the dessert came, a chestnut rum ice cream with sweet potato cream and powdered meringue, Dudley was thoroughly enjoying himself. He was not full, but the abundance of sake heightened his mood. Since the meal was paid for when he originally made the reservation, Mariko never questioned him again about Bradley Cooper and Jennifer Lawrence's absence. And when he broke into a rousing rendition of, *Please Hello* from Stephen Sondheim's *Pacific Overtures*, the other guests clapped and even Mr. Lalicon cracked a toothy smile.

"Sayonara, everyone," Dudley said, bowing himself out of the restaurant. Mary Jordan was hanging on his arm. They were laughing and to anyone passing by they would think this was a couple celebrating their twentieth wedding anniversary.

When the Uber driver arrived to take Dudley to the airport, she said, "I wish you didn't have to go back so early." She was leaning against him. She was more than a little drunk on all the sake they drank. "Come on. Take an early flight out tomorrow. I'll make it worth your while," she said biting his ear.

"Ooo don't do that. If I miss my flight, I will be in so much trouble," he mumbled into her hair.

Mary stepped back and blinked, suddenly fully alert. "Trouble? I thought you said you had to get back because you had an 8:00 am meeting with Bruce Willis's assistant. To finalize the interview."

"I did? I mean I do. I do," Dudley said, stumbling over his words.

She pushed him. "What the hell, George. What's going on?"

"Nothing. I swear," he said, but she knew he was lying.

The Uber driver rolled down the passenger window. "Are we ready to go?"

Mary Jordan looked at George, and there was a sadness there that she did not think she could ever feel again. "What did I tell you, George? What I told you was rule number one. Never lie to me."

She jumped into the back seat of the car, told the driver her home address, and leaned back, closing her eyes, fighting the tears.

"Hey," George said as his ride, and his girl drove away. "Mary."

His flight back to Los Angeles took seven hours. It taxied in at LAX at a little after 9:00 pm PST. The sake finally caught up with him and he slept most of the way. When he was not sleeping, he was thinking about Mary, and Kelli, and what his mother said. That most of all.

Kelli Lee had been waiting in the baggage area for over an hour. She did not want to miss him. When she finally saw Dudley coming down the escalator, she took off running. He saw her coming and all thoughts of breaking up with her vanished. She was wearing a dark blue crop top, black jeans, and Nike running shoes. Her hair was in a ponytail, and it bounced behind her. She looked young and sexy. Which is exactly what she was. She jumped into his arms as soon as he hit the bottom step. "You made it! You made it. Oh, my Archie baby. I love you."

"I missed you too Kelli." He kissed her and then placed an arm around her waist. They went to the baggage carousel to retrieve his bags. As they waited his hand moved up and down her side, her bare skin was like velvet. The feel of her was like a drug clouding his brain. He could not think of anything but being with her, touching her, loving her.

Maybe this is where I belong, he thought, during the cab ride back to her place. They sat close in the back seat. They were kissing and touching each other so much that the elderly man driving the cab was finding it hard to keep his eyes on the road. He adjusted his rear-view mirror for a better look. Dudley noticed and smiled.

But then his mother's voice intruded. What's next, Georgie? After you finish the book, where will you go? What will you do? Is your life out there now? *I'm sure I can get a writing job somewhere out here next year*, he thought. *But will it be as George Dudley or Archie Leach? I guess I could always legally change my name.* He laughed at that, and Kelli said, "What baby?"

"I was just thinking how funny life is. You never know what's going to happen next."

"That's how I live my entire life," she said innocently. Then she started to sing, "Tomorrow, tomorrow, I love ya, tomorrow." Dudley joined in with the harmony. "You're only a day… a… way!"

"Wonderful," the cab driver said. Kelli and George laughed. And he looked at her again, and thought, *I do love her*.

REFLECTIONS ON REPORT #20

I was never good at picking wives either. He is becoming like me.

Chapter 25
#Onhisass

REPORT #21

"It's not a big deal, Mr. Leach. People do it all the time," Ashley Lynn said to Dudley and Kelli. They were seated in Bruce Willis's double-wide trailer on the set of his latest movie, *An Eye for an Eye*. Ashley described it as a revenge-type action movie. "Bruce's daughter gets kidnapped, and he has to fight a bunch of bad guys to get her back," she said.

"So a Bruce Willis movie," Dudley said, sipping his iced coffee.

She laughed and said, "You're right."

"But you're sure he won't get mad? That I brought Kelli?"

"Not at all," she said. Then turning to appraise Kelli she said confidentially, "I know Bruce will be fine with it, you are just his type."

"She's not dessert, you know," Dudley said.

"You are so funny, Mr. Leach. Would you like something from craft services? Fruit? A granola bar?"

"Fruit and yogurt sound great."

"Hey, can I go with you?" Kelli asked. "I would love to see the set. I'm an actress, you know," she added.

"Okay. Sure. Just stay with me. Don't wander away," Ashley said.

The girls left and Dudley went to the bathroom. When he came out, Bruce Willis was seated at the small kitchen table. "Archie Leach. Did you wash your hands?"

"Oh shit," Dudley said and fell back into the bathroom.

"You okay in there?" Willis laughed.

"Yes. Yes, sorry. You just startled me," Dudley said nervously. "Wow. Bruce Willis."

"Where?" Willis said looking around, then he flashed his famous grin and said, "You better have a seat Leach before you destroy my entire trailer."

When Amy Andrews gave Dudley the list of actors he was going to interview back in November, there was only one name that worried him—Bruce Willis. The Moonlighting, Yippee Ki Yay, I See Dead People superstar was always one of George Dudley's heroes. He'd seen all of his movies, some more than once, and watched every episode of *Moonlighting* and could still quote some of David Addison's best lines.

And now here he was, sitting across from Bruce Willis. He didn't know what to do next.

"You okay, buddy? You look a little… off. You want to reschedule?"

Dudley blinked. *Reschedule?* "No. No. Ummm," he said, trying unsuccessfully to stop his hands from shaking. He reached for his small notebook, dropping it. "Damn, Sorry."

Dudley picked it up and said, "Okay, Mr. Willis. I just have a few questions."

"I hope you don't mind if I eat while we do this. I got to be back on set in thirty," Willis said opening a Styrofoam container.

"No. Of course not," Dudley said, flipping through his pages. "Okay. Found it. Question number one. Did you always consider yourself a matinee idol?"

Willis froze, his salad-filled fork inches from his mouth, and stared at Dudley. Then he shook his head and said emphatically, "NO!" Then under his breath, "What a stupid question." He checked his watch and willed it to move faster.

George Dudley almost cried. After all his work, he was going to blow the one interview he looked forward to. Now here he was, alone with Bruce Willis, just the two of them, and Willis couldn't care less. He started to breathe faster and decided to leave. *I can't do this*, he thought. *Plus, I don't need him for the book. He's no matinee idol, anyway.*

Dudley stood up and was about to apologize, as he had done so many, many times before in his life when Willis looked up and said, "Don't let the screen door hit ya." And if that was all he said, Dudley probably would have left—but then he laughed, and muttered, "Loser." George Dudley stopped. He knew that laugh. He'd heard Willis use it hundreds of times in his movies when he was mocking someone.

The old Dudley would have taken it and smiled. The old Dudley might have cried. The old Dudley would have left. But that Dudley was dead. Darcy had killed him. Murdoch had killed him. Bill Rawlings had killed him.

This was Dudley 2.0. No. This was Cary Grant, reborn, and Cary doesn't take shit from anybody He sat back and stared at Bruce Willis who was smirking again between mouthfuls of lettuce and blue cheese dressing. "Tick tock," Willis said, pointing at his watch.

Dudley closed his notebook and slipped it back into his pocket. He pulled out a cigarette, lit it, and leaned back.

"There's no smoking in here," Bruce Willis said.

Dudley ignored him. "You're right. You are no matinee idol," Dudley said forcefully. "Maybe when you were doing *Moonlighting*, but since then, not so much."

Bruce Willis lowered his fork and said evenly, "We should definitely reschedule."

Dudley laughed and said, "I'm just kidding Brucie. *Sixth Sense* is one of my favorite all-time movies. I like what David Harper said in Vanity Fair. 'It's not a great movie because of the surprise ending, it's a great movie because of Bruce Willis's understated performance'. I happen to agree with that."

Bruce Willis laughed, "Your interview style is very unusual, Archie."

Dudley smiled and put his cigarette out in his coffee cup. "But you do have one thing in common with matinee idols, you're very consistent. You choose your roles very carefully. They reflect your Bruce Willis's movie star image and you rarely deviate. *Red*, *Lucky Number Slevin*, *Sin City*, *Unbreakable*; the characters are interchangeable. Not to mention the never-ending Die Hard series."

Willis watched him. "I did some out of the box?"

"True. I did like *Moonrise Kingdom*."

"Exactly."

"You also did *North* and *Rock the Kasbah*!" Dudley returned. "And *Bonfire of the Vanities*."

"Hey. That wasn't my fault!" Willis cried defensively.

"I admit you did give it your best effort, but you were horribly miscast. Even Tom Wolfe said so."

"Really?"

"Brucie baby. We're both adults here," Dudley said leaning in. "You're an actor. You like to work. I admire that. But my question for you is, why? Why do you keep working so much?"

For the first time since the interview started, Bruce Willis felt uneasy. George pressed, "You've done over one hundred movies. You are world famous. You're a multi-millionaire. What else is there?"

Bruce Willis put his fork down. Touched his napkin to his lips and said, "Respect."

"Excuse me?" Dudley said.

"I want their respect. Hollywood. History," he said and there was a vulnerability in his voice Dudley hadn't heard before.

"I never wanted to be the next Burt Reynolds. I wanted to be the next Paul Newman. Bob Redford. I want to be remembered as a great actor. Not a great movie star," he said looking up at Dudley. "You know like Anthony Hopkins or Bobby DeNiro. Duval. Pacino. Brando for Christ's sake. Why am I never in that conversation?"

"I don't know, Bruce," Dudley said consolingly. "But I do have a suggestion."

Willis looked up hopefully, but just then the door opened, and Ashley and Kelli came in. "Sorry, Bruce. We got caught in the lunch crowd with the extras. I brought you a yogurt cup with walnuts."

Kelli sat next to Dudley and said, "You probably don't remember me Mr. Willis, but I was in *A Good Day to Die Hard* with you. I was an extra, but you got me a few lines in the bank scene. I was very grateful. Helped me get my SAG card."

"You're an actress?" Willis said, trying to regain his composure.

"Mostly independent stuff," Kelli said shyly. "Nothing you would have heard of."

"Pretty and modest," Willis said, his old charm reasserting itself.

Dudley watched the exchange warily, holding onto Kelli's hand. She suddenly pulled it away and playfully slapped Bruce Willis's arm. "Oh, you jokester," she said.

"How's the interview going?" Ashley said.

"We were just finishing up." Bruce Willis looked at Dudley then turned his full attention back to Kelli. "Are you busy right now?"

"We have to go," Dudley said. But Kelli shook her head.

"We don't have any plans, right Archie?" Kelli said.

"Ashley," Willis said, but his eyes never left Kelli Lee. "Did that girl ever show up? The one in the restaurant scene we're shooting this afternoon."

"Kyle got one of the extras to step in."

"Tell him I want Kelli to do it. Stand up honey," Willis said to Kelli. "What size are you, a six?"

"Four, actually," Kelli said, not believing what was happening.

He stood and placed his hand around her waist, guiding her toward the door. "Take her to Kyle then get her a script, Ashley."

"Oh, wait. Is this really happening? I'm going to be in a major movie?" Kelli said hopping up and down. Bruce Willis had not removed his hand from her waist.

"Not unless you don't get your cute ass out of here right now," Willis said, smiling.

Kelli threw her arms around his neck and kissed his cheek. "Oh, thank you. Thank you."

"C'mon dearie," Ashley said. "Let's go make you a star."

Bruce Willis watched them cross the parking lot and enter a tent. Then he pointed at Kelli and said, "I remember her now. She was that little Asian kid that kept telling everybody 'This is my first movie. This is my first movie'." Then he closed the door, turned back to Dudley, and said callously, "I think I tapped that."

No one would have considered George Dudley a violent man. In his entire life, he was only in one fight, and that was a drunken bar fight which consisted more of grabbing and pushing than actual fisticuffs. So, when Dudley swung a right cross into Bruce Willis's left eye, he was more shocked than the actor. Willis fell back onto the kitchen floor, motionless.

"I knocked out Bruce Willis," Dudley said, then he pushed open the door and ran for Kelli's car, saying a silent prayer of gratitude that he drove and still had the keys.

Once he was on the highway and his heart rate had slowed down, the only thought that kept banging around in his head was, *Amy is going to be really mad about this one.*

When I was a young man, I got into a few scraps. As I recall they were either about women or money. Sometimes both. Looking back, I could have avoided most of them. Most of them were with my mates. After, we'd laugh and go on as if nothing serious happened. Very few blokes needed a good thrashing. Unlike this guy. He deserved a good shot in the eye. If it wasn't for Kay's warning, I might have had a swing at him myself.

Even so, he shouldn't have done it. I feel a little responsible.

Sorry, George.

Chapter 26
We're Getting the Old Band
Back Together

Kelli didn't come home that night. He left her a half dozen messages but her only response was a single text at 11:15. *[middle finger emoji] You are an asshole. Move out of my house, now. Thanks for stealing my car! [puke emoji]*

At midnight, he called a cab and spent the night at the Hilton near the airport. His next interview, assuming Amy didn't fire him after she found out about the Bruce Willis fight, was with Ryan Reynolds in Ponte Vedra Florida, about two hours north of Orlando. His plan was to return to Orlando, stay with his mom, and keep his head down for the next couple of weeks.

He certainly didn't expect a knock on his hotel door at 8:00 am the next morning.

His first thought was Bruce Willis had hired some local muscle to track him down and break his legs. So, when he peeked out the spy hole and saw a purple beret, a lump jumped up into his throat.

"Open the door, dear boy. Your iced coffee is melting." Dudley opened the door, tears running down his face.

"Oh, Georgie, come to Daddy," Albert Poots said. He held George Dudley with one hand while balancing the coffee tray in his other. "I heard you had another eventful night," the Colonel said, closing the door.

"How..."

"It's a small town, dear boy. Everybody knows. You can't knock out Bruce Willis and not expect headlines. Twitter's blowing up. Someone snapped a photo after you ran off. Doesn't someone always snap a photo nowadays? *#OnHisAss* is trending like crazy."

"Oh shit."

"They had to shut down production for the day," Albert said. He opened the minibar and removed a 50 ml Baileys Irish cream bottle. "Your little lady friend made out okay. She not only got added to the cast call sheet, but she was also seen in Kyle whatshisname's Audi, heading toward the beach around ten-ish. I assume she does not live on the beach?"

"No," Dudley said quietly. He sat on the edge of his bed.

"Lucky for you, Henri has a lady friend who works the night desk here at the Hilton. Like I said, small town."

"Oh, Albert. I don't know what to do," he said, his face in his hands. "I don't know what to do."

The Colonel abruptly put his coffee cup down, rushed at Dudley, grabbed his arms, and shook him violently. "You can act like a man!" Then he slapped him. "What's the matter with you?"

Dudley was stunned, then he started laughing. "That was an excellent Brando, Albert."

"Thank you, Georgie. *The Godfather* is one of my dream roles."

"I guess now you're going to make me an offer I can't refuse?" Dudley asked.

"Actually I am. What you need Georgie boy, is some serious R&R, and time to reflect on the next steps."

"You sound like my mom."

"I'll take that as a compliment," the Colonel said pleasantly. "Now get your things. I hate hotel rooms. They're depressing and full of bad memories."

They were back at Henri's home in thirty minutes. Uva had breakfast waiting for them: scrambled eggs, blueberry waffles, two sausage links, fruit salad, and orange juice. "Let me know if you need anything else, Mr. Leach," she said and returned to the kitchen.

"What's wrong with her?" Dudley said.

"She missed you, sweetheart," Henri said entering the patio. "We all did." She crossed to him and kissed his cheek.

"I really messed up, Henri," Dudley said.

"You need to be more specific, Georgie. We talking about your fight with Bruce Willis? Your girlfriend dumping you? Your wife divorcing you?"

"Or is it, Mary Jordan?" the Colonel added, batting his eyes at George and throwing him a kiss.

"Oh, my God. Am I on *The Truman Show*? Are hidden cameras following me around day and night? How do you know all this?" Dudley said, genuinely dismayed.

"Albert here has become Facebook friends with your mother, Elsie."

"Mom's on Facebook?"

"For a few years apparently," the Colonel said, nibbling on the fruit salad. "She talks to her grandkids mostly. Post photos. Very charming."

"Can this day get any weirder," Dudley moaned.

"Uva? Can we get a carafe of mimosas?" Albert yelled. "And use the good stuff, please. I think we're going to be here a while."

"What did mom say about Mary?" George asked, and there was worry in his voice.

"Interesting, don't you think Colonel?" Henri stated.

"Very telling," the Colonel returned.

"Of all your problems, you start with her."

"Well…" Dudley said evasively.

"Well, indeed," Henri replied. "Curiouser and curiouser."

"Cried Alice," Dudley said automatically.

"Very good, George," Henri said. "Most people think that's a Cheshire Cat quote."

"I'm depressed Henri, not brain dead."

"That's good George because you need to put those neurons to work. Your little metamorphosis is at a crossroads. Your Archie Leach/Cary Grant creation is getting serious traction out here. You're getting known, which I think is contrary to your original plan. You're Jekyll and Hyde persona is causing problems for the real George Dudley."

Henri sipped her black coffee. "Your Grant persona enjoys confrontation. This was an oversight on my part," Henri admitted. "I should have remembered Cary Grant was an alpha male and more than willing to lock horns with the biggest Ram in the room. Your problem is those Rams are internationally known. It's headline news when they fart, let alone get into fights."

"The thing with Bruce was spontaneous. But I still can't explain what happened with George Clooney," Dudley explained.

"I can tell you. You hit on his wife," the Colonel said.

"Can you control him?" Henri asked pointedly.

"I don't know. It's an out-of-body experience. Once it starts, he takes over," Dudley explained. "But I like it. He's the me I always wanted to be. Confidant. Cool. Admired. Sexy. It's intoxicating."

"But it's not really you, dear boy," the Colonel pointed out.

"Isn't it? Didn't you think it was unusual how fast I picked it all up? From mealy mouth George to cocksure Cary, in just thirty days? Maybe it was always there, and I just had to let the fear go."

"There is nothing to fear but fear itself," Albert said in an awful Franklin D. Roosevelt impersonation.

"You're not helping Albert," Henri chided him.

"But maybe George is right, Henri," Albert said. "Maybe this self-assured personality was always there, and we just gave him the confidence to let it out. To trust it, and to hell with the consequences."

"And what consequences they have been," Henri moaned. "They'll never invite us back to Casa Clooney again."

"But he got Steven's private number," Albert countered. "And Oprah loves him. And Bradley." Henri shook his head, unconvinced.

"And the books going well, too. Elsie heard through Mary that Amy is incredibly happy with the latest draft. Isn't that right, Georgie?"

"Yes. Amy told me that last week," Dudley said.

"So you see Henri, sometimes change is for the better," the Colonel concluded.

Henri Harrison eyed Dudley and asked. "Are you happier now, George?"

"That's the million-dollar question, isn't it, Henri," Dudley said. "And I think the answer is yes. I feel more in control of my life. The old me always took it on the chin. Don't rock the boat. Safe and steady. My wife said I had no presence or inner fire. I think those are euphemisms for boring."

"Wives can be so mean," Albert Poots said. "And sometimes perceptive."

"I wasn't trying to be boring," Dudley continued. "I just didn't like confrontations. Maybe that's why I became a writer, working alone and remote. Theater was my only real emotional outlet. But even there, I never fought for roles. I was unremarkable. Just silly old, George."

"The man who wanted to be Cary Grant," Henri mocked him.

"Watch it, Henri," Dudley said menacingly. "Even Victor Frankenstein never mocked his creature."

"That's my point, George," Henri said rising out of her chair. "Are you George Dudley or Cary Grant? You can't be both."

Like Bill Rawlings couldn't be both Atticus Finch and Gregory Peck, George thought. *He became a weaker version of both.* "I'm becoming something new. Henri, and I'm still trying to figure out how to walk."

"I don't know about walking, but this new you knows how to throw a punch." The Colonel was looking at his cell phone. "#OnHisAss is trending number three right now, behind Free Britney and that Korean Girl band."

"Oh, fuck me."

"Entertainment Tonight scooped everybody," Albert said. "Their new reporter was the one who took that photo. Elliott Moore."

"Elliott Moore?" Dudley cried. "Oh, my God. It can't be my Elliott. Do they have a photo of him?"

Albert Poots scrolled and finally said, "Yes." He pointed his phone screen at Dudley. Looking back at him was his old boss.

"Oh, just kill me now."

REFLECTIONS ON REPORT #22

There has been a lot written about the fact I took LSD while in therapy. What isn't known is we discussed this very theme. Who am I? Archie Leach? Cary Grant? Or something I used to call Cary Leach, my monster. My creature.

Like George Dudley, I couldn't control him most days. Ask my ex-wives. He liked the cameras. He craved the attention, and he was desperate for approval.

Why didn't I ever win an Oscar, was another common topic.

Oh, dear. I shouldn't have typed that.

I need to make sure to edit that before I send this is.

Chapter 27
Everybody Loves Ryan

1

"No. No. No, George. How could you?" Amy screamed. "This could ruin everything."

Dudley pulled his cell phone away from his ear. "I didn't know he'd be there, Amy. What are the odds Elliot and I end up on the same movie set four months after we were fired? I didn't even know he was in Hollywood. What are we going to do?"

"I don't know. Barry's working on it right now."

"Keep me posted, and I'll let you know if I hear from Murdoch," Dudley said.

"Either way stop in before your Ryan Reynolds interview next week. We'll regroup."

"Okay. I'm really sorry, Amy," Dudley said, sadly.

"You punched Bruce Willis," she said amazed. "Who the hell are you, George Dudley?"

"I'm working on that as we speak, Amy. Bye now." He hung up. "Well, that could have been worse."

"Now call Mary," the Colonel said placing a check by Amy's name on his notepad. There was already a check with Bruce Willis and Kelli Lee's names. Dudley left an apology for the former and well wishes for the latter. There was nothing more to say to his ex-wife so that only left Mary Jordan on his list of people I need to apologize to.

She picked up on the first ring. "I didn't think you'd have the nerve to call me again," Mary said harshly.

"I'd like you to give me one more chance."

"You already have two strikes, slugger. One more and you're out, for good."

George Dudley closed his eyes, and at in that moment, he knew what he wanted. It wasn't fame. It wasn't riches, it wasn't the envy of men or the love of women, he wanted the love of one woman. She had to give him another chance, but he had hurt her. She didn't trust him anymore.

So he needed a secret weapon. And lucky for George Dudley, he had one.

"Ryan Reynolds," he said.

Mary was silent. "What did you say?"

"I said Ryan Reynolds is the guest speaker at the Hope North charity event next week at the TPC. I have two tickets."

She still did not speak right away. Then she said, "Ryan Reynolds, the actor?"

"The one and only: *Deadpool. The Proposal… Van Wilder.*"

"Oh, I love that movie," she sighed.

"I know you do. I took you to see it."

"Ryan Reynolds. Really? You're not just saying that are you?"

"I have to interview him for the book, so he got me tickets," Dudley said.

When she went silent again, he said, "Mary? Did you hear me?" The silence continued. "I got VIP tickets to the Players Championship too."

"With a preferred parking pass?"

"The Nicklaus entrance at hole sixteen. Remember we played there once?"

"I beat you by two strokes," she said.

"I also lost six balls."

"Hell of a day for you."

"I've had worst."

"Not as bad as Bruce Willis," she added quickly.

"You heard about that, huh?"

"Actually, I laughed my ass off. You never hit anything bigger than a fly in your life," she laughed. "Why did you hit him?"

"That's a story best told in person," he said.

"Okay. Golf, Ryan Reynolds, and the truth. It's a deal. Pick me up at 7. Plus, you buy breakfast." She promptly hung up.

"Well, that could have been worse," Dudley repeated, and Albert laughed.

"Well done, lover boy. That wasn't safe and steady or boring," Henri added. "Neither was it cocksure, smooth, or debonaire. See what I mean?"

Dudley smiled. "It was just me."

"That girl is special, George," Albert said taking his hand. "I believe she's the one. Your soulmate. Your life partner. You're happily ever after. I just have one last thing to tell you."

"What's that Albert?" Dudley said, hopefully.

"Don't blow it."

2

It was perfect golf weather. Not a cloud in the sky, a cool breeze coming off the ocean, and the humidity decided to take the day off. It was moving day and the sixty-six players who made the cut felt anything was possible. The conditions had been tough the first two days with lightning-fast greens and a constant 20-mile-an-hour headwind playing havoc with their aim. The cut score was even par and the three coleaders were sitting at six under. And for the best field in golf, it was anybody's tournament to win.

Dudley and Mary followed their two favorite players, Sergio Garcia and Phil Mickelson but neither of them was able to break par that gorgeous Saturday morning. After fours in the sun, they left the TPC at Sawgrass and drove up A1A to their hotel, the Casa Marina. They showered together, made love and both were very, very satisfied.

"We fit," she said after, her head on his chest.

"Like peanut butter and jelly," Dudley said.

Mary sat up. "Who's the jelly?" she said.

"Me?"

"Good answer, Mr. Dudley."

"We better get dressed. Dinner's at 7:00," he said.

"When are you talking to Ryan?" she asked, getting out of bed.

"Around 8:30. After his speech."

Dudley slipped easily into his tuxedo. Mary took a little longer, but the wait was worth it. She was wearing a floor-length evening gown, cut low in the front, that hugged her curves.

"What would you call that color? Light green?" he asked.

"Sage. Why?"

174

"I was just wondering if it would go with this," he said holding out a long, flat jewelry box.

"What's that?" she said, nervously.

He opened it and said, "An expensive accessory."

The string of Mikimoto pearls glimmered on a dark sea of green velvet. Mary's hands went to her mouth, and she gasped. "Oh, my God, George. They're gorgeous."

"Turn around. Let's see how they look."

She pulled her hair to the side, and he attached the delicate clasp behind her neck. She moved to the floor-length mirror to see how they looked. She was not disappointed. She touched them gently and said, "They're beautiful, George."

"You're beautiful," he said coming up behind her.

She spun and threw her arms around his neck. "You surprised me," she cried. "Oh shit, now I have to redo my eyes." She ran into the bedroom and shut the door.

He moved to the balcony window and looked out at the Atlantic Ocean. *Is this happiness?* he thought. *Did Cary do this or me?* He kept expecting the Cary Grant persona to assert itself, but he had not sensed even a hint of it. That was the most surprising thing. It was always right there.

But today, he felt no connection at all. *Was it gone?* he thought.

"Okay. I'm ready," Mary said bustling out of the bathroom, all smiles and giddy. She opened the door, turned to him, and said, "I hope Ryan Reynolds likes it."

"Hey!" He chased her down the hallway, both of them laughing like little kids.

3

"I have to be honest with you folks," Ryan Reynolds said from behind the podium. "It was my wife that got me involved with Hope North. She came home from work and said she just found out about Hope North and wanted to talk about it. I thought she was being asked to do a new Hospital drama. Hope North. I said, being the clueless spouse that I am, 'Don't you think you're a little busy to take on a series?' I thought I was being supportive."

He points to his forehead. "This is where the book she threw hit me. I still have the scar. I said 'Ow', and she said, 'I'm serious Ryan. Hope North is a school in Uganda'."

Ryan Reynolds looked out over his audience. A perplexed look on his face. "I knew better than to say the first thing that popped into my head. Or the second. Or the third. Instead, I said the right thing, 'Really? I never heard of it'."

"This answer was rewarded with a smile and a folder full of brochures and info sheets being dropped into my lap. As I leafed through the pages she said, 'Hope North is educating and healing the young victims of Uganda's civil war, including orphans and former child soldiers, empowering them to become voices for peace and development. Founded in 1998 by artist and former child soldier Okello Sam, Hope North is an accredited secondary school located on a 40-acre campus with an international arts center, vocational training, and a working farm. Over 1,500 vulnerable youth have lived at Hope North, and today 255 incredible youth are working toward their degrees and planning careers. These youth in turn are contributing to peacebuilding by organizing educational theater and soccer tournaments throughout the north, an area destroyed by years of war, reaching thousands more'."

A slide came up on the twenty-foot screen behind him. It was a classroom with smiling, engaged Uganda children. "And they need our help," he said.

He looked out over the well-dressed crowd. The elite of North Florida smiled. "You're a good-looking crowd, you know that. Give yourself a hand for being good-looking and rich in America," he said and started them clapping. They were laughing and smashing their hands together when he pulled up the next slide, a classic World War 2 Sherman tank riding through a deserted village, with ten fatigue-wearing soldiers crowded on top, mostly boys between twelve and sixteen. And next to this monument to war, a lone shoeless girl, carrying a schoolbag.

"For over thirty years, this has been the norm in Uganda; national wars, insurrections, civil wars, and insurgency. And who suffers the most? The politicians? The leaders? The government? No, the children. The least important. The displaced and discarded. While power transfers hands the children despair about their future. Is military service their only option?"

A new slide this time: the HOPE NORTH logo.

"Let me tell you how you can help the children of Uganda find a better tomorrow."

4

George Dudley and Mary Jordan were escorted to a small banquet room. Reynolds and his wife, Blake Lively were seated at the head of a white linen-covered table. He waved to them while sipping coffee from a porcelain cup. Blake stood and extended her hand, "Hi, Archie. Nice to meet you." Then, noticing Mary she said, "Wow, who's this goddess you got with you?"

"Blake, this is Mary Jordan. Mary this is…"

"I know who she is Geor… Archie. Hi Blake. I love your movies," Mary said, a huge grin on her face.

"Thank you, Mary. Which is your favorite?"

"That's easy. *Age of Adaline*. hands down," Mary said.

"That's true," Dudley said. "She bought the DVD and everything."

"Well, that makes me happy," Blake Lively said. Then she punched Reynolds in the arm. "See? I told you people liked that movie. Thank you, Mary. You may stay."

"The queen has spoken," Reynolds said.

"Long live the queen," Dudley added.

"Since we are playing, what's your favorite film of mine?" Reynolds asked Mary.

"Oh. Well, um. Haha," Mary stammered.

Blake laughed loudly. "That's what you get superstar. She can't think of one!"

"No. No, I love your movies, Mr. Reynolds. All of them," Mary said desperately.

"That's true too. She does tend to watch them with the sound off though," Dudley added, laughing.

"Shut up, Archie!" Mary said embarrassed. "*Van Wilder*. I like *Van Wilder*." Mary said.

"Thank you, Mary. I may do a sequel, in your honor," he joked.

Blake stood and knelt next to Mary. "Hey, pretty lady, let me see those pearls."

Mary looked up and said, "He just gave them to me. It was a surprise," and then she was crying.

Blake wrapped her arms around her and smiled.

"Hey, Arch. Why don't we go for a walk? Leave the ladies in peace," Reynolds said, moving out the door.

Dudley followed. Once they were in the hallway he said, "That was a hell of a speech earlier."

"Did you like it? Blake wrote most of it. The rest I just adlibbed."

"Just like your roles," Dudley said promptly. Reynolds looked at him. "Don't you appreciate what talent God has given you?"

"Are we still just talking, or am I on the clock here? Did we start?" Reynolds asked, confused.

They were standing on a balcony overlooking the eighteenth green. The grounds crew were preparing the golf course for the next day. Golf carts were escorting people around the grounds, and an army of waiters were serving dinner to the charity guests below.

"Of all the actors I've interviewed, you fit the model for a matinee idol better than any of them."

"Is that a compliment or an insult?" Reynolds replied warily.

"I'm just trying to figure out your motivation. You're world famous. Your movies are great box office. You're highly in demand, yet you play you more than any other actor I know. You've perfected this cynical performer who actually comments on your role, while you're doing it. In the movie."

"That's called adlibbing."

"I don't know if there is a name for what you do, but whatever it is, I can't deny, audiences eat it up."

"What can I say? I'm charming," Reynolds smirked.

"Just like a matinee idol," Dudley smirked back.

"Is that a bad thing? Back in the day, that was what actors wanted to be."

"I don't know if it's a good or bad thing. It's just something I discovered while working on this book. Do you want to be a serious actor? Or do you just want a big-box office? Do you want to win awards from your peers? Or do you want girls throwing their panties at you? Which is it?"

"You know Cooper warned me about you. He said, be careful, dude. This guy will get inside your head," Reynolds said wagging a finger at Dudley.

"What is it you want, Ryan?" Dudley asked simply.

"To enjoy it while it lasts," he said honestly. "I'm the emperor and one day soon those idiots are going to realize I got no clothes on. I'm winging it, man. Every part. Every film. I'm a no-talent bullshit artist. I'm Harold Hill, and I'm here to organize the River City Boys Band. Ta-Tada!" He turned away then and stared out over the famous golf course. He gripped the side of the railing and swayed. "I'm just trying to enjoy it for as long as it lasts."

"Hey, Ryan," Dudley said softly. "I want to tell you two things. First, you are a good actor. I know. I'm an actor too, and I know good from bad. But what I can't figure out is what you're afraid of. You can take a risk or two. Do Shakespeare. Do Ibsen. No, do Eugene O'Neil."

"I love *Moon for the Misbegotten*," Reynolds admitted.

"Do it. Off-Broadway. Off-Off-Broadway. Prove it to them you're a real actor. Hell, prove it to yourself."

"But I hate memorizing lines," he whined. "Movies are easy, a couple pages a day. But a play? Two hours. Eighty or ninety pages? I'd lose it."

"Every actor says that. In the beginning," Dudley agreed. "But by opening, you'll get it. I'd pay good money to see that."

Transformations are miraculous things. To watch with your own eyes a thing you knew very well, change into something totally different was special and unique. That night on a balcony overlooking the famous seventeenth green at the TPC at Sawgrass, George Dudley watched Ryan Reynolds speak a line, with total sincerity.

"Thank you, Archie," he said. "What's the other thing?"

"I'm not putting any of this in the book."

"You wanna make out?" Reynolds said, reaching for him, and Dudley laughed. "I'm serious. Pucker up. I'll do you right here in front of God and the PGA Tour. Just say the word."

"Come on. Let's go back. The girls probably think we're playing a quick nine in the dark," Dudley said.

"Hey. Wait." Ryan Reynolds grabbed his arm. "I've been meaning to ask you, why'd you pop Bruce Willis? I mean, I admit I've wanted to do it for years. But what happened exactly? What did he say?"

Dudley looked at him and said softly and with a perfectly straight face, "He said he hated *Age of Adaline*."

They heard the girls before they saw them. "Oh, Ryan, you got to hear this. Tell him, Mary," Blake said laughing.

"About the cat in the soup?"

"Yes," she laughed even harder, tears streaming down her face.

"Do you smell that, Archie? Is that an illegal substance in the air?" Reynolds said looking for the joint.

"I had one in my bag," Mary said innocently.

"I thought we were saving that for the ride home?" Dudley complained.

"Sorry," and the girls laughed even louder.

"Hey, I found out why Archie punched Bruce Willis?" Reynolds blurted out.

"Really? He didn't even tell me." Mary Jordan said.

"Oh oh, I put my foot in it didn't I, Arch?"

"My name isn't Archie. It's George," Dudley said suddenly.

"George," Mary began.

"No, I'm tired of it all. Elliott is going to tell Murdoch and it'll all come out eventually. Plus, I'm tired of lying to people. Especially to people I like."

"I think I'm gonna cry," Reynolds said.

"Shut up, Ry. This is serious," Blake Lively said.

"I got fired from The Times in New York last year, and one of the conditions of my severance was a non-compete. I can't publish anything for a year. An old friend needed help on this Matinee Idol book, so we came up with a fake name so I could do these interviews."

George ran his hand threw his hair. "But I don't know how to lie. I've never been good at it. And I've met some great people these past few months and they think I'm Archie Leach, not George Dudley."

"Maybe you should change your name to Archie Leach?" Reynolds said. "It's actually better than Dudley."

"Ryan! But why are you telling us now, George?"

"Because I like you guys. And Bradley. And Jennifer. I want to be friends after the book is out and my term is up. Plus, it's been so damn confusing," he added.

"Well, thank you, George. I appreciate that. I like you too," Blake said.

"I already told him I'd make out with him, so…"

"And what about me Georgie? Why'd you lie to me?" Mary said.

"I punched Bruce Willis because I found out he fucked my girlfriend," he said honestly, grateful to be released from the burden of the lie.

"You have a girlfriend in LA?" Mary asked quietly.

"Had. We broke up that same day."

"But you were seeing her on Valentine's Day. That's why you had to get back." Mary said, putting the pieces together now.

"Yes."

Mary was on her feet now. She moved closer to Dudley and taking a batting stance she swung her arms and said, "Strike three." And George could see the tears in her eyes. Then she was holding her stomach. "I think I'm gonna be sick."

She ran from the room. Blake was right behind her. And all George Dudley could do was collapse in his chair, immobile.

"Wow. You are like right out of a movie."

"You don't know the half of it," Dudley said to himself.

"What is it you want George? You asked me the same question a little while ago," Reynolds said lighting the remains of the marijuana cigarette the girls left behind.

"A year ago, hell six months ago my answer would have been simple. I wanted to be Cary Grant."

"Who doesn't," Reynolds said taking a big toke.

"But you see, I did it. I changed everything. My glasses, my hair, my body, my clothes, the way I walk, the way I stand, even the way I talk to people. Especially women. That's where I got into trouble in LA with that actress."

"An actress. A common tale bucko," Reynolds said with his eyes closed.

"Are you listening?"

"Like a priest. Continue my son and I will absolve your sins," Reynold said.

"But there was a dark side I didn't count on. I became aggressive, even violent a few times. I lived fearlessly. I loved it, actually but there were consequences."

"Like punching out Bruce Willis."

"Like punching Bruce Willis. And the subsequent photo that may doom me," Dudley said pitifully.

"That may doom me," Reynolds mocked him. "Now you really do sound like a bad movie," and he giggled. "You want some?"

"No. I'll need a clear head when Mary comes back."

"If she comes back," Reynolds said.

"She has to. I'm her ride home."

"Ryan, get the car. We're driving Mary home." Blake and Mary came back into the room long enough to make the announcement, then they left just as quickly.

"Mary wait! We have to talk. I'm sorry," George Dudley pleaded.

"You certainly are," Mary said over her shoulder and the women disappeared down the stairs.

Reynolds clapped him on the shoulder. "Call me when you get back to LA, Archie. George. Cary. Whoever you are. All things considered; I like you too." He ran after his wife.

George was left alone. Naturally.

REFLECTIONS ON REPORT #23

I don't want to do this anymore.

Chapter 28
At Least Someone Is Happy

"Congratulations Cary!" Clarence said, popping the cork off a bottle of champagne. "I am so proud of you. Both of you. A job well done."

"I didn't do anything, sir. I just watched."

"Oh, don't sell yourself short," Clarence said, handing him a glass of champagne. "You did a remarkable job. Case closed."

"If you say so, Clarence." It had been three days since his last contact, but Cary Grant could not get George Dudley out of his thoughts. *What was he doing now? Did he talk to Mary? Would Murdoch sue him? What would people think when they discovered he'd been lying to them?*

"Cary?" Kay said, touching his arm.

"Why did he have to choose me?"

"What dear?"

"Dudley," Cary said. "Why couldn't he pick Bogie or Clark Gable? I was just trying to make a living, you know? I didn't want a legion of followers. I was ACTING!"

She put her arm around him. "Don't, Cary. You can't be responsible for what other people do. This was Dudley's decision and only he is responsible for the consequences."

"But people are getting hurt, Kay. In my name!"

"What is this?" Clarence said. "All you did was observe, Cary."

"No, Clarence. I didn't just observe. I started this," he said, kicking the filing cabinet.

"I don't understand. Kay, what's wrong with him?" Clarence said, moving behind his desk and picking up the final report. "Everyone here is happy. There's talk of wings for the both of you. Things could not have turned out better."

Cary put his hands down on Clarence's desk, leaning toward him. "Clarence, I'd like to go back down."

"Whatever for? It's done. You said it right here in Report #23, 'My name isn't Archie. Its George'. I almost cried when I read that."

Clarence was confused. He looked at Kay Kendall for help and she, "He got attached, sir. He's very fond of George Dudley."

"What does that have to do with anything?"

"George Dudley is still in trouble," Cary said.

"They are always in trouble, Cary. You know that." Then he sat down in his chair and crossed his arms. "Plus, we never interfere. Rule number one you know."

"Yeah, rule number one. You're like a broken record."

Clarence's face started to turn red. "Now see here, I will—"

"I got this, sir," Kay said, putting her arm around Cary's shoulder and leading him to the door.

"He just needs a little break. That's all."

"Exactly," Clarence said, clapping his hands. "Go swimming with Esther. Play cards with your buddies. They miss you, by the way. Tony Curtis was in here yesterday asking about you. He's organizing an *Operation Petticoat* reunion."

Cary smiled. "It'd be nice to see the old crew again."

"Good. Good. That's the old Cary we all know and love," Clarence said satisfied.

Ky walked him out of the building and across the street to A Little Slice of Heaven Park. She sat him down on one of the benches and held his hand.

"It's true you know," Kay started. "What Clarence said."

"What part?"

"They are always in trouble. That's what life is all about."

Cary turned to her. His face was tortured, and she was sure he was about to cry. "He blamed me for punching Bruce Willis as I possessed him or something, and he couldn't control it. But he liked it. The power. The confidence. I can see why Clarence and the twelve are worried about this. What if everyone did it? What if everyone became Cary Grant?"

"Well, I don't know about helping everyone, but I know one guy we can help. Come on." Taking his hand, she stood and started walking down the path to the Peer Review.

"What do you mean? Where are going?" And then he realized he was at the Peer Review building. "What are we doing here?"

"I think it's time for a little Divine Intervention," she said mischievously.

"But, Kay. What about Rule number one?"

"What can they do, Cary? Kill us? We're already dead."

He looked toward the floor and said, "Maybe they'll send us… you know. Down there."

"That's true. But I bet they have some rockin' bands!"

Chapter 29
Can Chris Pratt Play First Base?

1

"I don't mind the beard, Georgie boy. I don't mind the sulking. I don't even mind the longsuffering silences, but I must insist you bathe," Albert Poots said. Two weeks had passed since the Ryan Reynolds interview. Much had happened, and much had not happened, yet. Mary still refused to talk to him. Rupert Murdoch had sued him. Amy hadn't returned his emails. And his mother talked to Albert now more than him.

Elliott Moore broke the 'Archie Leach' story the same day Dudley returned to Los Angeles. His phone began ringing insistently and so often he had to put it on permanent mute. Eventually, he turned it off. When he checked the messages, they basically fell into two categories—righteous indignation (many from people he didn't even know) and interview requests. But nothing from Mary.

Elliott's broadcast, a ten-minute top-of-the-hour story on Entertainment Tonight, was surprisingly accurate. Dudley thought Tiffany Pierce, the girl who did not get the assistant editor job from Amy was probably a prime source. They started with the Bruce Willis shot, flat on his back in his trailer. Then Dudley's face filled the screen. Elliott must have pulled it from their old company website. Dudley cringed. He looked like Jerry Lewis in the original *Nutty Professor* movie. *Always hated that photo*, he thought, unconsciously pushing up his nonexistent glasses.

There was a live shot outside the *Orlando Magazine* offices of Elliott following Amy Andrews up to the front door. She was exquisitely dressed and gave the obligatory 'No comment'.

Rupert Murdoch was mentioned, but even Elliott wasn't stupid enough to antagonize the media mogul. *The old bastard would just buy the network and fire everybody*, Dudley thought.

He was grateful Elliott stayed away from his family but there was a juicy section with Kelli, who was not shy about giving her opinion. "I knew there was something wrong with him right from the start. Oh, he was sexy and great looking, but there was something not right there, you know? Like he was acting all the time. And I should know, I'm an actress myself." Elliott cut her off before she mentioned her personal website.

Surprisingly, the interview that hurt the most was Bradley Cooper and Jennifer Lawrence.

Dudley could not help but notice their disappointment. "I wondered if he was a real reporter. I mean it was the strangest interview I ever gave," Cooper said. "He was charming as hell though. I liked him," Jennifer Lawrence said.

"Yeah," Cooper added. "I guess he fooled us too."

Dudley turned off the TV, closed his eyes, and fell back into the bed, his home for the past fourteen days. There was a knock at his door. "Are you decent, dear boy?" the Colonel said.

"I'm dressed. I haven't been decent for a while, now."

"You have a phone call."

Dudley jumped up. "Is it Mary?"

"No. Sorry. It's your other Orlando girlfriend," he said and handed him the cordless phone.

"Hello?" Dudley croaked.

"You sound like shit," Amy Andrews said.

"Feel like shit," Dudley replied.

"I made a reservation for you with United. You depart at 11:15. Get your ass to the airport. You have a lunch appointment with Chris Pratt tomorrow over at Universal," Amy said rapidly.

"What?"

"We're back in business, you idiot. And it's all because of your friend Oprah," she said, admiration in her voice. "I'll tell you all about tomorrow. Meet me at the office at 9:00. Get going." She hung up.

"Good news?" the Colonel said. He was lingering in the doorway.

"Yes. Apparently, Oprah Winfrey did something. I'm interviewing Chris Pratt tomorrow," Dudley said still in shock.

"I'm happy for you, George," he said taking the phone back. "Try not to punch him."

2

"It was Graham Stedman who actually fixed things," Amy said, unable to keep the excitement out of her voice. She was pacing behind her desk again. "He had some kid from his legal department call Barry last week and requested everything we had: your non-compete, the contract, everything. Then he set up a four-way Zoom with Murdoch, Jeff Shell, the CEO of NBC Universal, and some English Lord, and before you can say *Expelliarmus*, it was over. The lawsuit was dismissed."

"An English Lord?"

"I know, right!" Amy replied. "Crazy."

"Crazy," he agreed, still in shock. He sipped his iced coffee.

Amy watched him. "I never know who's going to show up when we have these meetings, George."

Dudley merely nodded.

"I'm seeing a masseuse now. I get a massage every Friday. Feel a lot better."

"I'm glad, Amy. Apparently, Archie Leach didn't disappoint everyone he met," he admitted.

"Are you going to be all right to interview Pratt?"

"Yes. I want to finish this," Dudley said with some resolve.

"Glad to hear it. You've done a fantastic job, Georgie," Amy said kindly.

"Thanks, Amy. That means a lot coming from you," he said and then added, "Have you heard from Mary?"

"You really hurt her, George."

"I know."

"You may have lost her. Forever this time."

Dudley hung his head. Then he took a deep breath and stood up and snapped his finger over his head as if to ward away all troubles. And it worked. "Well, let's go see what Star-Lord has to say."

Media junkets suck. Chris Pratt and Bryce Dallas Howard had been cooped up in a small conference room all morning. The questions were starting to repeat themselves and Pratt was bored. His answers were getting more laughs than anything resembling artistic insight. "Then he said, that's no Stegosaurus, that's my wife!"

The small group of reporters exploded with laughter. Bryce Howard rolled her eyes.

"Hey, folks," Pratt said standing, "It's been really great to be here with you, but I gotta pee like a racehorse. Adios." He rose from the table, gave a quick wave, and left the room. Terri Fuchs, the PR specialist for Universal held the door for him. "I could not find a free room anywhere in this dump, so do you mind doing the interview in your room?"

"No problem," he said.

"I'll grab you a salad and meet you there, okay?"

"Right. Thanks, Terri," he said running into the men's room.

Dudley was doing his business at the urinal next to him. Pratt unzipped and nodded in the way men in bathrooms do. When they finished, they both stood side by side at the wash basin washing their hands. Pratt was watching Dudley in the mirror. "I know you."

"Maybe, but everybody knows you," Dudley said.

They dried their hands and Dudley followed him out of the men's room and into the elevator. When the doors opened on the second floor, Pratt got off and Dudley followed him. They took another dozen steps down the hallway when Pratt turned to him and said, "You want something buddy? Autograph? Urine sample?"

"No. But I would like to know something. Did you ever learn to play first base?"

"What?"

"In *Moneyball*. Did you ever learn to play first base?" Dudley asked.

Chris Pratt looked at him closely and then snapped his fingers. "Wait a minute. Hang on. I do know you. You're him."

Dudley felt Cary's surface. He didn't call him, but one moment he was not there, then the next, he was. His hand went to his pocket, his head turned slightly, and his voice changed, just a little bit.

"I don't know, am I?"

Chris Pratt laughed. "Your Archie Leach! You scared me there for a minute. I thought you were a nut job or something."

"Bruce Willis thinks I am," Dudley said, relaxing against the wall.

"Oh, my God. I saw that pic. Wow," he laughed. "Why did you do it?"

"He said *Passengers* was the worst movie he ever saw."

Pratt just stared at him, then he doubled over. His laugh echoed off the concrete walls. "Good one." He stopped at Suite 215, used his key, and entered the suite. "Come on. We should get started."

"We already have. And my name is George, not Archie," Dudley said, smiling sheepishly.

"Right. Right. I heard about that." Pratt threw himself on the couch. "How's that all working out?"

"Pretty well, actually," Dudley said.

"Good. Good. Sit down. What's your first question?" Chris Pratt said eagerly.

Dudley sat in the chair in front of the desk. "I already asked it. Did you ever learn to play first base?"

Pratt blinked. He chuckled and said, "I don't know, man. It was just a movie."

Dudley studied him. He leaned back and crossed his legs. "The book I'm writing is about matinee idols, past and present. During this process, I have discovered something interesting. Matinee Idols only care about two things, how they look and how big the box office receipts are. That's it. The role, the character, and the movie itself are superfluous. Matinee Idols simply show up on set and play The Matinee Idol. They smile; they joke; they get the girl and go home. Easy peasy." Dudley uncrossed his legs and leaned in. "My question to you Mr. Pratt, is that how you see yourself?"

"No," he said evasively.

Dudley pulled a sheet of paper from his jacket and looked at it. "I'm looking at your film career here and, I'm sorry but nothing stands out. Acting wise. Where's the *Raging Bull*, or *The Kings Speech*, or *The Pianist*, or *Shine*, *Philadelphia, Ray... My Left Foot?* Oh, my God, when I first saw that movie, I thought they got a guy with cerebral palsy to play the part."

Chris Pratt just stared at him. His arms were crossed, and he seemed to have sunk a little bit into the sofa. "You know how many unemployed actors there are? Do you know how many have followed this dream only to be left on the sidelines? I am one of the lucky few, my friend. I was twenty-one when I got my first paying gig. After that, it was audition after audition after audition. All day long. It was another five years before I got my first series. More auditions followed. Headshots. Meetings. Callbacks. Small parts. You see the pattern? I took whatever they offered. I was a working actor trying to pay my bills."

Pratt got up and took bottled water from the minibar, his anger rising. "We all have dreams of stardom. But that's the fantasy. The reality is it can end like that." He snapped his finger in Dudley's face. "If I hadn't gotten *Parks and Recreations*, we probably wouldn't be having this conversation. I didn't have a string of Broadway hits. I didn't get nominated for Best Supporting Actor for anything. I was expendable. There are a hundred Chris Pratt's out there. A Thousand. A million. I get on my knees every day and thank God I was chosen."

He was pacing now, clearly agitated. "Hell, there are guys from my high school who are better actors than me. But the ball landed in my glove. I had the winning numbers. And now I'm doing the best I can."

"Smiling and joking and getting the girl," Dudley said harshly.

"I'm a good actor." Chris Pratt was getting angry.

"Confidence is helpful. So is luck, Star-Lord."

He flopped back down on the couch. "Yeah, so I guess I'm the luckiest guy in the world."

"And there's my cover quote," Dudley said. He stood up. "Thanks for your time, Chris. And believe it or not, I really do enjoy your movies."

"Thank you," Pratt said, sullenly.

"Hey, I got your salad," Terri said coming in as Dudley left.

"I'm not hungry."

Chapter 30
Rainy Days and Mondays

1

"I just emailed you the final draft," Dudley said to Amy Andrews.

"Thank God," she said, gratefully. "We only got two months left. There's a big party after the Premiere of *Jurassic World Dominion* at Universal Studios. I promised them the book would be there."

"I hear Bob recovered," Dudley said.

"Yes, thank God. He won't be writing any time soon, but he's up and around."

"That's good news."

"Speaking of Bob, I showed him your draft of the book. He was impressed. He wants to share author credit with you."

Dudley smiled. "Thank you. Amy."

"You did good work, George. Let me know if you want to make it permanent," Amy Andrews said. "We could use you."

"That's tempting. Give me a little time to think about it. Bye now." He hung up.

"Georgie?" his mother yelled from the kitchen. "Your lunch is getting cold."

He left the patio and sat down at the kitchen table. "Looks like rain."

"*Rainy Days and Monday*'s always get me down," Elsie Dudley sang the old *Carpenters* tune.

"I don't need either to get me down lately."

"I noticed," she said, putting a plate of spaghetti in front of him. "Albert told me you'd been mopey lately, but I had no idea. Maybe you need drugs."

"Mom."

"Prescription. Maybe you need to see a head doctor," she said candidly. "Did wonders for Emma Cappelletti. Since her Herbie died, she wore the same house robe every day and never answered the phone. After two weeks with this Dr. lady, she's laughing again and back with living. They started her on Prozac, but it was Celexa that did the trick. Happiness through chemistry."

"I'll think about it, mom."

"Don't think too hard, your head will explode." Then she said suddenly, "Oh fudge. It's Monday. I have that computer seminar. What time is it? I'm going to be late." She grabbed her purse and headed for the door. "Bye, dear. Stay away from the cutlery."

He drove over to Ruth's Chris. He found a spot in the parking lot where he could watch the front door. Not too close, not too far. *Just right*, he thought and laughed. This was becoming a bad habit. He felt like a stalker or worse a lovesick teenager. He wasn't even sure what he wanted to happen. The fantasy, of course, is she would see him, rush across the parking lot, and throw herself into his arms, crying I Love You, I Love You, I Love You. But the more realistic scenario was the Orlando Police would haul him in for vagrancy or peeping George syndrome.

His cell phone rang. He picked it up without looking at the caller ID.

"Hi, Georgie. Miss me?"

"Kelli?"

"Hi, baby. Where are you? You in LA?" Her voice was intoxicating. His breath quickened and some other parts of his body were quickening too.

"No. Back here in Florida. Finishing up the book," he managed to croak out.

"I miss you," she said, full on sexy/baby voice.

Memories of her flat stomach and strong thighs rumbled through his mind. He closed his eyes.

"You thinking about my ass?" she whispered. He was. And her other parts.

A car honked on a nearby street. Dudley opened his eyes. "You said some not-too-nice stuff about me to Elliott Moore."

"Oh, baby, I had to say all that," suddenly the victim. "They paid me ten grand for that acting performance." Her laughter returned. "After the movie, Kyle and I broke up. His wife was such a bitch. So now I'm back home. I smoked some weed, started playing with myself, and thought of you."

A Lexus drove by, and Dudley's heart started to beat faster. He recognized the passenger. Mary. It pulled into one of the reserved spots by the front door. A silver-haired man got out of the driver's side, walked around the car, and opened Mary's door. She smiled as she exited and held his hand as they entered the restaurant.

I blew it, George thought. *She's moved on.* George opened the car door. *No. I'll go in there.*

Right now. Apologize. Tell her I've been acting like a jerk. Mary. Wait for me.

"Archie? Archie?"

He looked at his cell phone. *Kelli? She called me.*

"Are you there? Hello?"

All I have to do is walk inside. I know she'll forgive me. I know…

The gray-haired man was coming out of the restaurant. Mary was right behind him.

Now George. Go. This is a sign. She's coming out for… She kissed him. On the cheek, but she kissed him. And now she's hugging him and smiling. He said something and she threw her head back. Laughter. He made her laugh. Oh, Mary.

"ARCHIE!"

He coughed. "Yes. I'm here."

"Maybe I should have yelled, George." She said his name with real distaste.

"No, baby," George Dudley said, as he watched Mary blow the man a kiss as he drove away.

"We'll always be Kelli and Archie," he said watching Mary re-enter the restaurant, her image fading away into the darkness. "Can you pick me up at the airport tomorrow morning? I'll take the first flight out."

Kelli Lee screamed in joy. "Weeeee! Yes, yes. YES! My baby's coming home."

2

Mary came running out of the front door of the restaurant. "Uncle Andy!," she screamed. "You forgot your cell…" But he was too far away already. She watched as his Black LS 460 pulled out of the parking lot and zoomed smoothly into the four-lane traffic. Behind him, a silver Corolla stopped at the exit. Behind the wheel was a familiar profile. Mary raised her hand to shade her eyes to get a better look.

"George?"

3

Two weeks later, Dudley called Henri Harrison.

"Hello, stranger," Henri said. "Heard you were back in town. Problems with your cell service way out there in the boonies?"

"Don't be that way, Henri. I'm sorry I didn't call sooner," Dudley said.

"Forgiven," Henri said.

"Just like that?" Dudley said surprised.

"I got religion since you left. I'm in a forgiving mood," she quipped.

Dudley laughed, imagining Henri Harrison in the front pew of St. Catherine's Catholic Church commenting on the cut of Monsignor Danaher's vestments. "I need to ask you a serious question."

"I don't answer any questions that are serious, Georgie."

"I need a job. And I was wondering if it would be cool to call Steven Spielberg?"

"He gave you his private number, didn't he?" Henri asked.

"Yes, but I…"

"Let me repeat. HE GAVE YOU HIS PRIVATE NUMBER, DIDN'T HE?"

"You don't need to shout Henri," Dudley said.

"Apparently I do. I think there's something wrong with your head."

"My mom said the same thing."

"I love her more and more each day," Henri said. "Yes, call him. That's why they call it a 'private' number."

"I wasn't sure he meant it," Dudley said, concerned. "I mean, we only met one time."

195

"Honey, Steven Spielberg doesn't do anything he doesn't mean."

4

The Universal City Plaza Building was easy to find. Getting inside was another story. There were security checks, bag checks, a pat down, and at least three calls to persons unknown who needed to verify everything. Eventually, he was sitting at a large conference table on the thirty-sixth floor overlooking the San Fernando Valley Steven Spielberg sat across from him, a stack of manila folders in front of him. "You sure I can't get you something, George? Coffee? Water?"

"I'm fine thanks," Dudley said calmly. He was glad the Cary Grant side decided to show up today. Otherwise, he was sure he'd be in the bathroom throwing up right now, but that was one of the useful things about Cary, he always appeared calm and relaxed. Not a care in the world. Dudley smiled his big Cary Grant smile and said, "So what do you have there, Steven?"

"I have some spec-scripts that were sent to me by a friend of mine, but I'm not really knocked out by any of them. I know your background is nonfiction, but I thought a fresh perspective might help me chose the best one." Spielberg pushed the three folders across the gleaming laminated surface. Dudley caught them, deftly.

"Take a look at them and let's meet again next week. Give me your thoughts," Spielberg said, but Dudley immediately pushed all three folders back toward Spielberg who awkwardly caught them before they flew off the table. "Hey!"

"This is a test, Steven. I don't do tests," Dudley said pointedly. Before Spielberg could protest, he continued. "Plus, I'm not a screenwriter. Never even wrote a play. You don't need me to look at scripts, so why am I really here?"

Spielberg smiled, tossed the three folders in a trash can, and leaned across the table. "I want to know about Archie Leach."

Chapter 31
Divine Intervention—In Action

1

The house was empty and dark when Ryan Reynolds got home. It was just after midnight and Blake and the kids were staying at her mother's house for the night. He closed the garage and opened the door to the kitchen when a voice called out from the dark. "Don't turn on the light."

"Jesus Christ," Reynolds screamed. Dropping his keys.

"No, but He says hi," Cary said. "Sit down, Ryan. I don't know how much time I have."

"How did you get in my house? You better leave right now before I call the police," Reynolds said, moving back into the garage.

"Your friend George Dudley needs your help, Ryan."

"George who?"

"You know him as Archie Leach," Cary said. "He's in a spot of trouble right now and he needs your help."

"Who are you? Your voice sounds familiar."

"I'm Archie Leach. The original."

"The original," Reynolds laughed. "You're telling me you're Cary Grant?"

"The one and only. All men want to be me, all women want me, or some such nonsense. Now please, Ryan. I've never tried to make contact through the veil before and I don't know how much time I have."

"The veil?" Reynolds whole body tingled. "Are you telling me you're an... angel?"

"No. Nothing so grand. Just a dead guy trying to help a nice guy out of a jam."

"Sorry, but I don't believe you. Angels don't appear in front of people."

"Really? Don't you read your Bible? Gabriel and Mary? Peter's release from prison? Daniel and the lions? You think we just stopped visiting people two thousand years ago?"

"I…" Reynolds started, but for the first time in his life, he was speechless.

"Sit down, son. I need you to do something for me."

Reynolds switched on the kitchen light. "Oh, my God."

Cary Grant was standing in his kitchen doorway. He was in his favorite tuxedo, the one he wore with Ingrid Bergman in *Indiscreet*. He had his hand in his pocket and his other covered his eyes.

"Hey. I said leave the light off."

"It's really you. Cary Grant is my kitchen."

"Yes, I am, but I don't know for how long. I've never tried this before."

"Well, sit down. I have a million questions. Can you sit?" Reynolds asked him, pulling out a chair.

"Of course, I can sit. Ryan. Now calm yourself. We have a lot to go over and the clock is ticking."

"Okay. Okay. Easy there, big fella." Reynolds sat down. "You're awfully grumpy for a dead guy."

"I'm sorry Ryan, but I could get into a heap of trouble if I'm caught. This is not a sanctioned visit."

"Got it. But I need to know one thing before you leave."

"Fine. One thing. What is it?"

"What was it like working with Grace Kelly?"

Cary stared at him. "Are you serious? I travel here from Heaven, and all you want to know about is Grace?"

"Well, yeah. She's hot."

"Can we please be serious Ryan," Cary said, sitting down.

"Oh," Reynolds said, pointing at him.

"What?"

"I can… see through you."

Cary looked down at his ghostly hands, the checkered tablecloth showing through. "Oh damn. Okay, Ryan, we need to hurry this up. Your friend George Dudley is in trouble, and I need you to do something to help him."

"Oh, Dudley. Yea, I like him," Reynolds said. "What do you need, Mr. Grant? Money? A kidnapping? We going to storm the castle?"

"I need you to answer your phone."

"Now this is a nice surprise," Elsie Dudley said, greeting Henri Harrison and the Colonel at her front door.

"Well, my, my my," the Colonel said, taking her hand. "Miss Elsie, your pictures do not do you justice." He leaned over and kissed the back of her hand. Elsie curtsied.

"Flattery will get you everywhere, Albert," Elsie Dudley said. "And you must be Henri Harrison."

Henri bowed, "Good evening, Miss Elsie. Thank you for having us over on such short notice."

"Come on in. I have whipped up some canapes for you in the kitchen. Are you hungry?"

"I never refuse a meal."

"Your home is lovely," Henri said, entering the foyer.

"Thanks. I like it," Elsie said, taking Albert's hand. "My daughter keeps trying to get me to move into some condo on the beach, but I'll never move. This is my home."

"I love it," the Colonel said, squeezing her hand. "Where's the kitchen?"

"Oh, you are adorable Albert," she said pinching his cheek. "Was your flight alright?"

"Uneventful. We flew in yesterday to see our newest client," the Colonel said, "And I told Henri, since we were in Orlando, we had to stop in and see my newest friend."

"I'm so glad you did. Talking online is okay for this younger generation, but I prefer old fashion face to face."

"And it's such a nice face," the Colonel flirted.

"Oh, stop," Elsie said, but she was enjoying herself. She turned to Henri. "Albert said you were in town for work?"

"Our client, Jimmy Miller is playing Motel in the national touring company of *Fiddler on the Roof* with Alfred Molina. It opened last night at the Phillips Center," Henri added.

"I think we should hire that hunk who played the Constable," Albert said to Henri. "Couldn't take my eyes off of him."

"Down boy," Henri said.

"Well, I am so glad you called. Come in. Come in. I hope you're hungry." Elsie pushed open the kitchen door. She was greeted by a voice from the dark.

"Don't turn on the light," Kay Kendall said.

"Oh, my God. Henri, call 911," Elsie screamed.

"I'm not a thief. I'm an angel. And I need your help."

"Oh, my heart," Elsie said sitting down hard at the kitchen table.

"Don't worry Elsie. You don't die today. But someone you know is dying; inside. Your son George needs you."

"You know Georgie?"

"Please. Sit down," Kay said more forcibly. "I don't have a lot of time. Your son is in trouble, and I need your help. All three of you."

"Your voice sounds familiar. Who are you?" the Colonel said, switching on the kitchen.

Kay Kendall shrank against the refrigerator, trying to hide from the light.

"Grab her Henri," the Colonel called out.

"You grab her. You're closer," Henri said.

Albert Poots, also known as the Colonel, reached out for the intruder's arm, his hand went through her, finding nothing solid.

"Oh, piss and puss," he screamed, falling backward onto the floor.

"Be not afraid," Kay said, stepping forward. She raised her hands and spoke in a deep voice, "I come with great tidings of joy." Elsie screamed, then fainted.

Henri pushed herself into a corner and started to cry.

The Colonel covered his face and whimpered over and over, "We are not worthy. We are not worthy."

Kay dropped her arms and sat down at the kitchen table next to a slumped-over Elsie. "Damn. I thought some classic Bible quotes would help. I am so new to this."

The Colonel looked up and said, tentatively, "You're not going to smite us?"

"Smite you? I don't even know what that means," then she gestured to Elsie. "Could you please wake her up? I'm not sure what would happen if I tried to touch her."

The Colonel got to his feet and stood behind Elsie Dudley. "Elsie honey, wake up," he said, gently shaking her shoulders. "The angel of the Lord wants to speak to you."

"Oh, my God," Henri said.

"Don't frighten her Albert, I just need all three of you awake. I don't have much time," Kay said, and the Colonel could see the worry on her glowing face.

"Who are you?" Henri said, struggling to his feet.

"I'm Kay Kendall," she said.

"But Kay Kendall died in 1960," Henri said.

"1959, actually. September 5. Leukemia. I don't recommend it."

"I don't understand," Henri continued. "Why are you here in Elsie's kitchen? Don't these things usually happen in churches?"

"Or fields with shepherds watching over their flocks?" the Colonel added.

"Like I said. This is new to me, and I didn't have a lot of time, so I arranged for you to be here so I could talk about Mary and George."

"George? What about George?" Elsie said, coming out of her stupor. "Is he dead?"

"No."

"Then you've come for me? I'm ready," Elsie said dramatically and laid her hand over Kay's but it slipped through and smacked the table. She screamed. "Aahhhh!"

The Colonel screamed louder. "AAAAAAAHHHHHHHHHHHHHH!"

Kay sighed. "I told Cary he should have talked to you three. Ryan Reynolds would have been a cake walked compared to this."

"Cary? Cary Grant?" Henri said slowly, the pieces starting to fall into place. "This cannot be a coincidence. George had been fantasizing about Cary for months now."

"I know. He's been watching, George."

"Watching him," Elsie said, suspicious. "What for?"

"It was his assignment. He was sent to observe George and find out about his obsession with Cary. Our Boss says each person is special, just the way they are. Everyone trying to be Cary Grant, or any idol, would be… well, it would throw a monkey wrench in the big plan, and He doesn't want that."

"But He's God?" Elsie said, confused. "Why doesn't he just wave his magic wand?"

"Free will, dear," the Colonel said, holding her hand. "We can do whatever we want, remember. That's what living your life is all about."

"Thank you, Linus, now why don't you and the rest of the Peanuts gang put a sock in it," Henri said sharply. "We need to get back to the angel in the room?" Kay shimmered and her vision blurred.

"What was that?" the Colonel asked, frightened.

"I'm fading already. I don't have much time left. So please, listen to me. Your son needs you. He's in trouble. Now will you help me, or not?"

"She's a feisty little angel, isn't she, Henri," the Colonel said.

"I like it. And God help me, I believe her," Henri said.

"Don't worry dear, He will."

"Alright, Kay. Can we call you Kay? What do you need us to do?" Elsie said.

"Have you ever seen *Cinderella*?"

"Which version?" the Colonel queried.

3

One hour late. "Why have you never taken me to Ruth's Chris before," the Colonel whined. "I love this place."

"It's dark and smoky; of course, you like it," Henri quipped.

"Bitch."

"Cut it, girls. Here she comes," Elsie said, watching Mary Jordan work her way over to their table.

"Elsie, what a nice surprise," Mary said, kissing her cheek.

"I had a couple friends stop by," she said loudly, "and I wanted to take them to the best restaurant in Orlando." She finished expansively, waving her hand in the air.

Mary Jordan looked at her, a smile playing on her face. "Okay. Welcome."

The Colonel stood up, took Mary Jordan's hand, and kissed the back of it. "You, my dear, are exquisite."

"I can see why he likes you," Henri added.

"Excuse me?"

"Mary dear, can we talk after you close up? There's something I need to ask you?" Elsie said, clearly nervous.

"Are you okay, Elsie?" Mary asked, concerned. "You're acting like you've seen a ghost."

"Oh, Mary," Elsie said. "You have no idea."

The lights were on, and the wait staff was clearing the final tables when Mary Jordan returned.

"Why don't you three wise guys follow me? I thought we should use one of the private rooms."

Elsie, Henri, and Albert got in step behind her. The private room was small but comfortably furnished, a round table and four high-backed chairs set up around it. "I brought a bottle of Cognac. I think we're going to need it," she said, pouring for the four of them. "I take it this is a George Dudley intervention. Am I right?"

"What did I say? Perceptive."

"I'm a little surprised at you, Elsie," Mary said. "This is not your style."

"Trust me, Mary, I am so out of my comfort zone, I can't begin to explain. But I do know one thing, I'm not dying today. I have it on the highest authority."

"Okay, boys and girls. Enough beating around the bush. Out with it," Mary said annoyed.

"Do you love George?" Elsie Dudley asked suddenly.

"Yes," she said at once. Then she lowered her head and added, "God help me."

"He is dear. He is," the Colonel said, and Henri reached over and smacked his arm.

"We know Georgie loves you," Elsie said, and before Mary could interrupt, she took Mary's hand and said, "Yes, he has done some, questionable things lately, but I know he loves you, too."

"Does Kelli Lee know this?" Mary said, raising an eyebrow.

"I'll admit, she has bewitched him," the Colonel agreed.

"Men," Henri said, contemptuously.

"But if you can give him one more chance," Elsie started, then she cried out, "Oh, Mary, you two are just so good together!"

"I know Elsie," Mary replied. "But he can be such an asshole."

"That's the truth," Henri agreed.

"We have a plan," the Colonel said, excited. "You've heard about this big costume party Universal is planning, right?"

"Of course. After that, the dinosaur movie opens."

"That dinosaur movie," the Colonel smiled. "I love this girl."

"Well, George is going to be there. You know, because of the book," Elsie said.

"Okay."

"And you're going too," Elsie said excitedly.

"No, I'm not."

"Yes, you are," Elsie said forcibly, right back.

Mary took a deep breath and said, "Elsie, even if I did want to go to this spectacle, I don't have an invitation. You must know it's the hottest ticket in the town. Maybe the whole country."

"We know this," Henri said, winking at the Colonel.

"I mean everybody's going to be there. Chris Pratt and Dallas, obviously. George Clooney. Oprah, for God's sake. I even hear Steven Spielberg is making an appearance."

"You heard right," the Colonel said.

"Well, how the hell am I supposed to get a ticket?"

"Funny you should ask." The Colonel pulled out his cell phone. He touched a single number for those special contacts he had on speed dial and waited as the connection was made. Then he smiled and said sweetly into the phone, "Hello, dear, how are you?" Then he nodded and said, "She's right here." He handed the phone to Mary. "It's for you."

Mary Jordan stared at it dubiously. Then she grabbed the phone as if she couldn't be bothered and said, "Yes. Hello, this is Mary Jordan. Who am I speaking to?"

"Hi, Mary. It's Ryan Reynolds. How are you?" Ryan Reynolds said.

"Ryan?" she said unbelievingly. "Are you a part of this too? Whatever this is."

"I believe the technical term is, Divine Intervention," Reynolds said.

"I am so confused."

"Welcome to the club. Anyway, Blake and I can't make the big costume party thing in Orlando Land, so I was wondering if you wanted to use our invite?"

Mary Jordan was silent. She stared at the three coconspirators sitting around the table, they were all staring at her nodding and smiling. She mouthed silently, *What the Fuck Is Happening.*

"Mary? Hello? Ground control to Major Mary?"

"Yes. I'm still here Ryan," Mary said.

"You want the tickets or not girlfriend?" he asked.

"Yes. Thank you. I'd like that very much."

"Fabulous. I'll email it over to you now." Mary's phone beeped. She just received an email. She blinked.

"Well, my work here is done. Luv ya. Call us when you're out in L.A. I know Blake would love to see you. Hasta my way goes, moo cha chas." Reynolds hung up.

Mary checked her cell phone and opened Ryan's email. The invite was attached. She looked up and said, "I guess I'm going to the ball."

"Bibbidi-bobbidi-boo," the Colonel exclaimed.

"So I guess that makes you my fairy godmother?" Mary said, smiling.

"At your service," the Colonel stood and bowed.

"I guess all I need now is a dress," Mary said, innocently.

Henri, Albert, and Elsie shared a bemused look, and then Henri finally said, "Oh, dearie. We are way ahead of you."

Chapter 32
ET Live at Jurassic Park

REPORT #24—Addendum

1

"Welcome everyone. Welcome to an Entertainment Tonight special event, Live at Jurassic Park, here at the extraordinary Universal Studios Orlando. I'm Elliott Moore and I'll be your host for the next two hours as we interview the stars of the big new hit movie, Jurassic Park World Domination. I mean Dominion. *Jurassic World Dominion.* We'll also talk with the director, studio heads, and lots and lots of celebrities who have flown in from around the world to watch the premiere of this, latest in the iconic Jurassic Park franchise. Right now, we have the star of the movie, Chris Pratt. Hi Chris. How are you?"

"Well, I'm excited to be here, Elliott. We just watched the movie, and the place went nuts. Standing ovation. Mass hysteria. It was very exciting. I'm really stoked to be here in Orlando. Go MAGIC! Wooo!"

"Thank you, Chris. I guess we'll see you inside at the big costume party, Universal has planned?"

"Oh, yes, definitely."

"What costume are you planning to wear? Or is it a secret? You can tell me."

"No secret. I'm going dressed as a matinee idol. Yea, baby!"

"Well, what an original idea. I'm sure no one will guess it."

"Thank you, America. Go see *Jurassic World DO-MIN-ION*!"

"Chris Pratt, everybody. Next, we have a surprise guest, all the way from Hollywood California, Mr. Steven Spielberg. Welcome to ET, Steven. Get it? ET? Haha."

"Yea. Good one. Elliott, is it?"

"Elliott Moore, for Entertainment Tonight."

"Okay."

"So, Steven, I'm sure everyone wants to know, could you even imagine the longevity and huge success of the Jurassic franchise when you made that first movie almost thirty years ago?"

"Yes."

"So… so you could tell. You knew because it was just so… good?"

"Yes. Well put, Elliott."

"Okay. One last question, How do you get those Dinosaurs to look so realistic?"

"Magic."

"Steven Spielberg, everyone. Thanks, Steven. Thanks for the memories. Okay, I just got word that the main ballroom has just opened, and the guests are starting to arrive. We're going to go to a commercial break, while I change into my surprise costume. Don't go away."

2

"Oh, this is nice," Elsie said. "Thank you so much for bringing me, Mary."

"No big deal. The invite was for two, and Henri and Albert had their own invites," Mary said sweetly. "Plus, who else would I take? You're the biggest movie buff I know."

"Pre-1960, every film after that sucked. Except for *The Godfather* and *Forest Gump*. I just love Tom Hanks. But who cares? Look at this place!" The entrance to the banquet hall was shaped like a cave. The craftsmanship was so good, Elsie thought they carted in real rocks to create it.

"Don't touch the set, ma'am," the security guard told her. "Tickets, please."

Mary handed over the invite, still expecting to be thrown out on her ear, but the guard simply nodded and waved them in. Elsie was wearing a Wicked Witch of the West outfit, complete with a towering conical back hat. "Thank you, my pretty, hahaha," Elsie said. Then to Mary, "I've been working on my Margaret Hamilton all week."

"Henri said to meet them at the bar by the T-Rex," Mary said, scanning the room. "There they are."

"Elsie, you look great," the Colonel said. He was dressed as Harold Hill from *Music Man*, complete with a porkpie straw hat.

"You too, Albert. But look at Henri," she said in awe. "Oh, my God."

Henri Harrison had blackmailed a costumer at Warner Brothers studios to get her hands on the white dress Audrey Hepburn wore for the Ascot Races scene from *My Fair Lady*. Complete with the giant oval white hat with plumes.

"HOW do you DO?" she said, imitating Hepburn's halting upper-crust British accent.

"Oh, Henri. You look glorious," Mary said.

"And where is your costume?" Henri asked her, eyeing her shapely figure in the elegant sage gown she wore to the Hope North charity event over two months ago.

"I know the plan," Mary said smiling. "I'll put it on when the time is right."

"You know your cue?" the Colonel asked.

"Is the Pope Catholic?" Mary replied.

"All right. Let's find a table. I am starving," the Colonel said.

"When are you not," Henri said.

3

"And we are back. Lawrence Olivier is here for Entertainment Tonight. No, I'm just kidding. It's me, Elliott Moore dressed as *Hamlet*, from that famous old Olivier movie. Sorry, I was late, putting on tights is hard. Haha. But seriously folks, as you can see, I'm standing here on the bandstand overlooking this massive hall the staff here at Universal has transformed into Jurassic Island for our big costume party. Everybody who's anybody is here, tonight."

"And speaking of which, here's Bradley Cooper and Jennifer Lawrence, all the way from Hollywood. Hi guys. Enjoying the party?"

"The best one I've been to all day," Jennifer said, laughing.

"Hell of a setup. You could fit a 747 in here," Cooper said.

"Along with a double-decker, eh?" Elliott said, smiling.

"A what?" Jennifer asked, puzzled.

"A double-decker. You know? The bus. Two stories," he tried valiantly to explain. "Ah, forget it. It's a British thing. Anyway, what did you think of the movie?"

"What movie?" Jennifer asked.

"The… Jurassic World Domain… Dominion," Elliott said expansively.

"Oh. Slept through it. Sorry," she said.

"We had a long flight," Cooper said. "But we plan to see it on the flight back home!" he said directly into the camera with fake enthusiasm.

"Okay. Well, thanks for stopping by. I guess they left their costumes on the plane. Next, we have Amy Andrews of Orlando Publications, the proud publishers of the official movie tie-in book—*The Matinee Idol Mystique*. Oh, sexy title."

"Thank you, Elliott. It's an honor to be here," Amy said nervously.

"I see you came as Cleopatra. Nice asp. Haha. Say, I should have dressed as Julius Caesar. We could have done a scene together. 'Out, out damn spot'."

"I think that's from Macbeth."

"Is it? All those Shakespeare plays sound the same to me. But hey, look at this book. You got Chris Pratt on the cover. He's saying, 'I'm the luckiest guy in the world'. Oh, how true that is," Elliot said.

"Yes. He told that to our author, George Dudley."

"And speaking of my old friend George, here he is now. Hi George. Long time, no see."

"Not long enough Elliott. How's your camera?" Dudley said, balling his fists.

"What a jokester. And who's this lovely vision next to you?"

"Hello, Elliott," Kelli Lee said, moving in front of George, staring directly into the camera. "I'm Kelli Lee and I'm dressed as a flapper." She then proceeded to shake her hips so the fringe on the bottom of her short skirt flipped around her hips suggestively.

"Very nice," Elliott said moving past her. "But George. What the heck are you wearing?"

"Yea. Funny story Elliott. I came here in a black Armani tuxedo. The one Cary Grant wore in, well pretty much all his movies. But as I was walking by the kitchen, a server rushed out with two giant jugs of margaritas. 32 ounces! And he spilled them both on me. I was drenched."

"Oh no."

"But that's not the worst part. When I was in the bathroom drying off, someone stole my tux. The only thing I could find in there to wear was this old-time football jersey and pants."

Amy Andrews looked off to her right where the kitchen doors were located. Standing next to them was Ricky, Mary's bartender from Ruth's Chris. She gave him a thumbs-up sign.

"They're a bit large on you George. What movie are they from? *Leatherheads*? That old *Knute Rockne* movie?"

"They're from *It's a Wonderful Life*," Amy said quickly. "It's what Jimmy Stewart wore after he and Donna Reed fell into the pool." Then George Dudley noticed Amy doing the oddest thing.

She raised her right hand straight up into the air like she wanted to be called on in class.

"Hey, I think you're right," Elliott said. "What was that old song they were singing?"

Then, as if on cue, because it was, the hall was filled with the opening notes of *Buffalo Gals*. At the same time, a spotlight hit a young woman walking onto the dance floor, situated just beneath the bandstand where George and Elliott were standing. She was wearing an oversized white bathrobe with the capital letters BFHS stenciled on the back. She was bouncing to the beat. Not exactly dancing, but clearly having a good time.

The whole room stared at her. Henri and Albert, standing by the DJ, held each other and Elsie crossed her fingers. But all George Dudley could do was stare, his mouth opened. "Mary?"

Then he felt a gentle nudge from behind him, courtesy of Amy Andrews, and suddenly George was moving down the stairs to the dance floor. Kelli Lee started to protest, but Amy grabbed her from behind.

George Dudley approached Mary Jordan. The music continued to play, and Mary started to hum along with the song. After a beat, Dudley realized what was happening and moved in front of her and badly harmonized with her at the end of the lyric. '…and dance by the light of the moon'.

They smiled and held hands and George asked Mary, "What is you want, Mary? You want the moon?"

"No, George, I just want you."

REFLECTIONS ON REPORT #24

Don't you just love a happy ending?

Chapter 33
Cary and Kay

"You're in a lot of trouble young man," Clarence said, hotly. He was pacing behind his desk and his wings were open and shaking violently. Another angel sat in his chair, an old man with a magnificent white beard. He was using one hand to lean on his chain, in the other he held a manila folder. The name GEORGE DUDLEY was stenciled on it.

"I know, sir," Cary said, his head down.

"No. No, I don't think you do," Clarence said pointing a finger at him. "You broke the Cardinal Rule. The Big One. Numero Uno. Never, ever, EVER interfere with people's lives."

"Sorry, sir."

"Sorry, won't cut it," Clarence continued. "Now we must reset their life meters, change their dates… the paperwork, Cary. The paperwork."

"I'll help you with the filings, sir," Kay said, stepping forward.

"No, no, no. You will do no such thing," Clarence said, raising his voice. "You will clear out your desk, young lady. Post haste!"

"Now see here, Clarence," Cary said, defending her. "This was all my idea. You can't punish, Kay."

"She appeared before three people, Cary. Three. Plus, we know it was her idea. You think anything happens up here that we don't know about?"

"I am terribly sorry, sir. Is there anything I can do?"

"Do? Haven't you done enough already? There's talk of sending you down. The both of you." Kay cringed and started to cry. Cary put an arm around her and said, "If that's your decision, Clarence, then so be it. But I'll tell you this. If I had to do it all over again, I wouldn't change a thing. George Dudley is my friend. He may not know it, but he is. I saw a friend in trouble, and I acted. He'd lost so much and thought he was a failure, so he wanted to

"

change his whole life. But he isn't a failure. He's just a regular guy who had a few setbacks and lost his way. You said it yourself Clarence, no man is a failure who has friends. George Dudley's no failure. George does have friends, Amy, Henri, the Colonel, his mom… and me. And if that means an eternity on the hot seat… well, it was worth it."

Clarence felt ashamed. To have his own words thrown back at him, hurt him deeply. He cleared his throat and said, "I know you meant well Cary, but there are rules—"

"Yes, Clarence, but you are forgetting the Eleventh Commandment that our Lord gave us, that supersedes all rules," the gray-haired man said, rising out of his chair, "Love one another, just as I have loved you. And that is exactly what our boy Cary did. He so loved his fellow man that he was willing to sacrifice himself. That kind of behavior should not be punished but rewarded."

"Thank you, St. Peter," Cary said, bowing his head.

"Please. Call me Pete. We don't stand too much on ceremony around here. Right, Clarence?"

"Yes, sir. Trying to keep up with the times."

St. Peter picked up a new folder off Clarence's desk and gave it to Cary. "I have another task for you. Actually, it's for you and Miss Kendall. The boys were very impressed with the work you two did. I took great pride in reading your reports to them when we had our monthly supper. Even Jesus chuckled a time or two."

Cary was speechless. Kay elbowed him and then asked, "So am I still fired?"

"Let's say, you're on temporary assignment," St. Peter said, genially. "You two are going to be quite busy for the next few decades."

After they left, Cary and Kay walked back to her condo. They sat on her patio, still holding the unopened folder.

"Well, that could have been worse," Kay said, sipping her Merlot.

"Yes. I didn't even have to do penance," he said, clinking glasses with her.

"The old Cary Grant charm works again," she said, raising her glass, toasting him.

"You know Kay Kendall, we make a pretty good team."

"You're just noticing that."

He dropped the folder and kissed her. *Oh, well, Heaven can wait.*

Epilogue
The Man Who Wanted to Be Cary Grant

Thanksgiving

"Where's your grandmother?" Dudley said to his daughter, December Stanton. "She's supposed to bring the pies."

"She's with Paul. God knows where they could be," Decey said, holding her four-month-old baby close to her breast.

"Maybe little Archibald knows where they are," Dudley said, tickling his grandson.

"Dad, he can't speak yet," Decey said, laughing.

"What's the matter with him? You better get that checked out as soon as you get home," Dudley said. "New York still has doctors, right?"

"Almost as many as lawyers," Gabriel Stanton said. "You want me to hold him down, darling?"

"Thanks. He weighs a ton."

"Who weighs a ton? I resemble that remark," the Colonel said.

"Oh, Albert," Decey said. "You are my favorite of all my dad's new friends."

"Of course, I am," the Colonel said, leaning back in Dudley's leather recliner. "But I do not babysit. So don't get any ideas."

"I really wished Henri could have been here," Dudley said.

"Duty calls, dear boy," the Colonel said with pride. "Old Jimmy Miller finally made the big leagues—*Guardians of the Galaxy 3*. Henri is closing the deal tomorrow."

"That's great news."

"Speaking of news, how's the script coming along?" the Colonel asked.

"Steven keeps making changes," Dudley said, nibbling on some stuffing. "Yesterday he said he wanted to change the title to *The Man Who Wanted to*

Be Cary Grant. I said it wouldn't fit on a movie marquee. Anyway, it's almost done. They've already started looking for someone to play the lead."

"Who they got in mind?"

"I know they're talking to David Harbour and Hugh Jackman. But nothing's set. But Bradley and Ryan are on board."

"Grandma's back!" Decey yelled from the front door.

"Finally. Honey, let's eat," Dudley yelled.

"Be right there," Mary Jordan Dudley said. Then into her phone. "Okay, Uncle Andy. Just tell him when he wakes up that I love him. You're still coming over, right? I'll save you a plate. Okay. See you soon."

Dudley kissed her when she entered the kitchen. "Did you talk to your father?"

"No. Uncle Andy says he was having a good day, but he was napping now. He'll be by later."

"Nice. I want to take his Lexus out for a test drive. I'm thinking about getting one myself," George said.

"Okay, everybody, get your drinks and sit down," Mary called out.

"It all looks great, Mary," Paul said.

"Well, December helped," she replied, sitting down. "George, you want to say grace?"

"I would love to."

He spoke words of love and God and family out loud, but inside, he sent a secret prayer of thanks to his own guardian angels, Cary Grant and Kay Kendall.

THE END